PRAISE FOR *AFTER MIDNIGHT*
AND IRMGARD KEUN

"Brief, important, and haunting." —PENELOPE LIVELY

"Explosive . . . Even reading *After Midnight* today feels dangerous . . . Keun has an amazing gift for exposing the conflict at the heart of the average citizen, whose naïveté is eventually and sometimes violently stripped away . . . Haunts far beyond its final page."

—JESSA CRISPIN, NPR

"I cannot think of anything else that conjures up so powerfully the atmosphere of a nation turned insane . . . One of those pieces of fiction that illuminate fact." —*THE SUNDAY TELEGRAPH*

"Acerbically observed by this youthful, clever, undeceived eye . . . This miniature portrait, rightly republished, is distinguished not only for its unfamiliar slant but for its style which is of a remarkable simplicity and purity, crystalline yet acid; a glass of spring water laced with bitter lemon." —*THE JEWISH CHRONICLE*

"The overwhelming power of Keun's work lies in her surprisingly raw, witty, and resonant feminine voices." —JENNY MCPHEE, *BOOKSLUT*

"Keun was possessed of a spectacular talent. She managed to convey the political horrors she lived through with the lightest possible touch, even flashes of humor . . . Her work stands as a brilliant record of the era she survived." —EMILY ST. JOHN MANDEL, *THE MILLIONS*

GILGI

IRMGARD KEUN (1905–1982) was born in Berlin and raised in
Cologne, where she studied to be an actress. However, reputedly
inspired by a meeting with Alfred Döblin, the author of *Berlin Alex-
anderplatz*, she turned to writing, and became an instant sensation
with her first novel, *Gilgi, One of Us*, published in 1931 when she was
just twenty-six. A year later, her second novel, *The Artificial Silk Girl*,
was an even bigger bestseller. The rising Nazi party censured Keun,
however, and her books were included in the infamous "burning
of the books" in 1933. After being arrested and interrogated by the
Gestapo, Keun left her husband and escaped Germany. While wandering in exile, Keun conducted an eighteen-month affair with the
writer Joseph Roth and wrote the novels *After Midnight* and *Child
of All Nations*. In 1940, Keun staged her suicide and, under a false
identity, reentered Germany, where she lived in hiding until the end
of the war. Her work was rediscovered in the late seventies, reviving
her reputation in Germany.

GEOFF WILKES, a Lecturer in German Studies at the University
of Queensland, has written extensively on the literature and society
of the Weimar Republic and the Third Reich, with special attention to Irmgard Keun and Hans Fallada. He is the author of *Hans
Fallada's Crisis Novels 1931–1947*.

THE NEVERSINK LIBRARY

I was by no means the only reader of books on board the Neversink. Several other sailors were diligent readers, though their studies did not lie in the way of belles-lettres. Their favourite authors were such as you may find at the book-stalls around Fulton Market; they were slightly physiological in their nature. My book experiences on board of the frigate proved an example of a fact which every book-lover must have experienced before me, namely, that though public libraries have an imposing air, and doubtless contain invaluable volumes, yet, somehow, the books that prove most agreeable, grateful, and companionable, are those we pick up by chance here and there; those which seem put into our hands by Providence; those which pretend to little, but abound in much. —HERMAN MELVILLE, *WHITE JACKET*

GILGI,
ONE OF US

IRMGARD KEUN

TRANSLATION AND AFTERWORD
BY GEOFF WILKES

MELVILLE HOUSE PUBLISHING
BROOKLYN · LONDON

GILGI, ONE OF US

Originally published in German as *Gilgi,*
eine von uns by Universitas, Berlin, 1931
Copyright © by Ullstein Buchverlage GmbH, Berlin
Published in 1979 by Classen Verlag
Afterword copyright © 2013 by Geoff Wilkes

First Melville House printing: November 2013

Melville House Publishing   8 Blackstock Mews
    145 Plymouth Street   and   Islington
    Brooklyn, NY 11201   London N4 2BT

mhpbooks.com facebook.com/mhpbooks   @melvillehouse

Library of Congress Control Number: 2013950829

ISBN: 978-1-61219-277-2

Design by Christopher King

Printed in the United States of America
1 3 5 7 9 10 8 6 4 2

GILGI,
ONE OF US

SHE'S HOLDING IT FIRMLY IN HER HANDS, HER little life, the girl Gilgi. She calls herself Gilgi, her name is Gisela. The two *i*'s are better suited to slim legs and narrow hips like a child's, to tiny fashionable hats which contrive mysteriously to stay perched on the very top of her head. When she's twenty-five, she'll call herself Gisela. But she's not at that point quite yet.

Six-thirty on a winter morning. The girl Gilgi has got out of bed. Stands in her cold room, stretches, holds it, opens her eyes to drive the sleep out. Stands at the wide-open window and does her exercises. Touches her toes: up—down, up—down. The fingertips brush the floor while the legs remain straight. That's the right way to do it. Up—down, up—down.

The girl Gilgi bends and straightens for the last time. Slips her pyjamas off, throws a towel around her shoulders and runs to the bathroom. Runs into a voice in the dark hallway which hasn't woken up yet. "Really, Jilgi, in your bare feet on the icy lin-o-le-um! You'll catch your death."

"Morning, Mother," Gilgi calls, and considers whether she should shower in hot water before the cold, just for today. Away with temptation. No exceptions will be made. Gilgi lets the ice-cold water play over her narrow shoulders, her little convex stomach, her thin, muscle-hardened limbs. She presses her lips together in a firm, narrow line and counts to thirty in her head.

One—two—three—four. Don't count so fast. Slowly, nice and slowly: fifteen—sixteen—seventeen. She trembles a little, and is a little proud (as she is every morning) of her modest courage and self-control. Keep to the daily plan. Don't deviate from the system. Don't slacken. Not in the smallest trifle.

The girl Gilgi stands in front of the mirror. Fastens a black suede belt firmly around the thick gray woollen sweater, hums the words of a melancholy hit song (she's in a good mood), and looks at herself with an objective pleasure.

Give me your hand, dear, once more in farewell / Good ni-hight, good ni-hight ... Rubs a touch of Nivea Creme on her eyebrows, so that they're nice and bright, a touch of powder on the tip of her nose. Nothing more. Make-up isn't for the morning, rouge and lipstick are reserved for the evening.

Give me your hand, dear, once more ... A mirror like this is a friendly thing when you're twenty years old and have a clear, unlined face. A face which you look after. Looked after is better than pretty, it's your own achievement.

Ti-ta—ta-ti-ta ... An assessing glance at the austerely impersonal room. White-painted bedstead, white chest of drawers, a table, two chairs, a peaceful pattern of little flowers on the wallpaper, and a little painting in a nondescript frame which—washed-out and unattractive as a girl whose man has left her—no longer cares to draw attention to itself. You should've got rid of it long ago, this sentimental blot of color. Gilgi raises her arm for the attack. Lets it fall again. Well, what's the point? The thing was a present from Mother, some time or other. She'd be offended if you chucked it out. Let it stay up there. It's not doing any harm. It's nothing to do with you, this room. Because you don't live here, you just sleep in this virginal white bed. Give me your hand, dear, once more in fare ... Three pairs of chamois-leather gloves, two collars, and a blouse to be washed. Gilgi jams them under her arm and heads for the bathroom. The door's locked. A man's voice, roughened by decades in bars, sounds out: "Jus' a moment, Jilgi, almost finished." Gilgi wanders up and down the hallway. And only because she's got nothing at all to do right this minute, she thinks about Olga's brother. A nice boy. What was his first name again? She can't remember. He kissed her last night, in the car. He's leaving today. A pity? Nah. But it was nice yesterday, with him. She hadn't kissed a man for ages. There are so few that you like. The undiscriminating years between seventeen and nineteen are over. He was a nice boy. It was a nice kiss. But that was all. You don't feel it anymore. That's as it should be.

The bathroom door opens with a bang. A rotund figure in whitish underthings rushes past Gilgi, trailing aromas of Kaloderma soap and Pebeco toothpaste, which fill the hallway.

"Morn', Jilgi."

"Morning, Father." Gilgi promptly forgets Olga's brother and the kiss and devotes herself to Lux soap flakes, chamois-leather gloves, collars, and silk blouse. Give me your hand, dear, once more in ...

A quarter-hour later, Gilgi is sitting in the living-room. Primordial furniture. Imposing sideboard, manufactured around nineteen hundred. Tablecloth with web-like embroidery and little cross-stitched flowers. Faded green lampshade with fringes made from glass beads. Green plush sofa. Above it, a cloth rectangle: Our Little Nest By God Is Blessed. The letters wobble, as though they were embroidered by an epileptic, and cornflowers wind around them, as though they're doing Saint Vitus' dance. Or maybe it's bindweed. And someone once gave this thing as a gift. Someone once accepted this thing and said: "Thank you." Above the cloth rectangle, an epic painting: Washington. He's standing in an unsteady boat which is making its laborious way through ice-floes, and he's waving a flag at least the size of a bedsheet. Admirable. Not the painting, but Washington. Good luck trying to do what he's doing: standing tall and proud like a gladiator in a little, storm-tossed boat, looking boldly forward, and waving a flag at least the size of a bedsheet. Only Washington could do that.

America For Ever. Germany Wants To See You. Deutschland, Deutschland über alles ... If you like, you can believe that Washington, who's painted in straight lines as though the artist used a ruler, is a representative of German heroism. Frau Kron believes that. She inherited the painting. For her, Washington, Ziethen, Bismarck, Theodor Körner, Napoleon, Peter the Great, Gneisenau, all blur into one. She knows as much about one as she knows about the next, which is to say: nothing. But the painting is patriotic, and that's what counts. Deutschland, Deutschland ...

Our Little Nest By God Is Blessed. The family is together. Father, mother, and daughter. They're drinking coffee. Their own blend: one-fourth coffee beans, one-fourth chicory, one-fourth barley, one-fourth Carlsbad Coffee Spices. The liquid looks brown, is hot, tastes dreadful, and is drunk without demur. By Herr Kron for the sake of his kidneys and of economy, by Frau Kron for the sake of her heart and of economy, by Gilgi out of resignation. And anyway, habit has broken the resistance of all three.

All three are eating rolls with good butter. Only Herr Kron (Carnival Novelties, Wholesale) eats an egg. That egg is more than nourishment. It's a symbol. A concession to masculine superiority. A monarch's badge of office, a kind of emperor's orb.

No-one speaks. Everyone is earnestly and dully occupied with their own concerns. The complete lack of conversation testifies to the family's decency and legitimacy. Herr and Frau Kron have stuck together through years of honorable tedium to their silver wedding anniversary. They love each other and are faithful to each other, something which has become a matter of routine, and no longer needs to be discussed, or felt. Something which has been carefully packed away in the nineteenth-century sideboard, a little tarnished like the wedding silver in the neighboring drawer. The tedium is the cornerstone of the stability of their relationship, and the fact that they have nothing to say to each other means that they feel no uneasiness about each other.

Herr Kron is reading the *Cologne Advertiser*. His reddish-brown, reasonably well-kept right hand raises the coffee cup to his mouth at regular intervals. His round face with its fresh complexion shows the shocked and anxious expression which all habitual newspaper-readers should assume. No decent person could possibly look pleased when reading: Polish Infantry on German Soil. Disgraceful, that is. "European Manifesto": Briand Proposes Declaration in Support of European Peace and Reconstruction at Closing Session of European Council. The explanation which follows this is a bit complicated for Herr Kron, which is a reason to look doubly anxious. Can you trust Briand? You can't trust anyone. Next: Scandal in Budget Committee—Precious Stones Smuggled to Poland—Witnesses Named in Tausend Fraud Case—Robbery at Dairy. Nothing but unedifying reports. Heaven knows that, for the good of his health, the honest newspaper-reader has to accept sad news items with gloomy satisfaction, letting them stimulate his digestion. More Kruschen Salts stories: Bishop of Leitmeritz Dead—Another Weapons Cache Unearthed—and here . . . Herr Kron reads it aloud, in a voice that betrays his nightly beer-drinking: "Trag-e-dy on the Treptow Bridge, a woman an' her child jumped into the water."

"Both killed?" Frau Kron asks, almost hopefully. It's not callousness. It's just that she enjoys the shuddering sympathy which news of deaths and scandals provokes in her.

"Nah, jus' the child," Herr Kron reports. He speaks the true Cologne dialect, partly out of pride in his hometown, partly for the good of his business. Mother saved, child dead. Frau Kron's shuddering sympathy drops by half, leaving her dissatisfied. She immerses herself in the advertising supplement, in search of consolation. Stock Clearance Sale. Uding's Shoes—Our Display Windows Say It All. Bursch's Carpets—Final Three Days—High-Quality Goods. Frau Kron reads. She's stocky and shapeless. The skin on her arms and breasts is honorably slack and tired. She's gray and unattractive and has no desire to be otherwise. She can afford to grow old. Her dark-blue woollen dress has a light-gray collar and cuffs, and there's an ivory brooch at her throat—remnants of vanity. She sits on the green plush sofa, reading the advertising supplement of the *Cologne Advertiser*, pressing her broad, fleshy thumb onto the bread crumbs on the table and absent-mindedly putting them into her mouth. Above her, Washington is flourishing his flag which is at least the size of a bedsheet.

With swift but deliberate, graceful movements Gilgi drinks a cup of coffee, eats a thinly spread bread roll—because you don't want to get fat—lights a cigarette, draws on it three, four, five times, stubs it out on her saucer, and stands up.

"S'long, Father."

"S'long, Jilgi." Herr Kron looks up, wants to say something, to be friendly, to take an interest, he opens his mouth: he can't think of anything. He closes his mouth and looks down again.

"S'long, Mother." Gilgi brushes her hand over Frau Kron's ham-like shoulder as she leaves the room.

"Jilgi," she hears from behind her, "aren't you comin' to coffee this afternoon at the Geisslers'?" Frau Kron is Hamburg born and bred, but in the interests of marital harmony she copies her husband's Rhineland dialect, with goodwill and poor results.

"No time," Gilgi calls out, closing the front door behind her.

No, she has no time to lose, not a minute. She wants to get on, she has to work. Her day is crammed full with work of all kinds, with each job pressing up hard against the next. She rarely finds even a small pause in which to catch her breath. Work. A hard word. Gilgi loves it for its hardness. And when she's not working for once, when she grants herself time for once to be pretty, to be young, to have fun—then it's purely for fun, purely for pleasure.

Work has a point, and fun has a point. Accompanying her mother to a *Kaffeeklatsch* would be neither fun nor work, but a pointless waste of time, and completely incompatible with Gilgi's character and her conscience.

Gilgi is sitting in the streetcar. Actually she wanted to walk, but she's run out of time. Next to her, in front of her, the line-up of office workers. Tired faces, discouraged faces. Each one resembles the next. Their daily routines are the same, their emotions are the same, they look mass-produced. Any new passengers—anyone else without a ticket? None of them like doing what they do. None of them like being what they are. Little pale girl with the nice legs, wouldn't you rather stay in bed and have a proper sleep? Suntanned girl with the hiking shoes, looks like it'll be a nice day today—wouldn't you rather take a long walk in the city forest and feed the tame deer with the chestnuts you collected in the fall?

Anyone else without a ticket—anyone else without a ticket? They're riding to work. Day after day, to work. Each day resembles the next. Dingadingding—they get off, they get on. They ride the streetcar. Ride and ride. Eight-hour day, typewriter, steno pad, salary cut, end of the month—always the same thing, always the same thing. Yesterday, today, tomorrow—and in ten years.

You young ones, the ones under thirty, is this dispirited early-morning face all you've got too? It's Sunday tomorrow. Won't little images of your desires light up your eyes this afternoon? I mean, young man, you don't buy yourself such a beautiful, lustrous yellow necktie if you don't secretly believe that one day you'll be the boss, with your own car and a foreign bank account, do you? I mean, nice girl from a good family, you wouldn't put on that pretty necklace if you weren't hoping that a man would come and say that it suits you perfectly, would you? Little red-head, would you have spent twenty marks on that perm if you weren't dreaming of a beauty pageant and a film contract? Greta Garbo was a salesclerk once too. The ride to work. Day after day. Will something come to break the monotony of the days? What? Mr. Douglas Fairbanks, a lottery win, a film contract, the dreamed-of promotion, the shower of gold from heaven? Will that come? No. Is there no prospect of a change or a break? Yes, there is. What is it? Illness, rationalization, unemployment. But you're still riding to work. Yes, still. That's good.

Gilgi looks out the window. The hopeless people in the streetcar—no, she has nothing in common with them, she doesn't belong with them, she doesn't want to belong with them. They're gray and tired and lifeless. And if they're not lifeless, they're waiting for a miracle. Gilgi isn't lifeless, and she doesn't believe in miracles. She only believes in what she creates and what she earns. She isn't satisfied, but she's pleased. She's earning money.

You people in the streetcar, aren't you happy?

We're so tired.

But you're earning money, aren't you?

It's so little.

You could turn that little into more.

That's so hard.

That's what makes it fun.

It's not fun.

Times are tough. No-one likes being what they are. No-one likes doing what they do.

Aren't any of you young like me, aren't any of you happy like me? Yes! One—two—three faces. Young, firm features, hard little lines on the forehead, chin thrust out to take on the world, alert eyes.

Gilgi wraps her hand around the edges of her little case. She holds on tightly. The sharp little movement is like a handshake. Yes, after all! Not I—but we. We! She lifts her head, and her eyes sparkle. You—you—you and I: we'll make it.

Tick-tick-tick—rrrrrrrr—with reference to your letter of the 18th of ... tick-tick-tick—rrrrrrrr ... enclosed please find ... tick-tick-tick ... following our telephone conversation yesterday we wish to inform you ...

The steno-typist Gilgi is typing the ninth letter for the firm of Reuter & Weber, Hosiery and Lingerie (Wholesale). Her typing is quick, clean, and error-free. Her little brown hands, her well-kept fingers with their short nails, belong to the machine, and the machine belongs to them.

Tick-tick-tick—rrrrrrrr ... the steno-typist Gilgi goes in to the boss and puts the letters on his desk for him to sign.

"Wait, please," Herr Reuter says, then reads each letter before inscribing his name with a somewhat forced vigor under the typed "Yours faithfully." Gilgi waits. The pale winter sun draws circles on the yellow cupboard, on the coarse cork matting, and on Herr Reuter's fuzzy egg-shaped head.

"Sit down, please," Herr Reuter says. Gilgi bypasses the good leather armchair where the clients sit, removes a few files and papers from the simple cane chair, and sits down.

She gazes ahead of her incuriously, with her composed, expressionless professional countenance.

"Do you always look so unhappy?" Herr Reuter asks. That's how it starts.

"I don't look in the least unhappy."

Gilgi is an experienced girl. She knows men, and what they variously want and don't want, and how this is betrayed by the tone of their voices, their expressions, and their movements. If a man and a boss like Herr Reuter speaks in an uncertain voice, he's in love, and if he's in love, he wants something. Sooner or later. If he doesn't get what he wants, he's surprised, offended, and angry. The atmosphere between her and Herr Reuter has been building up for some time. Now it's about to explode. Her colleague Fräulein Müller told her that Frau Reuter is away at the moment. That will accelerate the process.

Gilgi weighs things up. She has no desire to start a relationship with Herr Reuter, and she has no desire to mess up her job in his firm, and perhaps even to lose it. He's a good boss. He pays overtime, treats his office staff well, is pleasant and courteous. Gilgi has had worse bosses.

She answers Herr Reuter's questions politely, and decides to be slow on the uptake for as long as she possibly can. Lunch with him today? Unfortunately she has so little time. Herr Reuter becomes a little more insistent, and Gilgi promises to meet him after work, at two o'clock in the "Schwerthof" restaurant. Resisting too strongly might perhaps make her appear less harmless than she'd like.

A few hours later Gilgi is sitting with Herr Reuter in the "Schwerthof." They're up to coffee. Herr Reuter is smoking his first cigarette. He's showing Gilgi photos of his wife and his child, as married men do when they're prepared, despite minor pangs of conscience, to be unfaithful. "A most charming woman," Gilgi says.

Herr Reuter smokes his second cigarette. The pictures of his wife and child have found their way back into his wallet. He talks a lot. Now and then Gilgi says Yes or No.

Herr Reuter smokes his third cigarette, and mentions in passing that he can't have such really interesting conversations with his wife as he can with her. "Ohhh?" Gilgi replies. "Yes," Herr Reuter says, and strokes the back of her hand a few times. "How young you are, I could be your father, missy." He expects a vigorous disclaimer. Gilgi just smiles innocently, which Herr Reuter interprets in his favor.

He smokes his fourth cigarette. Suddenly he's overcome by the urge to feel unhappy. His marriage is a failure, his life is a mess, he's an old fool, his job is just buying and selling. He employs bitterness, self-mockery, and a touch of pathos. When he gets to "I should get away from it all," he throws his shoulders back so firmly that he endangers the seams of his jacket, then orders two liqueurs. Gilgi prefers not to drink alcohol so early in the day.

Herr Reuter smokes his fifth cigarette. His hand strays onto Gilgi's knee, and she removes it gently. "I feel so alone, couldn't you be a little bit nice to me, child?" She likes him very much, Gilgi says, and looks at him with the tolerant pity which women feel for men whose attentions are simultaneously annoying and flattering.

As Herr Reuter is about to light his sixth cigarette, Gilgi announces that she has to go. No, she can't stay, not a minute longer. She has her English class at four o'clock. "You're an ambitious girl," Herr Reuter says, disappointedly and admiringly.

Yes, she'll meet him again tomorrow night at the Cathedral Hotel. Gilgi is friendly, pleasant, and accommodating. She has her plan ready. The waiter comes, and Gilgi insists on paying for her own lunch. She gets her way, and says goodbye to Herr Reuter, leaving him with the pleasant feeling of being loved "for himself."

A few minutes later she's on the phone to Olga.

"Hello, marzipan girl, I'd like you to come by, around eleven tonight; I have to work till then."

"Love to, Gilgi," Olga says in her round, friendly voice. "Is something up?"

"Nooo, nothing at all. I'd just like to ask you for a small favor."

"Well, tell me what it is!" Olga is so nosy, Olga always wants to know everything right away.

"It can wait till eleven, Olga. See you."

"See you."

How nice that you've got Olga. Olga is the brightest color in Gilgi's life. And if she didn't have such a distaste for the word "romance," you could say: for Gilgi, Olga represents romance. She's looking forward to Olga's visit. But you're not to think about it beforehand. Your hour of laughter at eleven tonight has to be earned first.

Gilgi sits in the Berlitz School. "Learn Foreign Languages!" Gilgi is learning Spanish, English, French. Three lessons straight. When she finally makes it to her little attic room in Mittelstrasse, her head is buzzing with foreign words. "I want to be happy" … "sous les toits de Paris" … the dry instruction in foreign business correspondence is dissolved by the bright melodies of hit songs. "I want to be happy" ... Gilgi looks longingly at the wide, padded divan. She's a little tired, should she ... just for a half-hour ...? No time. "I want to be happy" ... Gilgi winds up the gramophone. Richard Tauber as a pick-me-up. I kiss your hand, madame ... She takes a samovar from the cupboard and brews tea. Takes off her jumper and skirt, hangs them carefully on the hook on the door, and slips into a yellow silk kimono. This little room is where she feels at home. She rented it so that she could work in peace. She pays for it, and it belongs to her. She had the walls hung with brown hessian. She bought the furniture gradually, piece by piece: divan, desk, cupboard, chair. Bought it all entirely with her own earnings. She did overtime to pay for the little Erika-brand typewriter and the gramophone.

She winds up the gramophone again: For it can't last forever ... Haven't you made something of yourself? You'll make even more of yourself. She sits down at the desk, rests her head with its short brown hair on her hands, and for the time it takes to smoke a cigarette she does nothing at all. Thinks things over a little: so far, she's saved twelve hundred marks. In a year from now, she can go to Paris for three months, to London for three months, and to Granada for three months. Maybe by herself, maybe with Olga. But she's going. She's calculated everything, and decided everything, exactly. If you can speak three foreign languages perfectly, then you're more or less guaranteed against unemployment. And maybe one day she'll give up office work anyway. She has other prospects. Has a talent for designing and making clothes like few others. When the young lady Gilgi goes out in the evening, men's and women's heads turn; and if she said she bought her dresses from Damm or Gerstel, people might believe her, although she's made everything herself. She owns three evening gowns, and none of them cost more than twenty marks. Maybe she'll open a small fashion studio one day in Paris or Berlin, maybe—maybe—oh, she's still young, and she's open to all ways of providing for herself, except as a wife, a film actress, or a beauty queen.

She reaches into the desk drawer and pulls out a pile of manuscript, an exercise book, and a battered novel: Jerome, *Three Men in a Boat*. She's translating it into German, just for practice, at the moment. Maybe later she'll find a way of translating for money. Gilgi writes. Writes, reads, crosses out, writes—until Olga arrives.

Pretty Olga, beautiful Olga! Suddenly, the austere little workroom smells like a summer garden, and Gilgi's hard little face becomes softer and younger. Happy Olga! A well-disposed God attached a champagne cork to her soul. Whatever happens, Olga won't go under. She has the most delightful blond hair, the softest, most radiant blonde's face. She has the most carefree eyes, blue-gray, with cheeky little flecks in the iris. She has the lazy, langorous movements of a harem-girl, and the intellect of a Jewish essayist. She has no ties to anything or anyone, she's the most independent being that Gilgi can imagine. She admires Olga, although she has neither the ability nor the desire ever to be anything like her.

"Do you want tea, marzipan girl? Apples, mandarins, bananas? I've got them all here." How pretty you look, Olga! Gilgi can't bring herself to say the words, and instead scolds: "More dirty marks on your blouse! How disgustingly slovenly you are!" Olga is lying on the divan, playing with some mandarin-peel: "I've really got to get organized now, the Americans are coming to Berlin in the spring."

"Ahh." Gilgi is upset. So in the spring Olga will be in Berlin, and then she'll be traveling, here and there, who knows when she'll come back to Cologne. At the moment she's copying a few paintings in the Wallraf-Richartz Museum for an American family. As well as making loud posters for a cinema in Hohestrasse. Olga paints whatever people want. Whether she's a great artist is something which Gilgi can't judge. Olga herself says No. Perhaps she's right. When she needs money, she works; when she has money, she travels. Often unaccompanied, sometimes accompanied.

"You said you needed a favor, Gilgi?"

"Yes. You have to take a man off my hands."

"Is he a nice man?"

"Good off-the-peg stock—not your type."

"So what am I supposed to do with him?"

"He's my boss, he's in love. If he realizes that I don't like him, it'll make things difficult at the office. You have to divert his attention from me."

"Uh-huh. But if he's in love with you, then he won't let me ..." Gilgi assumes her best woman-of-the-world expression.

"The guy's not in love with me specifically, he's just decided recently to be in love—generally. His attraction to me is arbitrary, a product of his imagination ..."

"We'll change his mind," Olga says, discreetly pushing an apple-core behind the cushions of the divan. "So how shall we do it?" Gilgi outlines her plan briefly, Olga approves—only: "But how will I get rid of him again?"

"Oh, Olga!" Gilgi perches herself on the desk. "You're so much more of a lady than I am—not because you're already twenty-five—because you just are. Men don't push so hard so fast with you as they do with a little girl like me, and anyway, after a couple of weeks you can tell him that you're going on your travels." Olga makes a gesture with her hand to convey that she feels herself more than capable of dealing with a situation like that.

Somewhere in Cologne, Herr Reuter (Hosiery and Lingerie, Wholesale) is lying in the marital bed which his wife has forsaken, suffering from sleeplessness and the desire to be ten years younger. I've got a little brown-haired girl—it's touching to think how the little one is yearning for you . . .

In the attic room in Mittelstrasse Gilgi winds up the gramophone, Olga chooses the record: . . . If you're coming to Hawaii / If the . . . Neither of them finds Herr Reuter interesting enough to warrant another minute's conversation.

On Sunday Gilgi and Herr Reuter are sitting together in the Cathedral Hotel. Gilgi feels that she has eaten, Herr Reuter feels that he has dined. They're drinking Haut-Sauternes. With each glass, Herr Reuter's currant-black eyes narrow by fractions of a millimeter. The shape of Gilgi's little breasts is clearly visible under her blue-gray velvet dress, convincing Herr Reuter that Gilgi is "the" woman who understands him. He tells her this, and he believes it. He lays his emotional life out in front of her like an excited poker player slamming down his cards. That's the way he is. Gilgi acknowledges receipt of this information politely, and with a modicum of interest. You poor fool, if you were younger there'd be no need to waste any time on you. Stop it, enough with the lyricism, it doesn't go with the pimple on your chin. Why can't I just say: don't speculate if you can't accumulate, don't invest emotional capital in a doomed venture. I can't say that. You poor old man, your blend of Business Baroque would be destroyed by a simple No. All right, then! Ultimately all I care about is myself, isn't it? About the hundred-fifty marks which I earn in your office every month, about working without you getting in the way, without having to put up with your cotton-candy emotions—all right, then, sir!

"Your health!"—"Your health!" Clink-clink. Herr Reuter is holding Gilgi's hand, saying they shouldn't talk so much, it's time for them to ... stop talking so much. There are so many people around. Well, if you consider that they all need hosiery and lingerie, then you have to approve of them and like them, but if they weren't sitting here and still needed hosiery and lingerie—you'd like them even better. Waiters are also annoying when they're standing around with nothing to do. "Scusmewaitah [Excuse me, waiter], another bottle!" Gilgi chooses not to hear Herr Reuter's invitation to call him Friedrich; at this rate, it'll be Fritz next.

A lady walks by, scanning all the tables. A beautiful lady, a lustrous lady. "An acquaintance of mine," Gilgi says falteringly, while her left eye is flashing out the message: About time, Olga!

"Good evening, Fräulein Kron."

"Good evening, Fräulein Jahn. May I introduce ..."

"A pleasure," Herr Reuter says, lying.

"Arranged to meet some acquaintances—after the theater—not here yet—so embarrassing—" Olga's eyes express helplessness, her marzipan fingers run softly over the expensive Russian squirrel fur on which she has so far paid three installments. "Yes, if you . . ." Gilgi is visibly at a loss, disappointed, embarrassed. Herr Reuter comes to the rescue: "If you would like to sit with us until . . ." He's a gentleman. Not willingly. "If I may! It'll only be for a moment." Olga looks at Herr Reuter with boundless gratitude. He helps her out of her coat. He's a gentleman. Not unwillingly. He notices that other men envy him when they see Olga sitting down at his table. More supply creates more demand. Herr Reuter decides that Olga is beautiful. But she's in the way nevertheless, because Gilgi's little brown hand has now retreated into the unreachable distance.

Olga tells stories of her travels to Cairo and Luxor and Spitzbergen. Gilgi goes to the telephone cabinet to call home. When she returns, Herr Reuter no longer thinks Olga is in the way.

After a while, Gilgi disappears to the bathroom for a quarter-hour. Herr Reuter remembers that, actually, he prefers blondes. He becomes witty. Olga looks at him admiringly, and Herr Reuter becomes convinced that he has underestimated himself his whole life long. Gilgi comes back, sits there quietly and modestly, and lets Olga outshine her. She's an unremarkable little girl. Herr Reuter recalls some rather rusty principles: not to get romantically involved with one's employees, and so on.

Gilgi goes into the foyer for ten minutes in search of a newspaper. Olga's fresh, rosy blonde's skin shimmers through cream-colored lace, convincing Herr Reuter that Olga is "the" woman who understands him.

A half-hour later he escorts the ladies home: first Gilgi, then Olga.

EARLY IN THE MORNING, A QUARTER-HOUR before the alarm clock is due to ring, Frau Kron comes into Gilgi's room and sits down on the side of her bed. She strokes Gilgi's bare arms and narrow, little-girl's shoulders with her honest, roughened housewife's hands. For a moment Gilgi prefers not to feel surprised by these unexpected caresses, nor to repel them. The familiar closeness of her mother's body, the faint aroma of laundry soap on her hands, give Gilgi a feeling of primitive comfort like a baby animal which is safe in its nest.

"Jilgi, my child, you do love me, don't you?"

"What's going on?" Gilgi sits bolt upright, looking startled and mistrustful.

"You do love me, don't you, Jilgi?"

Gilgi looks at her mother: her puffy cheeks are blazing red, as they do after particularly energetic washing or cake-baking days. Gilgi realizes that the question is only a starting point, heaven knows of what. Odd starting point. Superfluous question. She's never thought about whether she loves her mother. She looks at Frau Kron's broad, fleshy back with compassion.

"Jilgi, you turn twenty-one today."

"I know."

"Well," Frau Kron says, and "Well" again, before falling silent. Her full, pale lips start to tremble.

"Spit it out, Mother." Frau Kron remains silent. Impatiently, Gilgi pushes her long, slender feet out from under the covers—she could at least do her exercises.

"Jilgi!" Frau Kron's voice is shrill and dry. "You see, you're not our child."

Gilgi forgets to breathe.

"What—did—you—just—say?"

"You're not our child."

"I see!" Gilgi doesn't quite understand. Ten minutes later, she does understand. "I see," she says again.

Keep standing firmly on your two feet, make sure you don't waver. If that's all it is. Her face is indifferent, she's reacting on the inside.

"I'll be at the breakfast table in twenty minutes, Mother."

Frau Kron understands that she's supposed to leave. "Don't let it worry you, child."

"No," Gilgi says, bending over to touch her toes. Frau Kron leaves.

Keep standing solidly on your two feet. Up—down. If that's how it is, that's all right with her. She just wonders why this revelation was held back until her twenty-first birthday, specifically. She has no intention of letting something like this disturb her equilibrium. Is she supposed to be devastated? Are powerful displays of emotion expected from her? Is she required to do something in particular? How does one behave in a case like this?

Her mother is a little seamstress. Father unknown. She comes from proletarian stock. She's happy about that, because she's never set any store in belonging to bourgeois society.

Gilgi walks into the plush room. The Washington, the cloth rectangle, Herr Kron reading the newspaper—everything is just as alien to her as it always was. No more, no less. On the table, the usual ring-shaped birthday cake with its nice, regular, wavy top. On the arm of the sofa, Frau Kron's presents: long white kid gloves and a length of dark-blue silk for a dress (all bought together with Gilgi), and, on her own initiative, a bottle of *eau de cologne* and an impossible handbag, which also contains Herr Kron's invariable birthday present of a fifty-mark note.

"Thanks, Father." Gilgi takes Herr Kron's hand. He looks up from his newspaper.

"I hope the next year is a happy one for you, Jilgi, with good health, and—jus' forget what Mother told you before."

"I already have, father."

"Well, tha's all right, then."

"Thanks, Mother." Gilgi kisses Frau Kron on the temple.

"D'you like your presents, child? The silk won't shrink when you make it up. What d'you think of the handbag?"

"Quite beautiful, Mother." Gilgi picks up the handbag. Mother is looking so nervous and expectant, you have to say something more, but what, what, what? "Quite beautiful, really qui . . ." She's expecting something, she was worried, now you have to say something, something loving and kind, but you can't just do that to order, you can't do it precisely because it's expected, your tongue feels as heavy as lead, heavier and heavier . . . "I—I mean—quite beautiful, really . . . I mean, I'm—so happy, Mother—really." Gilgi breathes out and sinks into her chair. How do other people always know exactly the right words to say at the right time?

"Eat, Jilgi, drink, Jilgi." Eat, Gilgi, drink, Gilgi. She forces some birthday cake down, isn't really hungry. Eat, Gilgi, drink, Gilgi! Damned decent of these people. For twenty-one years they've given me accommodation, food, and drink. Got me an education. That man there who's reading the newspaper, and who has no actual responsibility for me, gives me fifty marks every year. Why? That fat woman there, she cried for five nights and couldn't sleep that time I had scarlet fever. Why? Eat, Gilgi, drink, Gilgi. And what about me? How have I paid them? Dammit, I have debts.

"Another piece of cake, Jilgi?"

"No, thanks, Mother." Should I go to a *Kaffeeklatsch* with her some time soon? Pointless waste of time. Should I spend every evening at home now? Pointless waste of time. Being with you two is always a pointless waste of time. Was, is, and ever shall be. Eat, Gilgi, drink, Gilgi. And for sure, if I spill even half a tear now, I'll smash everything up.

Gilgi has gone to see her friend Pit.

"Pit, my birth was a mistake."

"Lots of them are."

"Don't you think children ought to be grateful to their parents?"

"For what?"

"For money and feelings and all kinds of things."

"Gilgi, you know I don't have time for stupid conversations."

Eat, Gilgi, drink, Gilgi. She's perched on the decrepit camp bed, her legs crossed, her chin resting on her hands.

"I'm freezing, Pit."

"Then you'll have to go somewhere where it's warmer." Pit is unfriendly; he usually is. Gilgi doesn't mind.—Poor

guy. He never has any money. He's studying econom-
ics—and he earns his living by tutoring. Now and then he
plays the piano in seedy bars. Sometimes he doesn't have
enough to eat. They've been friends for years. She likes
him, you can rely on him.

Pit is sitting at the table, with books and notepads in
front of him, and a pot of black tea. Gilgi knows he can't
offer her any, because he only possesses one cup. Pit isn't
equipped for visitors.

Gilgi looks around the bare, unadorned room, a shabby
room in the old part of Cologne. She sees Pit's mop of red
hair, his white face with the sharp, angry lines around the
mouth, his small, intelligent eyes. Pit's crazy! Everything
could be so easy for him. His father has the best house
in Marienburg, has money and a famous name. Pit is his
only son—

"Why did you leave home, Pit?"

"What business is that of yours?" He doesn't like being
asked.

"What is it that you want, anyway? If it's help with
your bourgeois problems, I'll throw you out!" Gilgi pulls
the blanket up over her knees, exposing the neatly folded
nightshirt of white cotton with red trimming which lies
under the pillow. "Touching," Gilgi laughs. Red-faced,
Pit gets up and shoves the nightshirt back under the pillow. He gives Gilgi a poisonous look: "Who told you to
make yourself so free with the place?" Steer clear of these
women, he has no use for these women, he can get along
just fine without them, they shouldn't come to him and sit
on his bed. His hands are trembling; he'd like to hit that
girl there. Slowly he goes back to the table, pushing his
hips into the edge. Box her ears, right and left. Box her

ears. Disgusting. I have to keep a clear head, my intellect is weak enough as it is.

"Pit, I meant to ask you something, I might leave home entirely and set up on my own."

"Should've done that ages ago." Why can't she pull her skirt down? There, at the top of her stocking, you can see a strip of white skin. I'm a pig. Box someone's ears.

"Pit, I don't know if it's the right thing to treat the parents ..."

"The right thing!" Snap! Pit has destroyed a pencil, broken it clean in two. "If you want to do the right thing, love your parents, your fatherland, and its dogs! Marry and have children. Every embryo should come under the anti-abortion law. The state wants children, the earth doesn't have enough unemployed people yet." Pit is talking himself into a rage.

"Stop it, Pit, there's no need to be so nasty, I can read the satirical papers in a café if I feel like it." You want to ask the man something, but he's only got all that Socialist stuff in his head. I don't understand politics, it doesn't make sense to me. Gilgi runs all ten fingers through her hair. There's no talking to Pit today. She wanted to tell him her ridiculous story. For the last week, she's choked on every mouthful she's eaten at home. It can't go on like that, something has to be done. If they had brought her into the world, all right, then they could look after you, too, for as long as you can't look after yourself. But now! Yes, if you loved them and belonged to them, then you'd just pay them back with feelings. But to take, take, take—without being able to give anything—dammit, you feel like such a heel! And what if you left home now? That would hurt them so much, a fine way of thanking them! So you thought that Pit might know what to do, he sometimes hits upon the word that illuminates everything like a hundred-watt globe, but—no point at all, you'll have to help yourself, Gilgi!—she won't tell Pit her story.

Since when has she been so eager to talk about herself, anyway? A bad sign! Perhaps the ground is already starting to tremble under her feet? Rubbish, she's still standing firm.

Pit is decorating a sheet of paper with angular doodles. He's angry that he's said so much. If the girl would just leave! She's just sitting there, running her hand over her knee. She's wearing silk stockings and smelling of flowers and *eau de cologne*. "Are you planning to stay much longer?" Gilgi glances up. Why is he looking at her like that? Silly boy, what's wrong? She gets up and stands next to him. "You're crazy, you are." Her hand strokes his coarse, rust-red hair. She's the right sort of girl, a good comrade, she doesn't take it the wrong way when you're abrupt with her. Pit keeps quite still while Gilgi's hand strokes his hair, his face—her hand smells of violets—"Silly Pit, work alone isn't enough. Intellect is all very well, but there are all kinds of other things about people which are important, too, the road you're on might lead you right away from a full life." She'd like to say even more, but that's not so easy. Oh well, he'll have understood all right what she means. Find a nice girl who likes you, it doesn't have to be for all eternity.

"Ow, let go of my hand, Pit, you're hurting me."

"Go now, Gilgi."

"See you, Pit."

Gilgi stands in the street below, rubbing her wrist. What a grip that boy has! What a struggle he's making of his life! And she wanted to ask him for advice! He could do with some advice on his own account. Every man for himself, and God for all of us. Gilgi takes a little notebook from her handbag: Fräulein Margarethe Täschler, Thieboldstrasse. That's where you're going now. After all, you'll be interested to see the being who brought you into the world. Wasn't at all easy to get the name out of them at home; she found out the address herself.

You can feel the pre-Lenten carnival in the air ... How did you, pigeon, pigeon, pigeon / Get into our kitchen ... this year's hits by Willi Ostermann blare forth from a window somewhere. Gilgi walks along Cathedral Street, past Central Station—Saturday night—they're dawdling and teeming, rushing and chasing, she crosses Cathedral Square, has to hold on to her hat to stop it being blown away. Thank God, now she's outside the Savoy Hotel, it's less windy here. She smooths her trench coat and her hair, adjusts her little beret so that it sits properly again. Turns into Hohestrasse—people, people—they push their way along the narrow sidewalks, you can only make your way slowly. Obey the road rules! Walk on the right! You get quite jumpy when you're used to taking long, brisk strides. A few morose hookers are standing in a side passage, they look well-behaved, earnest and annoyed, if they weren't wearing make-up and using belladonna you could take them for unemployed telephone operators. Gilgi walks through Schilderstrasse. "Flowers—Flowers!" A little girl is standing at the corner, half-frozen. "Gimme a bunch." Yellow mimosa, who should she give them to? She'll take them to her mother, she might be pleased.

In Thieboldstrasse it's dirty and dark. It takes Gilgi a while to find the number on the right building. The lobby stinks of rotten fish and yesterday's laundry. Gilgi climbs

one staircase, another, the building is alive: somewhere a
woman is screeching, a child is crying, a man is cursing.
There's a *Cologne Advertiser* lying on a doormat: … And
we'll still hold the time-honored official stag party, even
if the whole Carnival disappears up its own … The spoil-
sports are just bashing their heads against Cologne's sense
of fun and tradition … Oh, the golden Rhineland humor!
"The asshole's boozed away all his unemploymen' money
again," a woman yells. The building is alive, the building
is breathing. Gilgi's legs feel heavy. Why did she come
here, what does she want here? Phew, she can't breathe.
No turning back. She sees a greasy little notice: Fräulein
Margarethe Täschler, ladies' dressmaker, ring twice. Gilgi
rings. She hears a drag—drag—drag getting closer—what
a stink there is in this building, I feel sick—tap—tap—
tap—I've still got time to …

"Who's there?" Why don't they open up?

"Is someone there?"

"Yes."

"Who?"

"Me."

"Who you wanna see?"

"Fräulein Täschler."

A safety chain rattles, the door opens: "Come in, Frollein, you gotta be real careful here, 'cos of the burglars. Jus'
the day before yesterday they attacked the poor woman
nex' door, people're so bad now'days, come on in, Frollein."
Is this her, is this her, is this her? Gilgi clutches the bunch
of mimosa to her chest. She doesn't feel like letting her
heart beat wildly, she doesn't feel like getting excited. It's a
room with a grubby bed, a gas stove opposite, with a few
cold fried potatoes sticking to a pan. Next to the window

there's a black tailor's dummy, a lady without internal organs. "That's how we live, that's how we live / That's how we live every day ..."

"Take a seat, Frollein." The woman sweeps a few dirty underthings from the chair. A classy girl! If she's come here for a dress—why else would she come here?

Fräulein Margarethe Täschler, ladies' dressmaker, ring twice—you have to look at her, Gilgi—you've come here to look at her. Take your eyes off the lady without internal organs, the old girl is standing in the corner chirping at the stove, behind which a mangy cat is lying. Misss, misss, misss—and she beckons with a horribly crooked finger, like the witch in "Hansel and Gretel." Misss, misss, misss— does the Frollein want to have a dress made? Misss, misss, misss. Everyone likes to make a good impression, now and then. One slips on a silk dressing gown, while the other entices a cat out of its hiding place. Misss, misss, misss— this is her, this is her. Gilgi holds fast to the bunch of mimosa and starts talking: yes, she heard about Fräulein Täschler, Fräulein Täschler was recommended to her, now she wants Fräulein Täschler to sew something for her, a dress with a little jacket, and she has brought the material along with her.

This is her. She's skinny and dried-up, and she has no face at all, she's lost it. She's got a bathing cap, a light-colored bathing cap on her head, with yellow-gray strands of hair protruding from it over her forehead. "I got the cap on 'cos of my headaches, I got a cold compress underneath." And Gilgi recommends aspirin and examines the fashion magazines that the witch-like fingers spread out in front of her. It's impossible to look up, it's impossible to look at a woman who has no face! Pan with fried potatoes stuck on, lady without internal organs, grubby bed, stink compounded of rancid margarine, damp walls, and rotten floorboards. *Elegant World*, Special Beauty Issue: the beautiful grandmother writes to her granddaughter: Carnival, oh, in my day it was still such fun and so delightful, the men always crowded around me even at masked balls, because they could still see my beautiful complexion (using Pfeilring's products was the secret) … Miss Germany 1931 … "you coulda won the title just as well, Frollein!" And the head with the bathing cap laughs, but the laughter isn't genuine, it's a lie. And the head bends down, and now it's right next to Gilgi's … I can't stand the smell anymore, I have to light a cigarette.

The light's bad, you can't see anything properly, how can she sew here! The non-face has red eyes, those aren't eyes, they're inflamed lids, and they hurt. The beautiful grandmother writes to her granddaughter … You, you, you—why do you put up with it? Why are you living here, why is this your life? If you're satisfied, someone should strangle you!

A gramophone is playing next door: Drink, drink, brother mine, drink … Why are you satisfied?—Leave all your troubles at home … Why? Drink, drink …

Accepted it, accepted it—I don't know anything different—I only know the song about the gray-lit hours—Is there anything that's worth the effort?

Gilgi offers Fräulein Täschler a cigarette. Unexpectedly, she takes it, leans against the bedpost, puffs away like a woman of the world, has a bathing cap on because of her headaches, has a wrinkled, dried-up body and no face. A crucifix hangs above the bed.

Gilgi's measurements are taken. Bust, waist, height.

When the wrinkled fingers fumble at her waist and the noxious breath wafts into her face, she becomes as gray and pale as the greasy hand-towel beside the washstand.

She could leave, but she doesn't want to. She starts a conversation with Fräulein Täschler. Fräulein Täschler is pleased to have someone to talk to. And she'll do well out of it, she'll charge twenty marks for the dress. Why shouldn't she be lucky for once and get some classy clients, some good payers? She'll decorate the seam on the jacket, that always looks nice. Before, the Frollein told her not to—but that doesn't matter. For her, decorative seams are a kind of article of faith, she won't give them up so easily.... Scorn all your worries and scorn all your woes / Your life will become ... I can't stand it here anymore—"Fräulein Täschler, wouldn't you like to have dinner with me in the bar on the corner? We're having such a nice chat, and I don't feel like going home yet."

Surely that will make her think. Something's going on, something's not right! But of course she'll accept, only— she takes care to speak elegantly: "Yerse, but someone like me can't afford to dine out in the evening."

"You'll be my guest, Fräulein Täschler." That's what she wanted to hear. She snatches the bathing cap and the compress from her head in one go. She fusses around for a good ten minutes, making pointless attempts to improve her appearance. She pushes what's left of a black comb through the remnants of her yellow-gray hair, she changes the brown blouse for a green one, and now she looks just as pitiful as before—as far as Gilgi's concerned. She herself considers it a marked change for the better when she looks in the battered mirror above the chest of drawers, and that's the main thing, after all. And because she's curious now, expecting something, she gradually develops something which looks like a face. A gray face with a chunky nose, inflamed eyelids, a narrow-lipped mouth, and awful teeth. The beautiful grandmother writes to her granddaughter ... To end up with a face like that! Why did you let such a thing happen to you? With a face like that, people can't love you, no matter how hard they try, it's impossible. They can sob, scream, laugh, sob—and what about my father! What could he possibly look like? And Gilgi feels her face becoming paler and her eyes retreating deep into their sockets.

I'll start to feel better now, she thinks, as Fräulein Täschler closes the door from the outside. The stink and the close air, they were what I couldn't stand. When they reach the street, she breathes in deeply. That doesn't help. She coughs, twice—there's something in her chest she can't shift. And there are vapors before her eyes, she can't see properly, maybe she's asleep, and it's all just a bad dream.

Then they're sitting in the bar on the corner. Fräulein Täschler has a small light ale and an open sandwich on the table in front of her. She's eating like a very elegant lady, with a knife and fork. Gilgi is drinking a double shot. Eating is impossible, she can't stop thinking about the cold, sticky remainder of the fried potatoes in the room up there, and she can't stop feeling that a chunk of those fried potatoes is in her mouth. Another shot! She downs it in one gulp. She shudders, but she still wants to retch. She has the sensation of having become completely removed from herself. There you are, on first-name terms with reality, and suddenly it's a stranger to you and you don't know how to approach it ... but that doesn't suit us, that doesn't suit us at all.

Gilgi drinks another shot, and another. She has absolutely no cause to shudder now, the stuff is going down
like water. Usually she's not interested in alcohol, or even
avoids it, but now she's pleasantly surprised that, just by
spending four lots of fifteen pfennigs, you can conjure up
such a nice bright red to replace the crappy black before
your eyes. Good for you! Right, now she'll just get to the
bottom of this, of how everything was and how it developed. What's there to be afraid of? She's holding her life
firmly in her hands, and it'll take a lot more than this business to make her lose her grip. And we'll put a stop to all
the soppy emotionalism we've been indulging in recently
while we're at it.

"Wow, Frollein, when I see you tossing 'em down like
that, I feel quite drunk myself. An' such rough liquor too!"
Fräulein Täschler orders herself a cherry brandy, and everything about her is so elegant that the Minister of Culture or President Hindenburg or Frau von Kardorff and
her political salon ... there's no point of comparison, because Germany simply hasn't seen such fearful elegance
since it abolished the monarchy in 1918.

"Didn't you have a child once?" Gilgi asks.

She's drunk five shots now, and they've removed any
desire for a roundabout approach. And I can tell you
straightaway that the tearful reunion scene between
mother and child, with or without embraces, is off.

Fräulein Täschler has had a face for the last half-hour,
and now she has eyes, too, tiny, glittering little points.
"What d'you mean, Frollein?"

Gilgi shrugs her shoulders. Answering a question with
a question, that's just what she wants to hear. "Well, you
had a child once, didn't you?"

"I?? Had a child?? You're quite mistaken." There are hostile lines around Fräulein Täschler's nose and mouth.

"Maybe you forgot," Gilgi suggests helpfully.

"I got a very good memory, Frollein, an' when you've always been a decent woman, it's easy to remember."

"Well, why not drink another cherry brandy, Fräulein Täschler!"

And now the words gush out of her like a waterfall, and she tosses the cherry brandy down as she goes, and overall she becomes just a tiny bit less elegant than Frau von Kardorff.

"I mean, Frollein, if you say standards're bad now'days, well, what I say is, there've always been all kinds, and our sort've always kept themselves decent, but the high-class people, well, I could tell you an in-ter-est-ing story if I wanted to." She pauses, and sighs: "Yerse, one is much too decen'!" The sigh unmistakably expresses regret.

Gilgi drinks another shot and decides that this can't go on. Is she supposed to sit here all night with Fräulein Ladies' Dressmaker Ring Twice, discussing problems of ethics? "Go on, drink another cherry brandy, Fräulein Täschler!" This business of looking for your mother runs into money! But now she wants to straighten it out, now she goes for broke.

"I thought you had a child, because I know a girl, she was adopted by a family—what's their name again? Kron—and she's twenty-one now . . ."

Whereupon Täschler leaps up, screeching, and a plate falls to the floor. So she's on the right track after all! It's only now that Gilgi notices how hard she's been hoping that the whole thing was a mistake, or a misunderstanding, or something—but whatever it was, not true.

"You're the child!" Täschler shouts as understanding dawns, and she subsides back onto her chair. Gilgi tries to work out if that was the voice of their common blood that just spoke. For the voice of their common blood to speak now would be in accordance with the rules. My blood is deaf and dumb, I should make an appointment with the doctor, or maybe I've just had too much to drink.

"Nah, nah, nah, I knew right away there was somethin' wrong about you. So you're the child!"

In Gilgi's head a fan is whirring, her hands are lying limply and tiredly in her lap. "So why did you say at first that you didn't have a child, it doesn't matter, it's not im-moral." That makes Täschler laugh, a shrill, tinny sound, with her head wobbling from one side to the other, it's em-barrassing to hear her, and even more embarrassing to watch her. And she laughs and giggles and sways back and forth on her chair. "Well, Frollein, we should have another little drink on the stren'th of it." Her laughter ends in a dry cough, saliva shines on her chin, her chunky nose is dot-ted with blackheads like a peewit's egg. Why did you turn into that! Whose fault is it, whose? Yours, no doubt about it, but not yours alone. Gilgi sees jagged red letters in a gray fog: What are you doing with your life? She doesn't move, she doesn't speak—what is there left to say?—she's not waiting for anything. She's an exclamation mark at the end of some red letters: What are you letting happen to your life!

Täschler tells her story. Her arms are spread out across the table. Gilgi listens.

"It's twenny-one years ago now, when I was sewin' in high-class homes. Always makin' old clothes into new ones, which a more expensive dressmaker wouldn't've

done. An' I can tell you, Frollein, I was a good-lookin'
girl. So I was workin' in this house, a mother an' daughter,
name of Kreil. Frollein, gimme your hand!" Gilgi gives it
to her. "Swear to me, Frollein, that you'll never tell anyone
else what I'm goin' to tell you."

"I swear to you," Gilgi says.

"Maybe we'll both make somethin' from it yet!" Täschler
has glittering little dots of eyes. "Right, the Kreils, it was
jus' the mother an' daughter, the old guy was dead. They
had tons of money, tons, I'm tellin' you! An' the daughter
was a nice girl, an' when she was about twenny, she got
involved with a guy, he was nothin' an' had nothin', an' the
old girl was against him, 'cos she wanted the daughter to
marry someone with a title, Count or Doctor or somethin'
like that. Anyway, the guy disappeared after a while, an'
everythin' would've been alright, but suddenly it turns out
that she's five months gone. You should've seen the old girl,
the way she kept her chin up an' got to work. Then one fine
day she came to me—I was livin' all by myself in a room
in Weyerstrasse. I didn' have any relatives, an' she knew
that, an' it suited her jus' fine. So she said that there was
this problem with her daughter, an' it had to be fixed, her
future'd be ruined if anyone found out, an' it wouldn' matter so much with me, the men of our class didn' care if a girl
had a child. An' she'd manage things so that afterwards the
child'd be mine, an' I was to get ten thousand marks. Think
of that—ten thousand marks, Frollein! An' she'd arrange
everythin'. Well, I'd've done lots of things for a hundred
marks, though not everythin', not by a long way, but for ten
thousand marks! When I heard that, I couldn' believe my
ears. An' then the old girl arranged everythin'. She rented
an apartment in Bayenthal, in a really out-of-the-way part,

an' the Frollein an' I lived there for the last three months.
An' the Frollein had to stay indoors all the time, she was
never ever allowed to go outside. I could go out sometimes, but then the old girl made me stuff a sofa cushion
up the front of my dress, so that the people in the place'd
all think I was havin' a little visitor soon. The old girl'd
thought of everythin'. An' the Frollein, she said nothin' at
all, she was jus' lyin' real quiet on the cheese lounge and
not sayin' Boo, it's like she was stunned, she jus' did whatever the old girl wanted. An' when the time came, there
was jus' a doctor there an' the old girl, no-one else. An' the
doctor, he probably knew there was somethin' fishy, but of
course he would've got money, too, and once he took that
he had to button his lip forever, 'cos he could've got into
real bad trouble himself. An' it all went well, and the Frollein spent the next week in bed, an' I had to stay in bed too
jus' in case. An' the kid was with me, such a sickly thing,
fed with the bottle. The Frollein was never ever allowed to
see the kid, an' the old girl wanted me to get used to it. It
was such a sickly thing, we thought it'd die, that would've
been best, 'cos then I would've had the ten thousand marks
all to myself an' not had to spend it looking after the kid.
An' after a week, well, they took the Frollein home to her
villa in Lindenthal, an' I took a room in a nice suburb, an'
moved in with the kid. But they didn' want me, because
of the kid, so I came here to Thieboldstrasse. An' the old
girl said that if anyone found out I could go to jail, so I
should jus' keep my mouth shut, an' not confess it to the
priest, either. An' then I went back to my customers an'
told everyone that I'd had a baby, that's why I'd been away
for three months, an' lots of them didn' want anythin' to
do with me anymore. An' then I went to Frau Kron, too, to
see if she had any work for me again. She'd just had a baby,

an' it was dead, an' Herr Kron was there an' was very unhappy, 'cos his wife'd wanted a baby so much, an' after this
difficult birth she could never have another one. An' then
we spoke about me an' my baby, an' Herr Kron pricked up
his ears, an' asked what I wanted with a child, 'cos it'd only
be a burden to me, an' he was quite right, an' then they
adopted the baby, an' it hadn' been baptized yet, either, I
mean it was only two weeks old, an' I hadn' sorted much
out yet. An' they organized all that, an' from one day to
the next the kid was gone. An' suddenly I had a whole lot
of money, which I never would've got by being legit. So I
went back to the good suburb an' had a good time, an' I got
engaged, too, but nothin' came of it. He drank like a fish,
an' when he'd got a thousand marks out of me, bit by bit,
then I thought, that's not love, an' broke it off. An' when
I only had five thousand or so left, then I came back to
Thieboldstrasse an' did dressmakin' again an' thought, you
can save that money for your old age. But it all disappeared
in the hipper—the hyperinflation, an' I was as poor as before. Then I remembered the old girl, Frau Kreil, an' asked
around, but she's been dead for ages, an' the Frollein got
married, just a year after the baby, to a very rich man, an'
they have a classy apartment in Kaiser Wilhelm Crescent.
An' that's your mother, Frollein—Magdalene Greif is her
name now. An' if you go to see her sometime, make sure
the husband doesn' see you, an' maybe she'll give you some
money, an' then you should think of me, 'cos I told you
everythin' about it, an' because I'm jus' a poor old woman
now, but don' say anythin' to her about me . . ." Gilgi is
rushing through the streets, she has to get to Pit, to tell
him what's happening, to talk to him. Couldn't Täschler
be helped a little? She's a pitiable creature, no doubt—and
probably there's not much more that can be done for her.

Gilgi crosses the New Market with long strides. The great clock is showing eleven, Pit won't be at home anymore, he'll be playing piano in a thirteenth-rate bar in one of those little streets near the Rhine by now. You can go there and wait till he's finished.

Gilgi has reached the Haymarket, with the Rhine in front of her. She swings right into the side-streets. Swell area. Little alley-ways, narrow, precarious houses. Now she's at the Old Market, with a magical little piece of the Middle Ages in front of her, but Gilgi has no particular love for the Middle Ages, today or any other day. She turns into an alley-way which leads down to the Rhine. Lintstrasse. This must be where Pit's playing. She hardly knows this area. The alley-way narrows as it approaches the Rhine. If you stretched your arms out, you could touch the houses on both sides with your fingertips. A police-man is patrolling somewhere, a woman with peroxided hair is waving from a window, some youths are strolling up and down, clearly feeling at home. Gilgi runs to the end of the alley-way, confused, she must have missed the bar— Breakfast Room—that can't be it. She turns around. Moves faster when a youth calls out something obscene to her. There it is—Wine Bar! She pushes the door open. Thank God—Pit's red mop of hair is the first thing she sees.

The marabou-bird said / The wise old marabou ... she taps him on the shoulder with her index finger: "I'd like to talk to you, I'll wait till you've finished." Pit's face be-trays neither surprise nor pleasure ... My dear girl, when you kiss / He does not need to look at ... "might be two o'clock," he grunts, without taking his fingers from the keys for so much as a second ... The marabou-bird said / The ... Gilgi sits down at a corner table.

What a depressing joint! Red-and-white paper streamers are hanging down from the ceiling, a few lanterns with
red paper shades are swaying back and forth over the piano. A fat bald man is stretched out at the bar, two traveling salesmen are sitting in the corner opposite to Gilgi,
one with a girl on his lap ... The marabou-bird ... Both
the traveling salesmen are shouting with laughter, probably because that's part of the experience, and because tomorrow they'll want to tell themselves and everyone else
what a great time they had. Two battered sample-cases are
lying neglected beneath the table.

A girl comes out from behind the bar, and asks Gilgi
more or less pleasantly what she'd like. "Cup of coffee."
They don't serve it. The cheapest thing she can order is
port wine. Fine, port wine. It's terrible how much money
she's spending today! She starts to feel uneasy, what's she
supposed to do here while she's waiting? Three more
hours! She digs some sandwiches out of her bag and starts
to eat, less from hunger than from boredom. Pit's playing the Song of the Pigeon ... How did you, pigeon, pigeon, pigeon ... the two traveling salesmen are singing
along, the waitress is singing too. One of the lanterns ex-
pires from enthusiasm, a breath of hometown pride wafts
through the room.

You should be in your loft / Our kitchen's not for you:
Get lost! / Take off! Take off! Take off! ... Gilgi is writing in
a little notebook. Income—Expenditures. You have to be
orderly. Especially in financial matters. "Like a sweet little
shopkeeper!" Olga says on those occasions when Gilgi
ponders for a half-hour about a fifty-pfennig purchase she
can't remember. Olga never has a clue what she's spent her
money on. She has no system, and no ability to organize

one. Whenever Gilgi thinks of Olga's finances, she feels faint. And whenever she hears Olga talking about money, she feels downright seasick. Income—Expenditures.

Maria, Maria, listen—do!
That Engelbert's not the man for you . . .

Bang! The door is thrown open, a multi-colored being sweeps in, alights next to Gilgi's table: "You don' mind, do you, Frollein?" and calls over to the bar: "Gimme a schnapps and five Ova cigarettes!"

The multi-colored being looks depressed. Gilgi offers it a cigarette. She packs her notebook away in her bag, chews on her sandwich and looks over the bright little hooker. Who sighs: "Nothin' happenin'," and Gilgi doesn't quite know if that means in general, or only in the bar.

"How did you end up here?" Gilgi doesn't answer. The hooker is wearing a coral necklace, her knitted jacket is mended neatly at the elbows—could she have done it herself?—she's put lots of polish on her broad, grubby fingernails, and she has no face, just as Fräulein Täschler had no face.

Maria, Maria, listen—do . . . What are these people to me, Gilgi thinks. Everyone is in the place where they belong. If their lives end up in the crapper, it's their own fault. "God, I almos' forgot again," the hooker laughs, "I was goin' to put my elbow on the table again, but that always ruins the mend in my jacket." She places her arms carefully on the table, like a well-behaved child in Sunday School. " 'S cold outside," she says.

Gilgi nods. "D'you want a sandwich?" she asks, friendly but uncertain, and points to the packet in front of her.

"God, if you've got enough of 'em." The hooker takes one, and Gilgi puts the next one in front of her, too, the hooker touched it with her finger, and Gilgi can't bear that. A girl as pretty as you / Deserves a real Prince Charm-ing too ...

The hooker chews, which she can only do on the left side, she has a big hole in a molar on her right. "Haven' been able to get it done yet, yeah, it's a lousy job I've got."

"So why'd you choose it?" Gilgi asks.

"I didn' actually choose it."

"So find a better one now." Gilgi feels vaguely that a girl who mends her knitted jacket neatly doesn't have to earn her living on the street. The hooker shrugs her shoulders: "God, I'm in it now, what'm I supposed to do?" Gilgi can't find an answer to that. Just don't stick your nose so high in the air, just don't always think it's so completely your own doing if you're something better. Say the Krons hadn't adopted her, say she'd been brought up by Täschler, back there in Thieboldstrasse, say she—better not to think about it at all — — —

" 'Lo, Gilgi." Pit gives her his hand and sits down at the table, clapping the hooker on the shoulder: "Well, how're things, little Lena?"

"How d'you think they are? They're crap." Lena gets up. "S'long, Pit—s'long, Frollein—gotta go."

"Pit," Gilgi begins after a pause, "Pit, you never told me what kind of man your father is, and what's your mother like, and—Pit, I'd like to tell you about — — —"

Pit jumps down her throat. "Why are you butting in on me here, what do you want? Since when have you been interested in conducting psychological studies?"

"Don't talk such garbage, Pit!" Gilgi looks pale and

tired: "You've got so angry recently, Pit." That's politics for
you, she thinks, it makes people so unpleasant, really nasty.

"Yes, I know, Gilgi." For a moment, Pit looks like a woe-
begone schoolboy. "Oh, you can't find me anything like
as disgusting as I find myself. I'm so full of bitterness and
hate, all I can see is injustice and prejudice." And then he
starts with his Socialism again, and all the things that have
to be changed, and Gilgi sits there on the lookout for a moment when she can interrupt him and tell him about the
things which are more important to her, and have more
to do with her, just now. All right, private capital can be
abolished for all she cares—and the anti-abortion law—
it should have been repealed ages ago, of course, though
maybe she owes her life to it—and the whole economic
system, yes—. Why do people who talk about politics
always have to make it so utterly complicated and confusing—and the revolution after the war was messed up—
"oh, Pit, I can't go on anymore!"

"What, you—you just go your way without caring,
without getting involved, Gilgi, did you actually read those
books about political economy which I gave you?"

"I don't understand them, Pit. I'm not terribly clever,
and when I start thinking about that stuff I lose my foot-
ing, I need whatever brains I've got for myself and my
career—"

"Your self-importance is disgusting!"

"Well, for crying out loud, who should I find important if not myself! I just don't believe, I think it's a damn
lie when someone says that he thinks of the community
first and himself second. Who is the community, anyway?
It has no face, it's not a human being you can love, and
therefore want to help. Shut up, Pit, I'm talking! You're so

terribly vain, you guys, you think that you're something special and that you're doing something special. You always see yourselves as heroes, and believe that the world couldn't run properly without you. And to be heroic, you need something which challenges you, which you can fight against, and if it doesn't exist you just invent it—"

"You can keep that lecture for those Nazi people." Pit stands up. "I'm sorry for you, Gilgi, if you can't understand that we won't find any peace until—what's the point of trying to explain it to you, you superficial little thing, you." Pit sits down at the piano again—Maria, Maria, listen—do . . .

That's Pit for you! Is it some kind of crime if you want to go your way quietly and decently and keeping well away from politics? And what exactly is there to stop him finding any peace? Maybe Pit's right after all—about this and that. Maybe you should—oh, it's better not to think about it, you don't know where it would lead if once you started. Gilgi rests her head on her hands. Red letters: What are you letting happen to your life? . . . Two by the Rhine / Two side by side / Your hand in mine . . . One of the traveling salesmen has fallen asleep, he's snoring, his head is wobbling, the red lanterns are wobbling, the piano is wobbling, the bust of Dante on it is wobbling. Dante in a dive like this! How did you, pigeon . . . With the tip of her tongue, Gilgi licks up a tear which has rolled down her face at the speed of a slow-motion film. She's surprised at herself for not being surprised at herself, and she'd think about that if it wasn't too complicated for her. Why is Pit so horrible to me? He's my best friend, after all! She still hasn't told him her story yet, but now she doesn't want to. The whole atmosphere here, the semi-darkness—she can't stand it anymore.

Gilgi pays for the port. Without giving Pit another glance, she walks past him to the door. Onto the street. She's going home. Home?

Anyway, Gilgi has other things to do besides looking for her parents. She decides not to worry about the matter for the moment. No doubt she'll find an opportunity to make the acquaintance of the Greif family sooner or later.

Gilgi is as gentle as a turtle-dove with the Krons. She's postponed her decision to leave home until after Carnival, and she's resolved to be as nice and pleasant as anyone possibly could be while she's still there. She takes her mother to the movies and the *Konditorei*. Doesn't complain when a film is sickeningly sentimental, and watches fearfully but silently as the massively overweight Frau Kron heedlessly devours whole mountain ranges of cream slices, chocolate cupcakes, and fruit tartlets.

They're expecting a visit from Frau Kron's sister and her two daughters from Hamburg. Their relatives want to experience Carnival in Cologne—and of course they haven't seen each other for ages. The three ladies from Hamburg will stay with the Krons. The house is bursting with excitement. A bed and a divan are moved into Gilgi's room—for her two cousins. Everything is turned upside down. An orgy of cleaning begins: "Hetty is so finicky," and Frau Kron wants to do honor to her household. When Gilgi gets home after work, she races through the rooms with the vacuum cleaner, hangs new curtains at the windows, waxes the parquet floor in the parlor. And she loves doing all of it. She has a heartfelt desire to make herself useful. But then she has to accompany her mother to the

station, to fetch the relatives, and she doesn't think that's
so useful.

Aunt Hetty and Young Gerda and Young Irene tumble
onto the platform with clamor and screeching and "No!"
and "Wow!" and a frenzy of embraces. Grown up so much!
And the children! Yes, who would've thought it—after
such a long time—and you're looking so good, Hetty!—
But not as good as you, Berta! When Aunt Hetty gives her
a juicy kiss, Gilgi feels like a cat which has been rubbed up
the wrong way. She'd very much like to wipe her mouth,
because it feels so wet above her top lip, but they're always
watching her.

"No, we can take the streetcar, Hetty." Frau Kron is a little overcome by it all, but she's still thinking economically.

"Of course, we've always wanted to see the Rhine—but
the War! And then the Occupation! You poor dears, how
you must have suffered." Aunt Hetty whispers, and looks
fearfully all around. Of course, the English troops have left,
but she's still not quite sure—you can never know . . . Frau
Kron's eyes express pain: "Yes, they were difficult times for
us, Hetty." Frau Kron enjoys being commiserated with.

Then they stop outside the cathedral. "Wow, isn't it
big!" Young Gerda is full of admiration. "You don't miss
much, do you, Gerda dear?" Gilgi says amiably. No, Young
Gerda and Young Irene don't have jobs, they help at home
a little—and they'll probably get married soon. Aunt Hetty
isn't in favor of the new ideas, though she picks out the
ones which suit her: for example, Young Gerda is twenty-
six and Young Irene is thirty, and before the war that
would have been old for an unmarried woman, but it's
not anymore.

Gilgi sits at home with her delightful relatives for the

whole evening. Young Irene and Young Gerda show off their Carnival costumes. Young Gerda skips around the room in her pixie costume—her legs are rather thick, but on the other hand she's quite small up top—and Young Irene wriggles cheekily on the arm of the green plush sofa, admiring her cute Pierrot outfit. While the girls aren't as beautiful as Aunt Hetty says, they're not quite as washed-out and unattractive as Frau Kron privately believes.

It's really time to go to bed, but they want to stay up until Herr Kron comes home. Aunt Hetty is lying on the sofa. She's been exhausted by the journey, her feet have swollen up—"quite takes it out of you, a train trip like that." Frau Kron is tired too. Young Gerda and Young Irene are still hopping around rather listlessly in their costumes. Gilgi borrowed a travel book from the library that morning—she'd like to read, but that would be considered impolite. Everyone is getting on everyone else's nerves a little, everyone would like to do something other than what she's doing just now. But everyone keeps smiling, preserving the impression that they have lots and lots in common.

Gilgi is kept awake half the night. Her cousins are overcome by the need to talk which usually arises when young women are lying in bed. Gilgi is on the chaise longue. There's a bed on her right—and a bed on her left. Young Gerda is lying on her right—and Young Irene on her left. The two silly cows fill the space above her with their mooing—chatter about dancing and men and maybe-they'll-get-engagedments. Whenever Young Irene mentions a certain Arthur, Young Gerda squeaks like a frog that's in the middle of being run over. Gilgi is vouchsafed confused explanations: well, Arthur is—and Arthur was—and Arthur will—"no, no, no, Renie, don't tell!" Gilgi tosses from one side to the other. Holds her nose: before Young Gerda went to bed, she made liberal applications of an anti-freckle ointment which is now polluting the whole room with its stink.

In the morning, Gilgi staggers out of her temporary bed, tired to death. Frau Kron had tapped on the door. Gilgi had turned off her alarm, because of course Young Gerda and Young Irene aren't to be woken. They're to have a nice long sleep in. Gilgi does her exercises. Now and then she casts baleful glances on the two sleeping beauties, with their knotted straw-blond hair, pasty faces, and slightly oily noses. Layabouts! An incitement to class hatred! These people who don't work, ambling so idiotically, frivolously, dozily through their lives—Gilgi can't stand them.

When she arrives at the office she feels good, and happy. She didn't ride on the streetcar, but walked, which takes just under an hour. Her clothes smell of the fresh air, and her face, which is usually pale brown, has a touch of red.

She's the first. She's come ten minutes too early. Oh, she's often there too early, and never a minute too late. She takes her steno pad out of the drawer almost lovingly. Slips the cloth cover off her typewriter, cleans the typeface of each key, and puts in a new ribbon. A new ribbon always gives her a little lift.

Fat Müller arrives, followed closely by little Behrend. "Morn."—"Morn." They sit next to Gilgi. They're both nice girls—a bit cheeky and careless, but not nasty.

Fat Müller puts a pile of sandwiches, a vacuum flask with coffee, and a cup without a handle on the table in front of her. Little Behrend is talking about last night.

"So then he says to me …" she whispers to Müller, which doesn't bother Gilgi a bit, the two are great friends, and anyway Behrend's experiences aren't of the kind to be confided to people who are just colleagues. Sometimes you might think that Behrend only has adventures the night before so that she can tell Müller about them the morning after. Müller is too fat and too passive to have adventures herself, she's satisfied just to hear about them—as though Behrend lives for her too. Crazy kid. Cute, with her curly black hair and her round brown eyes—a face like a squirrel. And she's always on the move, always has something going on, always has the latest hit song in her head and in her blood. Now she's sitting on the desk, dangling her pretty, cheeky legs: "… and then when the band plays—really sweet and schmaltzy—and I'm with a good-looking guy—well, I don't know what a girl's supposed to do, so that nothing happens afterwards …" She looks enquiringly at Gilgi. "You just can't say No," fat Mueller says triumphantly. Little Behrend makes a sour face, then she laughs: "No, I can't." She pirouettes over to Accounts and steals a few indelible pencils … For it can't last for-ehever … "just think, one day you're fifty and men don't want to kiss you anymore!" She tugs at her blouse—a gift from some guy. Why shouldn't some guy give her a blouse? That's not the sign of a bad girl, not by a long way. She can't buy anything for herself, has to give all her salary to her mother. Gilgi admires the blouse. It's very elegant—with hand-stitched embroidery—and doesn't go at all with the threadbare little skirt and the worn-out cheap shoes. Gilgi likes tarty little Behrend a thousand times more than her well-behaved cousins. She's as nippy and hard-working as an ant, and always happy and helpful.

After work Gilgi visits Olga. "My God, Olga, are you sick?"

Olga is lying in bed, with a wet handkerchief on her forehead, and melancholy in her eyes. "I'm not sick, it's just that I was at a masked ball, now I feel queasy."

Gilgi picks up a few articles of clothing from the floor and sits down on the side of Olga's bed: "Drank too much?"—"Never been so sober in all my life," Olga complains. "What was that? Why did I go? God, I'm living here like a combination of a Trappist monk and a Benedictine nun—I thought: have a little fun for once. Course, I must be suffering from advanced hardening of the arteries, deciding to go to a masked ball, of all things: the petty bourgeoisie stepping out—couples kissing like crazy, I won't be able to stand the sight of couples kissing for at least the next year—it stank of sweat and cold cigar ash, disgusting! I believe my hair still stinks of smoke even now ... could you hand me the bottle of lavender water from the table? What? It's on the floor? Is it broken? No? Well, there's no reason why it shouldn't have been on the floor. Aaach, I just find life so revolting." For a few seconds, Olga is dripping with *Weltschmerz*. For a few seconds only, then she throws out her arms, sits up with a jerk, the compress slips off, damp blond curls are stuck to Olga's forehead. She takes a photograph from under her pillow, shows it to Gilgi: a man's face, with good features. "Take a look at him, Gilgi—would you believe that I was married to him for six months?" No, Gilgi wouldn't. She makes an impatient gesture, she knows the story of Olga's marriage, and Olga has held Franzi's photo under her nose a hundred times before. "Oh, Franzi!" Olga slobbers on the picture. "I do love him, even now—but only when I'm not with him.

When we were together, it was terrible. He was as jealous as a touring-company Othello. Such a smart man, but—whatever you do—the point where being a man starts is the point where being smart stops. I became quite dazed. There was always shouting, shouting, shouting—about nothing. I mustn't look from the top down, nor from the bottom up, and sideways was completely out of the question. But you've got to be allowed to look, one way or another. I was already getting my first worry-lines, all my reserves of humor were used up, all . . ."

Gilgi snatches Olga's photo of Franzi away from her, stuffs it into the drawer of the night-table. She knows the story. "You're right, I'm chattering like an old washerwoman," and Olga jumps out of bed with both feet, fiddles with the radio set: six stations at once, three foreign and three German.

"Have you gone nuts, Olga?"

"Of course not—this is just how it should be: radio—Rrroma—Napoli—Wonderful! I've got the whole world in my room—Budapest—London—Amsterdam—Munich—let's see if we can add a few more stations to the list now." Gilgi protests vigorously. "Unimaginative creature!" Olga scolds, fishes in the depths of her wardrobe, re-emerges with a pair of light-colored suede shoes: "You don't seem to be in an overwhelmingly good mood either, young Gilgi! What? Relatives staying in the apartment? Dreadful. People who stay with their relatives deserve nothing better." Gilgi picks up a pair of stockings from the carpet. Olga is combing her short, blond curls at the mirror. "Oh, Gilgi, I'm looking forward to summer! I'll go to Majorca. You know, you can live fantastically cheaply there. Sun and air and blue sky—you get them all for free. And the people there talk a language that I don't understand. Can you imagine, Gilgi, how magical it is to hear just a melody of words, without understanding all the nonsense that lies behind them?"

Gilgi has pulled Olga's stockings over her hand and is looking reproachfully at the toe, where her fingers poke through. "Do you have any darning thread?"

"No.—Listen, Gilgi, if I get enough money, you can come with me, as my guest. Gilgi—doing nothing, lying in the sun—oh, you've got no idea how beautiful life can be."

"Olga, if you get some money, you'll have to save it. Don't you ever think about the future?"

"Yes, I do." Olga drops onto the bed next to Gilgi and pulls the holey stockings from her hand. "Give them to me. I have to put them on.—Do I think about my future? Take a look in the drawer of the night-table—there should still be a ticket for the lottery in aid of building the cathedral.—Will you come with me, Gilgi?"

"I can't, Olga." Gilgi has folded her hands on her knees. "I—you see, Olga—I can give so little, and that means I can't take anything. And I wouldn't have time, I have to work."

Olga strokes Gilgi's hair like a grandmother: "The sober soul of a little shopkeeper! If only you'd tell me what you're aiming for! What do you want—what do you wish for—what are you longing for?"

Gilgi pulls a face, as though she'd just drunk vinegar. Longing! A word which she can't stomach. "I want to work, want to get on, want to be self-supporting and independent—I have to get all of that step by step. At the moment I'm learning my languages—I'm saving money— maybe in a few years I'll have my own apartment, and maybe one day I'll see my way clear to setting up my own business."

"You poor little beast of burden! And you're wasting the best years of your young life working towards that!" Olga wants to express her sympathy by stroking Gilgi's hair again, but her hand touches empty space, Gilgi has thrown her head back angrily. "You don't need to feel sorry for me, Olga, I think my life's wonderful. I like the feeling of creating something. If someone gave me a million today, I'd—take it, but I wouldn't be overjoyed at all. I like the feeling of getting on by my own efforts." Gilgi jumps up, strides up and down the room, looking for the words. She wants to prove to Olga that she's happy, and has good reason to be. "I'm not talented, Olga—I can't paint pictures or write books, I'm Fräulein Average, but I don't see why that means I should give up. And what I can make of myself, I will make of myself. I'll always be working and always be learning something new, and I want to stay healthy and pretty for just as long as it's possible—I'll take up the breast-stroke again in summer, I—don't laugh like such an idiot, Olga—you've got to understand that it makes me happy when everything in my life is so well-ordered and well-regulated. And once I leave home, I'll be completely happy, once there's not a single person on earth that I have to pretend to or tell lies to about anything. And—Olga—yes, how can I explain it to you—the fact that my ambitions are never bigger than the chances of me achieving them is what makes me free, and ..."

"So it's a poor life after all," Olga says, shaking her head.

"But, Olga, it's so beautiful to have your life laid out in front of you like a neatly solved arithmetical problem!"

"It's awful." Olga is becoming heated. "I look forward

from one unforeseen thing to the next, I look forward to people that I haven't even met yet. I long to be alone, and then I long again for someone that I can really care about. You're so miserly with yourself, you heartless, egotistical little person—you don't care about anyone—but I still like you. Do you want my fur coat, Gilgi? How egotistical and cold you are, not wanting to let me give you anything. Do you want my coat, Gilgi?"

Gilgi has to laugh. "Pay the coat off first, Olga—what an irresponsible girl you are! Anyway, you shouldn't be talking to me when you're hungover like this."

"Yes, Gilgi, but you have to come to Maj ... Majorca—that reminds me! I'll have to get ready in flash—got a date at seven." Olga rushes to her wardrobe. "You can come with me, Gilgi. What? Well—I met Martin Bruck in Palma two years ago. You don't know him? No, he's not particularly famous. Wrote two books, quite good ones. We laughed together so much that we didn't have time to fall in love with each other. Anyway, the day before yesterday I ran into him unexpectedly in Komödienstrasse. He didn't say: 'Small world!' and as a reward I promised to meet him tonight. Come with me, we'll have a good time."

"I'd just be in the way."

"Don't be silly." Olga puts her hat on. "Don't you see that I'm wearing my black dress? If I'm going to a rendezvous with immoral intentions, I appear in pink or sky-blue."

Gilgi nods, Olga's black dress is incontrovertible proof. "I was going to do some work, Olga."

"Oh, come along, he's a nice guy, is Martin Bruck."

"All right, but for an hour at most."

He's already waiting for them outside the "Schwerthof." Nothing special, Gilgi decides, looks quite amusing, oh well.

"You don't exactly seem to be aiming at the elegance of Adolphe Menjou, Martin!"—"Not exactly, Olga!"—He laughs, slaps a battered little hat onto his thick dark hair, tries unsuccessfully to smooth out his crumpled overcoat, looks at his reflection in a shop window. "Don't look at yourself for too long, Martin, it might depress you!" Olga pushes her hand under his arm. "You'd do better to look at my unusually cute little friend—and don't pull a face as though you'd been tied to ten martyrs' stakes at once! How old are you now? Forty-three? Well, of course, at that age a man is as dependent on flattery as an ageing beauty queen. But I'll console you by saying that despite your ridiculous clothes you manage to look—if not elegantly dressed— then at least elegantly proportioned."

Olga leads the way to a little *Konditorei* in Aachen-strasse: "Not in the mood for a café-with-orchestra today. If I hear the Song of the Pigeon one more time, I'll go nuts." Martin is happy with that. He really likes this kind of touching little *Konditorei* with its sagging plush sofas and the poor, bare little marble-topped tables.

One—two—three hours go by. Gilgi, who only wanted to stay for an hour at most, is still sitting there. What's keeping her here? Her arms are lying on the cold marble top of the little table as though they're frozen in place. She knows so many men, but this Martin Bruck is different, completely different. Why does she like him? Yes, why? As if it were so easy to give yourself the right answer to that. He's not handsome, not big and strong, not elegant. He's dressed as carelessly and indifferently as someone who's finally accepted that he can't run around naked. He has such thoughtful hands, thin, frail fingers. His face is narrow and fleshless, his forehead is high and angular, his hair needs trimming at the back. A sharp nose, a soft, sensitive mouth, regular teeth shining with health, each one seeming to join in when Martin Bruck laughs, and dark, lively eyes, their expression constantly changing, and their gaze constantly roaming. He's of medium height, narrow in the shoulders and hips. His posture and gestures are sure and unconstrained. Nothing special, it's a mystery why I'm looking at him so closely.

It occurs to Olga that Gilgi has powdered her nose four times in two hours, it occurs to Gilgi herself that she wishes Olga wasn't sitting directly under the lamp, the light makes her hair glow even more than it already does. Tonight, at least, Olga shouldn't look quite so pretty.

Martin is funny and entertaining, pleased to be sitting here with a couple of pretty girls. And he has stories to tell! He's traveled even further than Olga has. Gilgi is amazed. "Yes, but home—where do you call home?"

Yes, this Martin Bruck doesn't call anywhere home—this vagabond, this idler, this man with empty pockets. He's always been a vagabond and an idler, his pockets have only been empty for a few weeks. Life was fun while they were full. He'd drifted around every continent, spent money on every continent. Everywhere was beautiful, everywhere had something new to offer, life everywhere was full of surprises. He'd only make himself unhappy for the sake of a change—so that he could be twice as happy again afterwards. In Stanleyville on the Congo he suffered a slight case of malaria, in Colombia a crocodile looking for change of diet chewed on his upper left thigh—both accidents which had no serious after-effects, and didn't cloud his enjoyment of life for a moment. For four years he led something approaching the life of a normal citizen. He wrote two books, which were a success in literary circles. They didn't earn him any money. But earning money wasn't the point. Instead of building a literary career, Martin decided that he'd worked enough. He wasn't ambitious. There would always be lots of other people who wrote much better books than he did. All right, then! It occurred to him that there were still countless countries, islands, rivers, and cities in the world which he hadn't seen yet. The restless wandering began anew. Everywhere he found friends, people who liked him, women and girls who were made happy by his first kiss and sad by his last. So for another ten years he lived entirely as he pleased—then he ran out of breath. He put the remainder of his capital into his brother's factory, and now he gets a monthly payment of two hundred marks. That means that he won't starve. He's never been a snob, he can do without luxury and elegance, he's used to hardships—what can go wrong? So now he'll wander around Europe for a change. Must still be enough interesting things here which don't cost much. Maybe he'll work again too. It's possible. Not probable.

Now he's in Cologne. A friend is letting him use his apartment while he's away in Russia for two years. Martin has set up house: he's hung a crumpled overcoat and two dusty suits in the elegant built-in wardrobe, and set up three huge crates of books in the library, where their rough light-colored wood is clashing discordantly with the prevailing notes of dark oak.—

Gilgi's imagination was always a well-behaved child: it was allowed to play in the street, but not to go beyond the corner. Now the well-behaved child is venturing a little further for once. Martin talks, and Gilgi sees: oceans, deserts, countries—but that's not the essence of what she's seeing, she'd like to make an accounting to herself—as she always does—to record her feelings in her own words. Oh, my little, gray words! That someone can speak so colorfully! She's sitting on a sphere that's damp with rain—there's a sun far, far away in the sky—with each hand you grab a sunbeam, wrap them around your wrists, quite tightly, let yourself be drawn upwards—how heavy you are! The sunbeams could tear—you're getting closer and closer to the sun's hot orange-red ball—it's getting warmer and warmer ... And somehow Martin Bruck's fingers brush Gilgi's hand, quite by chance—and even more by chance Gilgi's hand moves past the cups and the little milk-jugs, and now it's lying right there ... lying well within reach of—after all, your hand has to be lying somewhere. And Olga's eyes are shrouded in memory, she's thinking of Franzi—Gilgi likes Olga very much, she doesn't know Franzi, but she's pleased that he exists.

You have to show your relatives the city. Frau Kron has so little time. On the next day, Gilgi is picked up at the office by Aunt Hetty and the two silly cows. They inspect the Ringstrasse. "But the Jungfernstieg in Hamburg is nicer." Church of the Apostles, Hohestrasse, Wallraf-Richartz Museum. That doesn't interest them in the least, but if you come back from a visit to a strange town, you want to be able to say: we went to the museum.

Gilgi parts from these three delightful people at eight o'clock.

Kaiser Wilhelm Crescent. Greif. Magdalene Greif, née
Kreil. Once more, Gilgi climbs a staircase. There's no bad
smell here. Behind the doors, it's quiet. No yelling, no
cursing, no stinking, twice-breathed air paralyzing your
chest. Shameless, arrogant banisters—No Access For Mes-
sengers and Deliverymen!—a building for the upper crust.
Sticky fried potatoes—lady without internal organs. For a
few seconds, I believed that Täschler was my mother. Because I believed it, she was it, whether for a few seconds,
two, three, four—days—weeks—doesn't matter a damn.
Magdalene Greif, née Kreil. High-class building—disgustingly high-class building. I don't belong here. I don't
belong in Thieboldstrasse, either, but the stinking room
there—that had something to do with me. Why? Dear
God in heaven—Olga, Pit, mother—help me, I don't want
to think. So you wrap two sunbeams around your wrists—
You, the one with the cheeky strong teeth, with the lively
hands, the upright, unbowed neck—God, dear, dear, dear
God, I've already been standing here for ten minutes in
front of this ridiculous stained-glass window, I know that
I'm standing here, I'm not crazy! There's something wrong
with me—wrong with me—wrong with me. You think in
hit songs, feel with their rhythms, submerge yourself in
them—tam-tam-tam-ta—those songs: help you run away
and towards.

Gilgi climbs slowly—step by step. She doesn't know
yet what she'll say, has made no plan at all. It'll have to
be whatever the moment suggests. Her hand presses the
white doorbell calmly and firmly: a thin ringing. Sure to
be one of those disgustingly fat little dogs. A maid: "Can I
help you???"

"Like to speak to Frau Greif."

"Madam is traveling." Of course, it's one of those unfriendly buildings where the maids get such a weird idea
of their own social status, one which reflects their employers' incomes rather than their own wages.

"When is she returning?"

"Not for at least two months."

"So where is she?"

"In St. Moritz, and from there to Nice. Your name?"

"Isn't so important.—I'll come back in two months."

Gilgi feels hostility welling up inside her. One woman
in the gray dirt—one in the bright light—one is no less
valuable than the other. Gilgi leans over the banister.
With some people, they can't lean over bridges or banisters—without spitting. Gilgi spits.—It goes Click! when it
splashes on the cold marble down below. Gilgi is pleased.
That was a kind of tiny gesture for Täschler, a small expression of solidarity—not yet conscious—a Yes and a No.
Again: . . . Click.

Gilgi is sitting in her room. Now it's time to work. It
can't go on like this, you're not getting anything done.
The search for her mother, the stuff with her relatives, the
disturbances because of Carnival—it takes up an awful
amount of your time. Gilgi translates from *Three Men in
a Boat*. Now and then she rests her head on her hands,
staring into space: five minutes, ten minutes, fifteen minutes—what do you think you're doing? Do you think this
is work? Well, heck, surely you're allowed to think? What'll
she wear tomorrow? Will she be able to look just as pretty
as Olga? I have—I have a rendezvous—well, that's no
big deal!

Gilgi is waiting in the little *Konditorei* from the day before yesterday. Martin Bruck isn't there yet, but he's sure to be there soon. She's sitting with her back to the door: every time she hears a noise she turns her head, her neck is hurting already. And every noise at the door creates a wave of hope—and disappointment. No, she's never waited like this before, never like this. Will he come? Won't he come? The young lady Gilgi solves crossword puzzles and tries to convince herself that she would have spent an hour in a café today anyway. The young lady Gilgi is exquisite: her hands are manicured nicely, her eyebrows are drawn exactly, the bright georgette collar on her brown silk dress was cleaned with benzine this morning and is now radiant with self-conscious cleanliness. The colorful scarf is fragrant with chypre. The young lady Gilgi is so exquisite, she looks so pretty. But is there any point in looking so pretty just for yourself? Martin Bruck is bored with Cologne, he wanted to meet Olga and Gilgi today, but Olga said promptly that she didn't have time—nice Olga!—well, then he'd meet Gilgi by herself. And now Gilgi has kept the appointment faithfully, and that deadbeat isn't coming. That dirty dog! But of course you won't get angry. Of course it's only a man. But anyone who resolves not to get angry already is angry, and anyone who wouldn't get upset for anything in the world already is upset.

Right, she's leaving now. And if he does still come, it'll serve him right to find that she's no longer there. The dirty dog. Gilgi goes to her room. It happens that she throws an empty brass ashtray against the wall. But I'm not angry. Not a bit. On the contrary. Now I've got some lovely time to myself. And she sits down at the Erika-brand typewriter, the keys are flying. She types ten Spanish business letters—for practice. Never once looks up, never once rests her head on her hands to stare into space. Tick—tick—tick—rrrrrrrrr . . . .

Gilgi sees an advertisement in the daily paper. Someone is looking for a skilled typist for evening work. Something for me. I'll go and enquire. He gives the address. Please apply in person between seven and eight p.m.

"You were lucky," the pale woman says to Gilgi as they leave the big house in Lindenthal together. Of course I'm lucky, Gilgi thinks, walking with long, self-confident strides. She's got the job. With an elderly ex-officer who apparently steered his assets skillfully through the shoals of the hyperinflation, so that now he can write his memoirs of the war in peace and quiet. For about a month—he'll dictate to her every evening from seven to nine. A nice extra income. The man will pay fairly: one-fifty per hour. The fact that she'll bring her own typewriter gave her the victory over the other applicants. Maybe also that she made eyes at him a bit. Men over fifty nearly always like it when you look up at them prettily. It's also good to appeal to their protective instincts, to replace your solid self-confidence with an appealing helplessness at the appropriate moment. You've got to understand all that stuff. Gilgi understands it. The fact is that you're dependent on employers, and you can't get their attention without a few tricks. You don't succeed just because of your abilities, or just with tricks—but usually you succeed with both.

The pale woman walks along beside Gilgi: "When do you start the job?"

"Right after Ash Wednesday."

The pale woman sighs. "How I envy you! The firm where I worked went bust five months ago, and since then I haven't found anything else."

"But you're getting unemployment benefits, aren't you?"

The pale woman grimaces: "Which doesn't mean much! Anyway, it runs out next month, then they'll put me on emergency relief."

They stand beside each other at the streetcar stop without speaking. Gilgi feels uncomfortable. Perhaps the decent thing would be to give up the job now, so that the pale woman could have it. What kind of idea is that? Gilgi bites her lips. She has to make sure that she gets ahead—every man for himself—where would you end up if you gave in to every flabby prompting of sympathy?

The streetcar comes. They get on. The pale woman sits down next to Gilgi: "So you worked, just so that you had something to eat and drink and a place to sleep, and you thought that life couldn't ever be more miserable, but suddenly it's even more miserable, and there's nothing so bad that it couldn't get even worse—you know that now, like it's your only consolation."

"For two!" Gilgi says to the conductor, holding out her multi-ticket. And to the pale woman: "Had just one more trip left on it." The pale woman nods, quite satisfied. The thought that she had paid car-fare for nothing was what had been getting to her the most. Now at least she's having one free trip. Gilgi squints at her neighbor: patches on her dark overcoat have been rubbed bare—maybe you could, maybe you should ... Nonsense! She had an equal chance, didn't she? Did she? Did she really? With her wrinkled, old face, her sloppy posture, with her flat, dead eyes and her horrible clothes??? Who'll give her a job now? She's made a mess of her life, but when she was starting out, at least, she had an equal chance. Or maybe she didn't? Gilgi becomes less sure. The fact that people begin life with most unequal chances is not entirely clear for a moment—but then it's undeniable. A gross injustice, Gilgi decides. And if it was up to her ... but it's not up to her, and she has to accept that. When the streetcar reaches the cathedral the pale woman stands up, forgets to say goodbye to Gilgi, and shuffles on her bandy legs to the exit.

When Gilgi gets home, her two cousins fall upon her. Young Gerda is back in the Pierrot costume, and Young Irene in the pixie one.—"Hurry, hurry, hurry, Gilgi, we're leaving in a minute." Then Gilgi hears a scream from her parents' bedroom, and rushes in: Frau Kron has dropped a bottle of hair lotion—"it was still almost full, an' it cost three-fifty." She wrings her hands, standing there like Cologne's and Hamburg's answer to Niobe, a white paper chrysanthemum on her gray silk dress, a cute little red cracker-shaped hat on her freshly permed hair, a pained expression on her face. "I'll never buy that brand again!" No-one has ever been able to accuse Frau Kron of being a logical thinker. Gilgi gathers up the fragments of glass. Herr Kron, at the wash-stand, proclaims the Germanic folk-wisdom (which always bears repeating) that broken glass brings good luck! And devotes himself once more to pushing his canary-yellow tie through the matchbox cover which secures it when he dresses for Carnival. Aunt Hetty sweeps in: a most dramatic shawl around her square shoulders, three red poppies behind her ear—Carmen after a successful weight-loss program. "God, Gilgi isn't ready yet!"

Gilgi runs into her room. Saturday of Carnival—the beginning of Carnival. The whole family is going to a masked ball. Gilgi dresses in very short blue velvet trousers, a white silk blouse with a blue tie, black patent-leather pumps. All right, ready. Gloomily, she powders her bare legs. Ach, she has absolutely no desire to go along, absolutely none. She sits down on the side of the bed and lets her mind wander. If people would just leave her alone tonight. Because she's got something she wants to think about ... "Are you ready, Gilgi?"

"Yes, yes—in a minute." Pit says that she's a superficial little thing, Olga—that she doesn't love anyone. She cares a lot what Pit and Olga think. You shouldn't care what anyone thinks. Perhaps she really doesn't love anyone. And she doesn't want to, either. Doesn't want to feel empathy. Not with the Krons, not with Täschler, not with the pale unemployed woman. "A poor life," Olga says. Poor? If you're working—.—And then you wrap two sunbeams around your wrists, let yourself be drawn upwards—I want to stay down here, with my feet on the earth. You should probably talk to someone, but there wouldn't actually be any point. Because she doesn't have any words, to make herself understood.

How did you, pigeon—pigeon—pigeon / Get into our kitchen??? Ostermann's pressing ornithological question is being asked everywhere at this year's Carnival. Woohoo—What a night, what a night! ... Oh, once upon a time—a faithful hussar ... here we go, here we go—I'll call you naughty Lola ... "Waiter, a bottle of Moselle for me—Traben-Trarbacher Auslese—and some canapés ..."

"But, Paul, you just ate at home—"

"So what? I gotta have a good foundation to put the alcohol on."

"This'll be a great evening."

"That's what it's supposed to be.—Ya got a good seat, Hetty? Ya want a few more streamers, children?" Herr Kron is sitting with his loved ones around him, feeling proud and happy as someone who creates and sustains Cologne's Carnival. "Who's got the cloakroom check, Paul, you got the cloakroom checks?"—"Berta, stop yapping all the time, I got them in my pocket." It takes a while to re-assure Frau Kron. Young Gerda and Young Irene wriggle on their chairs, whoop happily when a man in a domino costume taps them on the head with a rattle, and throw streamers around rather awkwardly. You can't ask more of the first half-hour. The Beckers and the Wollhammers are sitting at the table with them, as previously arranged. The little Becker daughter flirts girlishly with Herr Kron. Frau Becker is proud of the child. She's engaged to a Daimler, though it's not there at the moment, and its owner isn't either. "A phenomenal car," Frau Becker explains dreamily. Aunt Hetty looks a little envious, her maternal procuress's expression appears: "Gerda dear, Irene dear—don't sit so quietly at the table—have a bit of a scamper through the rooms, children!" The children scamper off.

How did you, pigeon—pigeon—pigeon . . . "A heavenly car," Frau Becker says, sticking to the dream, she's an ultra-modern mother in her own way: Daimler, Daimler über a-halles . . . "The important thing is that a man is of good character," says Aunt Hetty. Character, character! If he's got a top-line car, that's character enough, you would think. Frau Becker wipes out her wine glass with Herr Becker's handkerchief before the wine is poured. Aunt Hetty follows suit, except that she uses the tablecloth. She wishes that Young Gerda, at least, could be settled soon. Even if it's only a motorcycle with a sidecar. The main thing is—that—you know. I see your daddy's nice and treats you right, my sweet / You know, that's just the kind of daddy that I'd like to meet ... Everyone drinks, everyone links arms and sways back and forth, everyone dances, everyone calls everyone else by their first names. Herr Kron pats Aunt Hetty on the behind in Carnivalistic excess, Frau Kron thinks that such japes are only appropriate after midnight ... Two by the Rhine / Two side by side / Your hand in mine ... We'll laugh and play / All through the day ... Come with me to the Rhine ... Here we go, here we go! Everyone is spending money, and wants something for it. If anyone doesn't get their money's worth, it's their own fault.

Gilgi is sitting beside Herr Becker. He pinches her thigh, she kicks his shin with moderate force: "Hands off."—"Go on, it's Carnival!"—"That's no reason for me to put up with your foolishness, Herr Becker."—"Call me Karl, call me—Karl ..."—"Pathetic." Herr Wollhammer wants to dance with Gilgi. They're separated in the crowd. Gilgi keeps dancing, with a domino who's exuding a powerful odor of mothballs. Gilgi can't help sneezing, once, twice, three times—"Have you got a cold?" the domino asks naively. Overcome by generosity, he drags her to the champagne bar. "Here's to you, lovely lady!" You see, usually he's rather earnest, tending to melancholy—just once a year—"there aren't many people who understand me ..." Gilgi stuffs confetti into her ears, but that doesn't stop her hearing the profound conversation between the pair next

to her, an Indian dancing girl and a maharajah with pad-
ding over an already impressive stomach—

"And when you're not at Carnival, what do you do?"

"Deal in oil and lubricants—but never mind that, child.
Let me kiss your rosebud mouth."

"If that's what you want, I can lend you my lipstick—"

"It's your mouth that I want—"

"Don't be in such a rush—on one glass of Moselblüm-
chen."

"Do you want champagne, child?"

"Less talk—more action!"

"I'm glad you said that—"

"Keep your hands off me—I meant the champagne."

"Stop playing hard to get, child—come on, it's Carnival—it only comes once a year . . ."

"What about my champagne?"

"How can you think of that now? Stop being so cold—
come on, it's Carnival . . ."

"You think that makes you better looking?"

"You've got no style—"

"When you look in the mirror, you'll see why . . ."

"I know I'm not handsome, child, but I have a gentle
heart—my soul . . ."

The dancing girl gets up: "The ones who yap about
their soul and their heart are the biggest pigs, and cheap
on top of it all." And on that line, she exits. The maharajah-
lubricants guy folds his hands on his double stomach, as
his faith in humanity shatters.

The domino-mothball guy tries to clasp Gilgi to his
manly chest, but she just sneezes, fends him off, and disappears into the crowd. The maharajah's and the domino's eyes meet. And as the domino is in the turpentine

business, it turns out that they have intellectual interests in common. "Ya wanna go get a glass of beer at the
other bar?"

"Yeah, let's go."

How did you, pigeon, pigeon, pigeon ... Gilgi pushes her
way through the dancing couples. It's not even midnight,
and the family won't head home until five in the morning, particularly with Young Gerda and Young Irene in the
party. She doesn't want to be here anymore. How did you,
pigeon ... Buzzing, scraping, screeching, laughing—you'd
have to be drunk, and desperate to fall in love, to enjoy it
here. Hell, the stink in a wild animal's cage at the zoo isn't
as bad as this smell of humanity in the mass. You're swal-
lowing dust and smoke with every breath. An exuberantly
tattooed youth grabs Gilgi around the waist: "Come on,
dance with me."—"Nah, don't feel like it."—"Why not—
come on, it's Carnival ..." Come on, it's Carnival, come
on, it's Carnival—stick it where the sun don't shine. Gilgi
brushes off the tattooed hand. Sets a course for the family
table and gets Herr Kron to give her the cloakroom check:
"Just want to get my compact out of my coat pocket."

A few minutes later she's standing on the street. Now
what? What does she actually want? She makes her way
over the rain-dampened pavement towards the New Market. Her hands are buried in the pockets of her black seal-
skin coat. Her bare legs are rather cold. She walks with
unwilling, ambling little steps. Where is she going? ...
how did you, pigeon ... She's uneasy, sour, depressed for
no reason. New Market, Mittelstrasse, Rudolph Square—
Aachenstrasse. A little *Konditorei*. Gilgi goes in and sits

down in a corner, has them bring her coffee and some magazines. It's quiet here, so for the moment she'll stay here. It's good that the little cafés are open all night now during Carnival. Gilgi flicks through the magazines ... For you too will betray me one day / You too, you too ... They should turn the gramophone off, you can't take that sweet schmaltzy stuff forever ... For you too will betray ... This is where we sat five days ago: Olga, me, and that Martin Bruck. And two days ago I waited here, and that idiot didn't come ... For you too will betray ...

"That's nice, little girl, finding you here. I figured you were kind of a regular here!" Martin Bruck is standing at Gilgi's table, well-dressed, unruffled, self-confident. "May I join you—or are you waiting for someone?"

"No, I'm not waiting for anyone," Gilgi manages to say, a fraction too quickly. But she promptly adds a friendly and conventional smile: "I'm pleased to see you: I have to apologize for not being here the day before yesterday."

"Weren't you? That's good. I only realized yesterday that I had completely forgotten our appointment." The boor, the graceless creep, the ... Gilgi can't make herself angry, she's too happy. Martin takes her hand, suddenly finding this little one exceptionally cute with her shining gray eyes, her cheekily lipsticked mouth—he takes her hat off: "I like you even better like that." Such a fresh guy! Gilgi has to laugh. No, she'll keep her coat on.

He wants her to talk to him, tell him about herself, he's interested in every detail. And Gilgi lays out for him the life of a very self-confident, very ambitious little girl. She tells him about Herr Reuter, about Pit, about the office, fat Müller, little Behrend. She even tells him about her search for her parents. About the Krons and Täschler. Oh, the

story hasn't bothered her for ages, she's not some sentimental goose, she doesn't need anyone, she gets by on her
own. She knows what she wants to do, and knows that she
can do what she wants to do. And the whole time she's telling Martin this, she grips his hand as though she was afraid
that he could suddenly stand up and disappear, never to be
seen again. He mustn't do that, he must stay with her, for
a long time yet ... "Yes, and a girl has never been in love?"
Martin Bruck frees his hand so that he can stroke Gilgi's
hair. Gilgi smiles patronizingly. Because in the end men
always ask the same dumb questions. "Of course a girl has
been in love—here and there—but a girl doesn't take it too
seriously, there are more important things. Men! They're
no big deal." And she quotes Olga: " 'Love is nice and it's
fun, but you should never take it seriously.' " Martin thinks
that really it's him who should be saying that kind of thing,
but at least such an uncomplicated way of looking at the
world suits him just fine.

As they get into the taxi, Martin asks: "Should I get
him to drive you to your masked ball, Fräulein Kron?"
Gilgi doesn't answer. It's lucky for Martin Bruck that it's
dark, Gilgi would never forgive him if he saw how much
she's blushing.

Where are we going? I shouldn't be doing this, I
shouldn't be in the taxi with him ... he's put his arm
around her shoulders—a man! That's no big deal.

A beautiful apartment. Thick carpets, bright cushions,
soft lighting. "All this belongs to you, Herr Bruck?"—"To
me?" He laughs: "Nothing in the world belongs to me, everything here belongs to a friend, he's gone to Russia for
two years, I'm supposed to keep an eye on things here, you
might say I'm a kind of superior concierge. I don't think I'll

be able to stand two years of it." He has to stand two years of it, he has to—Martin takes Gilgi's coat off: she stands in front of him like a slim boy, a Gainsborough painting come to life. "I like you, little Gilgi." Martin runs around busily. "What would you like to drink, young lady?"—I'm in luck! Life always has nice little surprises in store for its old friend Martin. What a figure the girl has! The legs just the right fraction too long, broader in the shoulders than in the hips. "Sit down, little Gilgi."

Gilgi stands motionless. He's already calling me Gilgi. How confident he is, how well he knows . . . If he's confident, I'll be even more confident. Gilgi is pale to the lips, makes an imperious little gesture with her hand: "You can save yourself the trouble, Herr Bruck. You don't need to tell me that you've brought me here to look at an interesting book or to taste a particularly old Scotch . . ." Martin swallows her words like an especially bitter pill. "Little one, we have to follow the rules for a short while, at least!" Gilgi walks to the table with unsteady little steps, takes a glass—"Silly little thing," Martin says softly, steps up behind her, strokes her shoulder gently and tenderly—"little girl, don't try so hard to cover your nervousness with boldness, I really like it when women are nervous." Klirrrr—Gilgi's glass falls to the floor. She wants to push away the hand that's stroking her shoulder, but doesn't even have the strength to lift her arm—it's all too fast—too fast—Fast? When you've been waiting for this for five long, long days?

MARTIN BRUCK IS WALKING THE STREETS, GOING nowhere in particular. Crappy weather, damp that sticks to you. If you look up: cloudy, dirty gray—if you look down: grubby pavement slippery with damp. The illuminated advertisements on Hohenzollernstrasse peer gloomily through the fog. Urban's Restaurants—Café Vienna. Jazz hits wash towards the entrances in little waves, which break on the shivering doormen. Inside, a few bored visitors from the provinces are dotted around on the red plush seats. Given the slightest opportunity, waiters talk about how bad business is, a married couple makes a great show of leaving one café because it serves coffee in nothing smaller than a pot. Top-quality head waiters have already been brought so low that they wear out the obsequiousness previously reserved for elegantly dressed regulars on mere passing trade. Only a cute little cigarette boy bolstered by inviolable self-esteem and class-consciousness is left to represent the Ringstrasse's claim to be a match for Berlin's Kurfürstendamm.

Martin drinks his coffee. Drops a two-mark coin on the table, without troubling—as he never troubles—to wait for his paltry eighty pfennigs change. Thrilled, the waiter accompanies this unusual customer to the door, believing him (despite all protests to the contrary) to be an American, promises him—from an urgent need to reciprocate his generosity—better weather next week, and recommends Dahmen's motorized city tour.

Martin turns into Ehrenstrasse. The housewives' El Dorado. Shop after shop. Butchers with invitingly illuminated and carefully arranged window displays. Pale posies of narcissi cowering between chunks of bloody meat. Fluffy little hares staring reproachfully out of dead, glassy eyes. From fish shops, silver-bellied pike and cod exude the stink that's their revenge. Ladies with string shopping-bags push past the display windows with their eyes searching for their quarry, like Sioux Indians on the warpath. Pale, worn-out women drag unwashed children along behind them, shabby unemployed men sniff at the warm, inviting aromas of bakeries in a vain attempt to feel like they've eaten. For no charge, a dealer in radios lets Tauber sing something terribly sad from Lehár's *Tsarevich* to the bustling street . . . In darkest night . . .

Ehrenstrasse becomes Breitestrasse. Someone called Rich can be poor, someone called Little can be big—just as this so-called broad street is narrow. Martin notes with surprise that there are people—depressed and depressing obstacles to traffic—who are veritably strolling amid the rush and hurry of these others who are eager to spend their money (or have no money to spend), as leisurely as the people who take the waters on the promenade in Wiesbaden or Carlsbad. Cologne on the Rhine, you're such a beautiful little city—Martin is freezing cold. His hands and face are wet with rain. A sad town. A sad country. The mouths open only to exhale bad temper and joyless-ness into the atmosphere. Tired eyes, glum faces. Chilled and gloomy, Martin ends up in a bar at the harbor, runs his hand over the bare, honest wooden table. Furniture like this—cracked, soaked in schnapps—makes him feel at home. He breathes in: this bar smells like every harbor bar in the world: it smells of cheap liquor and rough tobacco and moving-on-tomorrow. You could forget that you're in Cologne, in Germany. He'd like to forget it, but can't quite manage to. Never in his life has he felt himself so crushingly alone, so forlorn, so embarrassingly unnecessary. Whether you talk to waiters, cleaning women, street-car conductors, taxi-drivers, booksellers, bar owners, sales clerks—every third word is: "problems." Everyone's dissatisfied, everyone's complaining. A sad country, where you suck in pessimism with every breath. It seems as though, in this country, doing nothing couldn't be pleasant, but more likely oppressive. Having to economize isn't an unalloyed pleasure, either, he'd assumed that his needs were more modest than they actually are.

Martin stirs his toddy. He thinks about Gilgi, and his mood brightens. Nice, cheerful, little girl. He's pleased that Gilgi likes him, that she's attracted to him, it means a great deal to him today that someone really likes him, he feels much in need of recognition, support . . .

Gilgi is typing Herr Mahrenholz's memoirs of the war. A tedious, uninteresting job—in her opinion. Tick—tick—tick—perhaps Martin will pick me up when I finish—he has before. Martin! We understand each other perfectly—name and substance. Actually it's quite wrong to say: we understand each other, as if we've known each other for ages! An incomprehensible error. The warm, lively understanding of the first hours, days, weeks. We're more than ready to discover things in common, firmly united in the reciprocal joy of difference. We know a great deal about each other. We'll know less about each other when we start thinking about each other. What comes later—is intimacy. We mustn't mistake understanding for intimacy. Under- standing each other—at the right distance from intimacy, that'll take some doing. That'll really take some doing— similar words—implacably irreconcilable ideas. You don't create understanding, you understand each other, from the very first moment. "Too fast!" I thought—I'm really ashamed of having thought that. I was so stupid! Waiting is terribly immoral, because it's so pointless. Because you mustn't lie your desires out of existence . . . Gilgi's thoughts are fleeting, leaving nothing behind—she inspects them briefly and forgets them completely. They appear—they've disappeared—she doesn't know they were there.

Herr Mahrenholz dictates. Walks up and down. A fine figure of a man! As Frau Kron and Frau Wollhammer would say. Face with fresh color and regular features, im- pressively full white hair, exaggeratedly upright posture. If you look at him for too long, you get a pain in the small of your back. Well, I suppose you're in love, and can't look at any man without making unfavorable comparisons. Complete nonsense, what you're typing here: a little saber- rattling—Company, halt! Occasional philosophical obser- vations, which don't impress Gilgi, although she doesn't understand them.

As she's leaving the house, she sees Martin walking up and down on the other side of the street. She goes weak at the knees, feels painfully queasy—like you feel in an eleva- tor when it jerks into motion. "Martin!" She rushes across the bare, deserted roadway. Laughs idiotically and aim- lessly when he lifts her up—the thin little thing! I bet she doesn't weigh more than fifty kilos! He carries her a few steps to the next street-light: "You're very pale—I don't like you working so much! — — — Your new lipstick tastes good, like pineapple . . ."—"Put me down, Martin—mind my typewriter!"—"I wish it would fall apart"—"Oh, Martin!" A disheveled Gilgi looks at him reproachfully. "You mustn't damage it," she says warningly and mistrustfully as Martin takes the little typewriter-case from her hand.

"We're home again, Martin," Gilgi says with complete seriousness, without a trace of irony, as they walk into the beautiful big apartment. We're home again!

"Oh, I'm famished! Did you wait on dinner for me?— And you've laid the table, and arranged everything, so nicely! Martin, you're a model housewife. And champagne! But you don't need to ply me with seductive fizz anymore."

While they eat, she talks: "This Herr Mahrenholz? Definitely an attentive man. Nothing dangerous, I can handle him.—What? Oh, Martin, I don't think men are anything like as bad as people say. Of course most of them try their luck when a pretty young girl comes into their way—you can't blame them for that. Can you? I find it quite normal and natural. The main thing is that you know how to fob them off tactfully, without starting some great drama of outraged honor, like in that novel, *Tragedies at the Typewriter*!—No, not white bread—give me the rye loaf—the crust, got to chew something hard, otherwise I'll quite forget that I've got teeth in my kis . . . in my mouth.—Herr Mahrenholz's memoirs? A lot of crap, you'd die laughing if you read . . . I don't know much about literature anyway, and it doesn't mean a lot to me, either . . ."

"So what does mean a lot to you?"

"You do, Martin." No point in hiding it. She's finished with all the evasive strategies.

"Don't you read anything at all, little Gilgi?"

She lights herself a cigarette: "Please, Martin, do smoke Mokri cigarettes, there are coupon things in the packets which I can collect, when I've got a hundred-twenty they'll send me a fountain pen, and then I'll give it to you. Do I read? Yeees—I read newspapers, especially the fat Sunday editions and *Uhu* magazine, and I've read Remarque, I liked him. And then I read Jack London and Colin Ross and Bengt Berg. I read one by Berg just recently—about a little kid in Lapland who grew up quite alone, and had a harsh and sad childhood, and I could really understand that, those were real difficulties, not the kind of problems that are terribly superficial. Modern *Weltschmerz* makes me want to puke. You know, anyone who's healthy and has enough to eat simply doesn't have the right to be unhappy.—And, Martin—the worst ones are those old people who have thrown themselves into the new era. The ones who write about sport-oriented modern youth, driving cars, short skirts, short hair, and jazz, and have an amazing ability to hit the nail right next to the head. They're right behind the young people! As if the young people cared! And they puff themselves up with an authority they don't actually possess. The new generation! The new era! They act as though 'the new era' had made its bow before them: oh, please, do come with us, Herr X, we'd be completely lost without you. And then Herr X nods graciously and goes with them. Is terribly sympathetic and generous, and occasionally wipes a conservative tear from his eye." Gilgi stands up, gathers the empty plates and dishes and takes them into the kitchen. Comes back, sits on the arm of Martin's chair and lights herself a cigarette. "The old people! Either they abuse the new generation or they idealize it—it doesn't matter which: if those of us who are under thirty took ourselves half as seriously as they do—we would've all choked to death on our megalomania already. Yes, and they've choked themselves and us with their stodgy words and their endless chatter." Gilgi falls with a plop from the arm of Martin's chair—onto his lap. "They—they—they should all be injected with strychnine! They should be ashamed of how they talk about hearts and feelings, I—I'd rather stand naked in Cathedral Square—"—"Yes, but you don't mean me, you like me, little Gilgi?"—"Oh, you—as if you needed me to tell you that!"

He bends her head back—the light from the standard lamp shines brightly on her face. Her young face. Her young, young face. But nevertheless—here and there, under the eyes, on the forehead, around the corners of the mouth—they're not furrows and lines yet—no—just slight, distant hints, tiny prophecies that will reach their sad fulfillment in four, five, ten years—despite creams, despite ointments, despite almond-meal face-packs. Little girl, I'll have to be nice to you, you're so much poorer than I am. A thousand of my own thoughts, of others' thoughts, time, air, and desires have etched themselves into my face, boldly and without my permission—but no harm done, as long as a girl like you lets me kiss her. But what about when your expressionless little face is overwritten by time? And what if I kept you for a long time? If the little lines which are coming belonged to me then? What is there in you that would make me want to grow old—with you? Dutiful, stupid, bourgeois child—your work will make your face like a cobweb—why? To what end? So much resolve for so little return. So much obstinate ambition for such a trivial goal. Trrr—trrr—trrr the rain splashes against the

window-panes. It's a cold, sad, unfriendly country, this
Germany! You ought to have money still. You ought to
take your suitcase in one hand, the little girl in the other
hand—travel far away, to some place where there'll be
more light, more fun, much more sun, and teach her how
stupid and unimportant the whole time-consuming daily
grind here is.

"Are you tired, little one?—It can't go on like this, I feel
like such a brute! We won't see each other for a week."

"Not see each other for a week!! Martin! What do
you mean? Not see each other for a week??? Why? For
my sake?—Oh, Martin," Gilgi smiles with a kind of hopelessness—"what use would that be? What do you think—
would make me more tired: a sleepless night with you—or
a sleepless night by myself? Let's choose the lesser of two
evils—one should always think logically! Cheers!"

Olga picks Gilgi up from the office. "Why haven't you
come by, or telephoned?" She links arms with Gilgi, they
walk along together without speaking.

"I've got a half-hour at most," Gilgi says as she unlocks
the door to her little attic room. It's almost a fortnight
since she was here last. She has a shameful feeling of dis-
loyalty towards Olga, Pit, the room, the extra work she
gives herself, her whole life.

Olga pulls Gilgi down next to her on the divan, examines her with experienced eyes: unmistakable symptoms—
slightly drooping shoulders, restless eyes, uncharacteristic
softness around the mouth and chin.

"Martin?" Olga asks.

"Yes."

"Is it serious?"

"Yes."

"And?"

"What's that supposed to mean: 'And?' At the moment, I'm happy." Gilgi winds up the gramophone ... For it can't last forever ... Olga is disturbed to see a few tears dropping onto the record.

"So you've become sentimental recently?"

"Nonsense. Just nervous. All the racing around, all the—oh, all of it."

Office, home, work, love—how did she possibly manage all that before? It was different, completely different. She saw long tall Klaus, who was her boyfriend for six months two years ago, two or three times a week. Dancing, movies, summer excursions to the Rhine, canoeing, a weekend's brief magic—all quite pleasant, fun, and no reason to get excited. If you saw each other, that was fine—if not—well, you had other plans. Both of you. The guy and the girl. Working and getting ahead were still the most important things. You liked each other in a rather cool, undramatic way, and the possibility that a friendly attachment to a man could ever become important enough to disrupt Gilgi's program would have been the last thing on her mind. And now! Martin has disrupted her program. And the worst of it is that this disruption means more to her than the whole rest of the program.

"And you sit from nine to five in the office, then you rush home for a bit, from seven on you type for old Mahrenholz, and it's not until nine that you can enjoy being with Martin. Olga, you can probably imagine how quickly the time goes then—because the day only begins at nine p.m. Oh, and I've got to move out from the Krons', right away. If you don't come home till early morning during Carnival, nobody has the least objection. But after Carnival! If you're not at home late at night, it looks suspicious—everybody will notice. If I could just get away—! Only I can't see how to swing it."

Olga has a pensive, worried expression. Gilgi and Martin! An odd combination. As long as it turns out all right.

Gilgi is sitting at home, at the breakfast table. Herr Kron is reading his newspaper, Frau Kron is slurping her coffee, Gilgi is buttering her roll. No-one speaks. As usual. But this morning's silence gives Gilgi an uneasy feeling. Of course, they heard her coming home in the small hours again. "I slept at Olga's," she says, without being asked. Herr Kron grunts something indeterminate, Frau Kron picks up breadcrumbs from the table and doesn't say a word. The silence becomes embarrassing. Gilgi is blushing with shame and anger at her stupid excuse. Does she need to say anything? Isn't she independent, a grown woman? Can decide herself what she wants to do and not do?

Herr Kron folds up his newspaper and leaves the room, making a big point of not looking at his wife. As he pushes out the door, his broad back looks hostile and determined, suggesting: won't put up with it—not that kind of thing—in my house! And Gilgi thinks unhappily that from Herr Kron's point of view, he and his back are right. And of course both the Krons have spoken about her, about . . . it's intolerable to know that they've spoken about these things, so inexpressibly embarrassing.

"Gilgi," Frau Kron says suddenly, with a slightly plaintive undertone in her voice, and completely forgetting to adopt Cologne dialect. "Gilgi, you're not doing bad things, you're not bad, you're not that kind of girl, are you?" Gilgi clenches her hands until the knuckles stand out, waxy white on the skin. It's horrible, a conversation like this! She should have moved out of here ages ago. Her mother is drilling questioning looks into her face. It's unbearable. "You weren't with a man last night, were you, Gilgi?" Gilgi is ashamed unexpectedly—for her mother. How can she say such a thing, and in such a way? Reproach, sympathy, interest, curiosity—all justified—yes, yes, all justified—but so revolting. Everything between Martin and me is a matter for me and me alone. Why doesn't she understand that she shouldn't think about any part of it—I mean, I don't do that—I don't think about what goes on between her and her husband . . .

"Gilgi, you haven't done anything hateful, have you?"

"What you call hateful, Mother—always becomes hateful, only becomes hateful, when a third person thinks about it and talks about it." Gilgi is hoping desperately that her mother will understand that this conversation is impossible. But Frau Kron only hears the confirmation of what she feared. "Gilgi, I would never have thought that you . . . ," she's crying softly—"you were such a good girl, some man has hypnotized you, some man has seduced you, why didn't he come to the house like a respectable person?" Ach, God almighty, these touching efforts to absolve me of guilt—a guilt that doesn't even exist. And Gilgi wants so much to explain: that she loves Martin, that they're very happy when they're together, and that it's all the most simple, the most normal, the most natural thing in the world. But here in this room absolutely nothing is simple, here everything is terribly sinister and complicated and repulsively dramatic.

Her mother is sobbing. That should make you sorry, but it makes you angry. For God's sake, where's the tragedy here? Just stop it, would you? An unpleasant emotion rises within Gilgi: alienation—dislike—hostility. Frau Kron lifts her head: "Who is he, then? And, Gilgi"—her voice is bright with hope now—"will he marry you?"

Yes, that was just what I needed! Gilgi stands up. "Will he—marry me? I don't know. I won't marry him—I do know that."

Gilgi disappears into her room and bolts the door behind her. She fishes her big suitcase from the top of the wardrobe, and packs: clothes, underwear, shoes. She moves quickly, quietly, cautiously. In her parents' room next door, she can make out Herr Kron's rumbling beer-fed bass and Frau Kron's excited whispering. She has to leave—it's the only decent thing she can do. Oh, it's quite clear to her that her parents must be indignant about her behavior, they have the kind of rock-solid moral ideas which can't be overturned from one day to the next. She pauses in her packing: hears her father in the next room saying something about "laying down the law." My God, what a ridiculous, petty story. Moving more quickly now, she tosses underwear into the suitcase. A swift exit. It's the only solution. You simply can't stay here, be treated as an errant child, magnanimously forgiven when there's absolutely nothing to forgive.—The door-handle is pressed down from the other side: "Jilgi!"—Herr Kron's voice sounds annoyed. Finding the door bolted makes him furious: "Either you're home by eight tonight, or you need never come home again!" Heavy footsteps, and the front door closes with a loud bang.

Gilgi treads on the suitcase with both feet until the lock

catches. She opens the door quietly, hears Frau Kron having her ritual argument with the cleaning woman in the kitchen:

"An' if the butter isn't good enough for you . . ."

"In other houses . . ."

"I could get ten new cleaning women tomorrow."

"Carryin' the heavy trash cans downstairs an' draggin' coal up from the cellar an' then rancid butter for breakf—"

"The butter is not rancid."

"Yes, it is rancid . . ."

With a massive effort, Gilgi drags the heavy suitcase down the stairs, it's almost pulling her right shoulder from the socket, her hand hurts . . . an empty taxi is driving past outside—Stop! Stop!

"What's wrong, little Gilgi? You turn up in the middle of the night—with a huge suitcase?'

"It's nine in the morning, Martin." Gilgi smiles wanly and drops the suitcase with a thud in the middle of the room.

"I'm glad you're here," Martin says, simply and convincingly. Still not quite awake, he looks alternately at the uncharacteristically elegiac Gilgi-girl and at the suitcase. His hair is tangled, his left cheek is showing the pattern of the lace on his pillow, he's thrown an old, battered raincoat over his pyjamas. He looks a little like a refugee, an opera-prince in disguise, or a non-gentleman cracksman. Slowly he rubs the back of his hand over the hard stubble on his chin, and suddenly he's awake. "Wait a moment! Before you start what will doubtless be a lengthy explanation, I'd like to give you a kiss, and for that I need to wash and shave first." He rushes into the bathroom with the speed of Paavo Nurmi.

And Gilgi does something which she's never done before, something which is more disorienting and momentous for her than her flight from home: she telephones the office, is put through to Herr Reuter: "... I feel so sick and miserable ..."

"Not flu, I hope?"

"No, no, just ..."

"Stay in bed ..."

Yes, she'll be there tomorrow—

"A speedy recovery"—"Thank you." She hangs up, finds herself irresponsible, unfair, lazy, and slovenly. Sits down on her suitcase, cries for a while, then is pleased again because now she'll be spending the whole day with Martin, and has a bad conscience because she's pleased. Feels a sharp pang as the finality of her separation from the Krons gradually dawns on her, suddenly feels a quite pointless longing for the silly, green plush Washington room, and shudders at the thought of sitting there again— it's a terrible mess, everything inside her has become a battleground of bitterly conflicting emotions, everything is rolling, rushing, shaking, there's no fixed point—only Martin. He enters proudly carrying a tray, having used the brief interval not only to dress himself smartly, but also to brew coffee swiftly. Rolls, butter, jam, honey—it's all there. It takes only moments to arrange everything on the coffee table, and incidentally to break the handle off a cup. An exquisitely timed movement drops the honey-jar precisely on the narrow strip of parquet floor between the runner and the rug, where it quietly explodes into fragments.

"So, come here, little sad-eyed girl." He lifts her off the

suitcase, sets her on his lap—"you can stay there like that until my left leg goes to sleep again.— ... that's the way! She gives me a lecture the other day: anyone who's healthy and has enough to eat simply doesn't have the right to be unhappy—and now she's crying all over me, turning my lapels to mush."

"You're right, Martin." Gilgi lifts her face. Registers with pleasure and pride that he remembers even her modest remarks. "Well—you see ... and ... then ..." it turns into a long and more or less clear report. "And what really gets me down is precisely the fact that they were fair and decent to me, so that from pure, awful egotism I wish that I could do something really special for them too one day. And I like them, but there just isn't any common ground. I can't be honest and open with them, and always lying revolts me. If they doubt me, it's embarrassing, and if they believe me faithfully it's even more embarrassing." Oh no, she's not sad anymore, she's here with Martin, which is where she belongs. She's behaved like some sheltered innocent from a century ago, doesn't understand it herself. There's that theory of heredity, or whatever it's called; that's the only explanation for her attack of sentimentality. The Krons will realize that children always go their own way sooner or later, and they'll accept that. They won't be unhappy, Herr Kron won't be unhappy at all. He's only unhappy when a Carnival parade is cancelled or people don't laugh at his jokes, or if business is bad. Frau Kron's capacity for unhappiness is equally limited. And one day they won't be angry anymore, then she'll visit them quite often—and she has Martin, she has her work, tomorrow she'll be more punctual than ever at the office—everything will turn out right, everything is all right now. Gilgi slides off Martin's knees. "Just want to write my mother a quick letter."

"The one in St. Moritz?"

"No, of course not; the other one."

"I find your family situation rather complicated."

"Dear Mother," Gilgi writes—"Don't be sad. I won't be living with you and Father from now on, I don't want the way I live to upset you anymore. There's no need to worry about me, I'm working and I know how to make my own living. I'm very sad about how ungrateful I must seem to you both, and how ungrateful I in fact am. But if you need me sometime—I'll always do anything for you. Don't try to find me for the time being. I don't want to come back permanently. That's better for you both, and for me. I'll ring you up from time to time, and if you don't want to talk to me you can just hang up. But whenever you want— I'll come to see you. Don't be angry with me. If that's possible.   Your Gilgi

"If you're feeling good about things again by the time spring cleaning starts, and Father doesn't mind, then I'll come for four days and help you."

"Back in a minute, Martin." She stuffs the letter into her pocket. Runs into the street. Buys a quarter-kilo of almond roughs—Frau Kron's favorite candy—and a nickel-plated coffee-pot—the old china pot started to leak yesterday. She gets the sales clerk to make a parcel of the pot and the candy and put the letter on top: yes, the messenger will deliver it in the course of the morning.

A quarter-hour later, relieved and content, she's back at Martin's. "If I have to do something, I've always got to do it right away. Delaying things makes me ill.—Right—and now let's unpack—"

Martin's eyes look thoughtful. "Gilgi," he says, and puts his hands on her shoulders. She looks so disconcertingly young, the little one, and notwithstanding her habitually exaggerated independence she looks almost helpless. He can't offer her his insecure existence as a replacement for the security of her parents' home. "Little Gilgi, I'm delighted that you're with me now, but—don't you think you might've made a silly mistake? You shouldn't be doing this for my sake, you understand? And if you like, I'll sort out your problems at home, because after all I feel myself responsible for you."

All the softness disappears out of Gilgi's face, her voice sounds hard and bright: "I sort out my problems myself, and if I make silly mistakes—then I pay the price myself.—And I'll tell you something, Martin"—she shakes his hands off her shoulders almost roughly—"I won't tolerate people feeling responsible for me, that's the worst way people can insult me, I . . ."

"Well, don't get upset, my little canary bird." A cheerful Martin carries Gilgi's suitcase into the bedroom, rejoicing with all his characteristic insouciance at the advent of a nice, entertaining extra resident for the apartment. Gilgi trots slowly behind him:

"I'm still not certain at aaalll," she says, trying unsuccessfully to lengthen her short, straight nose by pulling on it, "I had absolutely no intention—there's absolutely no question of me living here—you know I've always been independent—I have my room—"

Ignoring these words completely, Martin opens the lid of the suitcase: "Look, your beautiful red evening dress! Think how happy my crumpled, ugly little overcoat will be to have this hanging beside it from now on—"

"That's only a slip, Martin—and, my evening dresses! There's no danger of me putting them in with your things. So that you can pull them off their hangers every time you take a suit out!—There's another wardrobe here—that's where they'll go—"

In the afternoon they're sitting in the library, in the middle of all the books they've emptied from the crates. With loving enthusiasm, Martin fishes volume after volume out of the chaos, reads a few pages aloud, thinks something is beautiful, explains to Gilgi why he thinks it's beautiful— "and you'll read that—and that—and that—because you're not nearly as one-dimensional and unimaginative as you make out, little Gilgi." He tries to convince her with her own kind of logic: "Whatever is beautiful brings pleasure. There are some things which can't be recognized as beautiful straightaway, you have to train a little bit first. Because you feel pleasure in the end, the training is worth it. It's precisely the pleasures which you earn for yourself that are the most profound, the most lasting, they belong to you. And you understand, don't you, that you can never have enough pleasures that belong to you?"

Gilgi nods and is ready to believe Martin blindly. A book which is held so tenderly in his elegant, slender fingers must surely be beautiful, even if it's not necessarily by Jack London, Bengt Berg, or Remarque. She thinks about it: "You know, maybe I've always preferred useful things to beautiful things, or more likely I've only found useful things beautiful.—But I'll learn all right."

"Yes, you will. There are less intelligent and less sensitive people than you, my cute little boy. And there are other ways—other areas—in which your eyes are closed like those of a new-born baby, but I'll teach you to see soon enough." He kisses the back of her neck and feels a childlike joy in the educational work he is beginning.

"Oh, Martin!" Gilgi picks up a Cervantes in the original from the rug—"do you speak Spanish, Martin? Wonderful. We'll read this book together, it'll be good practice for me, now I'm learning Spanish so that later ..."

The next morning, Gilgi wakes up to the feeling that something incredibly life-changing and important has happened. Martin is lying beside her. Every morning, when she wakes up, Martin will be lying beside her.

The calm sleep beside each other, no longer permeated by anxiety and agitation, will make the thin, chance thread which connects them stronger and more robust. She switches the light on, looks at the alarm clock: no, she doesn't need to get up for another half-hour. — — — It's pleasant to lie so quietly beside each other. You don't divide yourselves with thinking and speaking, you unite yourselves by breathing. You come very close to each other, belong very firmly together in this slumbering, soft-breathing quietness. His face is right next to her shoulder, his chin is already quite rough again. She puts her hand on his chest and observes its slight rise and fall with deep satisfaction. Cautiously, she feels around on his thigh: there's the scar from the crocodile that bit him. There's a kind of exaltation in lying beside a man who was bitten by a crocodile in Colombia. What if it had eaten him all up? Horrible. Really you have to be grateful to the crocodile for its restraint. Oh, it's so good that he's alive. And belongs to

me. A real live human being belongs to me. Tuck—tuck—
tuck, you can feel his pulse beating at his temples and in
his throat—a living human being belongs to me. I'll keep
him, I want to keep him . . .

Thump—thump—thump—what's that? "Martin!"—
she tugs at his shoulder—"Martin! Someone's knocking,
Martin!"—"Come in!" Martin calls, like someone who
under all circumstances will regard knocking as a problem that is entirely solved by calling "Come in!" The door
opens: a comfortable-looking female individual appears
with a tray: "Made the coffee like ya always . . ." The individual notices Gilgi. Each looks at the other with mild
surprise. Martin decides to be half-awake: "Don't drop the
tray, Frau Boss—and—if you would be so kind—an extra
cup for the lady!"

"Morning, my little Gilgi. What was that? Who's the
woman? She comes every other day to clean, and then for
reasons best known to herself she can't be dissuaded from
waking me at the crack of dawn with coffee. What? She
saw you? So why shouldn't the good woman see you? As
long as it's not her husband that you're in bed—"

Frau Boss is standing in the kitchen, turning a light,
fragile little cup between her honest, work-reddened fingers and meditating on her decision: to be offended or
tolerant. "It's only human," she says aloud, interrupting
her meditations. She enjoys pronouncing the "hu"—you
have to breathe out so vigorously—"it's only human." The
repetition acknowledges her allegiance not only to the re-
spiratory charm, but also to the meaning of the sentence.
There's no need to get het up, it's only human. Which is an
example of how the ethical sense is influenced by a prefer-
ence for aspirates.

"You seem so changed, Kron," little Behrend says at the office. Has she already noticed too? Gilgi makes the typewriter keys dance. I suppose it's nothing new if a woman is changed simply by love. The only bad thing is that one half of you has changed, while the other hasn't, and now you consist of two halves which don't fit together at any point, which are always struggling with each other, and neither wants to retreat even a hairsbreadth. Everything's fine, you thought, when you moved in with Martin. Nothing's fine. Maybe you want too much. You want to keep your whole life from before, with its joy in getting ahead, its well-oiled approach to work, with its strict allocation of time, its brilliantly functioning system. And you want another life on top of that, a life with Martin, a soft, contourless, heedless life. You don't want to give up the first life, and you can't give up the second one. Tick—tick—tick—and now you have to erase yet again, and that'll make one of those ugly marks on the carbon. Yes, and there you were thinking what a wonderfully competent girl you were, and now you don't think yourself worth the price of a typewriter ribbon. And who knows if Martin won't decide tomorrow or the day after that a girl like Olga is much better suited to him. And you can't collect your thoughts properly for work anymore. Can't help thinking, what's he doing now, what'll he do next, I won't see him until nine tonight—it's hours yet till then. But I should go to Mittelstrasse again today and do some of my own work. And when the time comes, I won't go after all.—And this morning he said goodbye to me so casually and last night . . . I'm supposed to ask Meier & Schröder's salesman to call—as if that mattered— . . . and we have the honor to ask you . . .

Herr Reuter is pale and anxious and now completely

uninterested in pretty girls. "You should have written that on a business postcard, Fräulein—then the postage would be less—we have to economize."

Economize! Fat Müller, who has a carefully cultivated nose for trouble, tells them about three checks which have bounced. "And Grossmann has gone bust, we'll lose money there, too, and one bankruptcy prompts the next." She picks up her sandwich gloomily, and you have the impression that she's not eating it, but interring it in her mouth, though with a certain gusto.

"Fräulein Kron, have you heard that Höhne has been given notice?" the quiet Wendt asks during the lunch-break. Höhne is the head bookkeeper. "Yes, it's because he has such a high salary, and Kaiser only gets a hundred-eighty and can easily do Höhne's work as well as his own."

"Höhne has three children, doesn't he?"

"The boss is sorry, too—but what can he do!" And they're all terribly considerate to Herr Höhne. Whenever they talk to him, they use a very gentle, lowered voice, as though to a sick man who isn't supposed to find out that his case is hopeless, but who must inevitably work it out from the obtrusively tender care which people take of him. Gilgi could never stand Herr Höhne, because he's one of those silly slogan-men: it was better in the old days—under the Kaiser—the new era—the curse of moderniza-tion. Now she feels sorry for him. If the firm gets rid of him, who knows where he can get a job again.

When Gilgi leaves the office in the afternoon, Täschler is waiting to receive her. She's just what I needed. This is the second time she's been on guard outside the office, she's sniffed out where Gilgi works. She's the complete de-tective, sprung from the pages of an Edgar Wallace novel.

With her head weighed down by a startling hat, she trips along beside Gilgi. "Ya got anywhere?"

"No."

"Ya got any money yet?"

"No."

"I jus' don' know how I can go on," Täschler says. She's not whining in the least, she's talking quite calmly and objectively, and she's even smiling. A thin, crooked smile. And her hands look like wilted cabbage-leaves, and she walks like a dead woman. And if she cried and whined, it would make no impression at all. You can't stand that—other people's tears—or your own, either.—If only she'd cry. But no more than—I jus' don' know how I can go on. That sounds so convincing, and whether it's her own fault or someone else's—it remains the fact. How should you answer? There's no advice you can offer and no help you can give. You're quite powerless. There must be lots of people who don't know how they can go on, lots of people who are having a bad time. Collective misery—you've always closed your eyes to it. If you encounter an individual case, it pushes in behind your closed lids. It means something to you. Why? Yes, why! Because you're not made of stone.

"A three-mark coin is all I have on me!" You're ashamed and feel ridiculous—which is a big help! She doesn't even want to take it. "Oh, not from you—I mean, ya have to earn it yourself. But why don' ya go to your mother?" She's built herself a kind of tenement in the air and can't be coaxed out of it. "Go on, take it—here you are—my streetcar!" And Gilgi tries to press the coin into Täschler's hand—it falls to the ground—Gilgi jumps onto the departing streetcar; the conductor yells at her—let him yell as much as he likes. She sees the old woman kneeling on the busy street—crawling, searching the ground with groping hands and short-sighted eyes. She's scrabbling there among the pedestrians, her hat has slipped to the side . . . close your eyes, tight, tight, don't give in, don't give in, anyone who hits rock bottom has almost no chance of getting back up again, you don't have any damn time to waste now on slacking off and going soft — — —

"I can stay for an hour, Martin—I'm not going to my room today, I . . ."

"Don't you want to tell me where this mysterious room of yours is?"

"No, Martin. I must—it's—to do with my independence. I must have a place to work, I can't do it here where you're always around, and if I was in my room, I wouldn't have a moment's peace if I had to think that you could suddenly appear."

"Idée fixe."

"Well, let me have one."

"Gilgi," Martin says on Sunday morning, "you shouldn't go to the office anymore, the bed always gets so cold and uncomfortable for me when you get up so early." Gilgi shakes her head, so astonished that she can't think of an answer. What answer could anyone think of? Yes, that's a reason to give up your job in times like these, just to protect his right side from a draft. He's one-of-a-kind, this Martin! "Look, little Gilgi, the money I have isn't enough for one, which means that it won't be enough for two, either, what do you think—shouldn't we live together on my money?"

"What an idea, Martin!" Gilgi smiles with motherly superiority.

"Well, at least you shouldn't go to old man Mahrenholz anymore!"

"I'll be finished with him in three days anyway. Seriously, Martin—I really must earn money. You know, next year I'll have saved enough to go to Paris and to Spain. Martin, we'll go together, I don't see things properly if you're not there, you're my better eye. Olga says you can live terribly cheaply on Majorca, and in Paris we'll live in the *Quartier latin*—if we've saved carefully—you, too, Martin, you can put aside a set sum every month. I'll make some changes in this household here."

And Gilgi becomes energetic. Starts by giving Frau Boss her notice. She can do the little bit of washing-up and sweeping-out herself. Now she'll show Martin just how competent and productive she is. So much competence and productivity make him uneasy.

"Are these all of your shirts, Martin? Can't be worn anymore. What? I'll make new ones for you. I know how. What was that? Well, there's a sewing machine at the back of the store-room, I've been itching to use it for ages. What did you say? It doesn't matter how you look? It surely does. Never mind those old Greeks now, Martin, we're going out to buy material."

"You're so terribly impractical! Martin! Yes, are you nuts? Because we don't buy material in such an expensive shop—Henry Ford might, but I wouldn't bet on it—we go to one of those little places on an upper floor, Martin, where everything only costs half as much. You have to take into account the fact that the people are paying high rents on the shop and all kinds of other ... What? Boring? It's not at all boring, it's interesting, and useful to know.

"Would you like stripes, Martin? I think plain colors

are more elegant. Fräulein, this material won't shrink in the wash, will it? What did you say, Martin? You're happy with anything? We'll take shantung silk—because summer's coming soon, then you won't need a jacket when ...

"Martin, you've just got to have a new overcoat."

"What can you possibly have against my good old overcoat, that's served me so long and so faithfully? If you knew all the things we've been through together ..."

"That's just it, it's so obvious what the coat has been through."

"Doesn't matter, I don't want a new coat. Am I a gigolo?"

"You must learn to keep track, Martin, you must get into the habit of writing down your income and expenditures," Gilgi commands, purchases a little notebook, equips it with a little cord, and hangs it next to Martin's desk. Martin can never see it without shuddering inwardly. He goes on strike. "I don't have any income, and writing down just expenditures—that's no fun." Gilgi is frustrated to find that, despite all her efforts, she fails to establish a system for their joint financial affairs. It's incomprehensible to her that someone can create such a muddle just by existing. But Martin can. Without getting worried in the least. He's always spending money—on nothing. Only needs to walk around Ringstrasse in his horrible old overcoat for ten minutes and bingo!—his pocket is ten marks lighter. Heaven knows how he does it.

And he runs up debts too! The first time Gilgi comes across a few of his bills, she feels like crying. She goes secretly to the tobacconist's on the corner and pays the outstanding amount. Martin has found out by that night. It's their first fight. Martin rages, until Gilgi sits cowering in the corner of the club chair, all tiny and intimidated.

"What I do with my money is no business of yours—understood? What a tactless little thing you are. How much did you pay? What? Here it is. Who invited you to take care of my debts? Who gave you the right?" Gilgi crawls further and further back into the corner of the chair. She's desperately unhappy, but she's pleased that he's so angry. She loves him a thousand times more now, assuming that such a thing is actually possible.

"Well, don't cry." Martin comes closer, already appeased. He's surprised to find himself taking this funny, silly little thing so seriously. He lifts her onto the windowsill, he enjoys moving her around like a doll. She pulls a thick curtain of hair across her face:

"Don't look at me, Martin, I look so ugly when I've been crying.—Yes—give me the face-powder that's on the table—and the mirror." Well, if he's not supposed to look at her face, then he'll look at her legs. The slight, gentle curve of her calves is so beautiful, so perfect, and her knees are so finely chiseled, that you can admire them without feeling aroused. Martin admires these beautiful live artworks so thoroughly, and describes his admiration in such a silly, childish way, that Gilgi becomes jealous of her own legs. After all, they're not separate beings of some kind, they're part of her, and he's talking as though that's not so. "I wish you loved me, Martin—do you understand—me!" But of course he doesn't understand, and she can't explain it.

And Gilgi is drifting in the river of superfluous feelings. Superfluous? They were once, they seemed to be once. Isn't she happy? Of course she is. Often. But the hours of happiness come at a high price. The bill is presented promptly. Pay it! With what? With fear and twinges of pain. No, I don't think the price is too high, I just find the currency strange. Fear—pain! To whom should I pay them? Who profits from this odd currency? Gilgi feels the impersonal element in Martin's love. There's no doubt—he loves her, even takes her seriously—in his own way. But something's missing, the commonality of their inner and outer lives is missing. Gilgi thinks long and deeply—a difficult and unfamiliar job.

At night she lies awake for hours, with Martin close beside her. Her bare arm lies diagonally across his chest. Nevertheless, Martin is far away. You know so little about him. All attempts to co-ordinate him with her life somehow have failed so miserably. You should try it the other way around—to adapt yourself to him. Commonality is what counts. Our connection is so loose, so insubstantial. He might decide tomorrow that he's had enough of Cologne. What did he say yesterday: "We should go away from here—to Bergamo or to Scotland, I've got friends there, they'd be happy to have me, and if I bring you along they'll be twice as happy." Yes, and after that? He doesn't think about it. But it's completely impossible for her to abandon everything here. Impossible to be dependent on the hospitality of people that she's never met. To be dependent on Martin! On his money. When he doesn't have enough for himself. He has absolutely no idea how impractical he is, and he'll never change ...

And if you lie awake at night, you're tired during the day, and if you're tired—no, she's not doing her job badly. "Once a man appears, a woman becomes useless at work,"

Herr Höhne, the bookkeeper who'd got his notice, had always said. She'll prove him wrong, she'll prove everyone
who says that stuff wrong. Gilgi is two and three times as
conscientious as before. Only—what used to be a pleasure
is now a major effort, she's cramping up, if you like, but
after all that's her business alone. The letters which she
gives Herr Reuter to sign are cleanly and correctly typed,
no cause for complaint there. The fact that she's given up
her classes at the Berlitz School, that she hasn't been to her
room for weeks—don't think about that, put that right out
of your mind. You need the little bit of the afternoon that's
left to be together with Martin. You go for walks with him,
read books with him, try doggedly to agree that everything he finds beautiful is beautiful. Make quite inhuman
efforts to find that things which left you cold before are
beautiful, grit your teeth and try to force yourself. And has
it worked? Not so far.

"Oh, Martin, now you've spent all your money again!"

"Well, what if I have?" He shrugs his shoulders, and
you can tell that he doesn't want to talk about it, simply
doesn't want to admit that he'll start getting into debt
again—what's he going to pay with, he's getting in over his
head. But you still worry, because you belong to him. This
mess, this confusion, it'll have to make him uncomfortable
one day, and when he's uncomfortable . . .

And Martin himself is surprised that he doesn't feel
even more uncomfortable. He's never heard the repulsive
word "money" as often in his life as he hears it from this
little girl. She's a well-meaning and pretty little thing. And
if he didn't like her so much, he wouldn't stay here another
hour. Seems almost to think that he's a con-man, the little
one. He'll pay his debts all right—sooner or later. After all,

he won't need much—later—when he's by himself again. But to economize while living with a pretty woman! Hell— he feels sick at the very idea. It's not the kind of thing he's used to. And he'd be much, much more in love with the little one if he could give her nice clothes and diamonds and soft furs ... that's just the way it is: the more brilliant and impressive a role you can play for someone, the more you love them. And his thoughts are a closed book to Gilgi, who wishes: if you could just talk sensibly with him—about money, about economizing, about practical things. You'd like to see your future stretching before you like a smooth, clear road—a stretch of a shared future— and you see nothing but a dark, messy thicket.

"My poor little Gilgi, you look pale—I've got a marvelous old Burgundy, we'll drink it tonight—you'll get the roses back in your cheeks, and you'll cheer up.—And one day I'll just pack you in my suitcase and set off with you."

"Martin," Gilgi says, sitting down in his lap—"if you did some work!" She blushes dark red, is afraid he'll be angry. He just laughs: "What kind of work should I do?" Well, if someone asks like that, what are you supposed to answer? "Anyway, I do work, little Gilgi." Yes, he does. Thank God, he does. It happens once or twice a week that Martin suffers an acute attack of work-fever and writes from the evening into the small hours. Those are happy hours, when Gilgi lies awake at night and hears Martin's pen scratching across the paper. Those are happy hours, when the place beside her in bed is empty—because Martin is "working." She used to think that there was nothing more despicable than a man who doesn't work. And Gilgi would rather identify all the most pathetic, miserable qualities in the world in herself than find the slightest

defect in Martin. He's succeeded in half-convincing her
that not working doesn't necessarily need to be contempt-
ible, and that even if Martin is a—a—a non-worker, then
this just proves that there are—non-workers who are wonderful people. This proof notwithstanding: she's prouder
and happier when Martin is working. And when Gilgi,
during one of her brief meetings with Olga, says in passing: "he always works through the night," then she believes
it, because she wants to believe it.

"Now then, now then—my little one—dissatisfied
with me?" She grips his thick hair: "Martin, I feel sorry
for the girls who fall in love with bald-headed men—can't
be much fun scrabbling around on a bare surface without finding anything—yes, Martin—what I mean is—I—
whether you want to work—to work for money!"

"You don't have to come at me with such demoral-
izing suggestions, little Gilgi.—Lived a rich man, died
a poor one!—Go and put your red dress on, put lipstick on—young, pretty women are made even prettier
by make-up—old and ugly ones even uglier. One of life's
delightful injustices. Go on, little Gilgi, make yourself
beautiful tonight.—I'm going out again—back in a half-
hour."—Where's he going? Gilgi doesn't need to ask. Martin has recently developed a complex about the Church of
the Apostles: "I've rarely seen such purity of style!" At least
three times each day, he goes out and looks at the Church
of the Apostles. Dear, good Church of the Apostles, I don't
really know what's so special about you, but if you just
help a little to keep Martin in Cologne, then I'll think that
you're one of the most beautiful things in the world.

Gilgi puts on her coral-red dress. It falls in soft folds to
her feet. Has a bright, cheerful color, radiant and festive.

She fastens a belt of gold thread around her waist.—She made this dress before she ever met Martin. How pointless, how dead it would have remained if his eyes hadn't brought it to life.—

She stands in front of the mirror, powders her shoulders and the back of her neck, looks slim and frail and estranged. Removed from the everyday. Removed from reality. White face with dark eyes, very red mouth—I'm very pretty today—now—I'm allowed to say it, because I don't belong to myself anymore. What I see in the mirror is what someone else has made out of me, I can't take pride in it.—I shouldn't look like this—so disconnected from the street, the dust, the workaday. I look differently from the way I think. She runs her fingers cautiously over the indistinct line of her hips. My body is estranged from me, it's way ahead of me in knowledge, experience now ...

She lifts her hands—slowly—my hands have become unfaithful to me, once they were familiar to me—and now? Soft, tired skin, carefully filed fingernails, gleaming with rosy polish. Four tender, pampered lover's fingers on each hand—plus the index fingers with their typewriter-hardened tips—ordinary, robust tools for work—you mustn't put polish on them, too, you mustn't do that to them. Eight smooth, elegant fingers, two coarse ones—you ugly ones with the blunt nails, you're still my favorites among all my ten fingers.—

"Martin, my two index fingers are all you've let me keep of myself."

"Drink, my little Gilgi." Yes, yes, I want to drink. To break this resistance just once.—That's a damned good head for alcohol you've got—another glass—and Martin tells his brilliant stories, has laughing teeth and young lively eyes, and really he is younger, a thousand years younger than me—and you've got to drink, maybe it'll make you that young, too—and if he wrote down the stories he's telling—then they'd make him money—and you know you shouldn't tell him that, but you have to ... and now: he's never spoken like that before ... "this cursed country—messes up everyone who lives here—money, money, money—always talking about money and earning money ...". Oh, and you decide that you're an inferior money-grubber, you'll never say another word about money, you'll let everything fall in a heap, it doesn't matter what happens after that—it just doesn't matter.

"I'll take you away from this ugly country, little Gilgi—soon—what is there to keep you here—? Only a hundred-fifty marks at the office?"—Oh, he's so sick and tired of this gray rainy country, these miserable clockwork people—he wants to get away, and he wants to take this shining little girl with him—if she's already so pretty here, just how pretty will she be somewhere else, freed from her eight-hour day, no more of that stupid, pointless business stuff in her head. He'll simply take out everything that's still his from his brother's factory—they'll be able to have a good time on that for a few years—and then? Well, who cares what—after all, his greatest skill has always been in expunging stupid, annoying What-Thens from his life.—"We'll have a wonderful life—when we're somewhere else you'll belong to me more than you do here."

"But I do belong to you, Martin—I only wish I belonged—to—you. Yes, I'm drinking it."

Yes, that's how he likes me—when I'm talking stupid stuff like that—God preserve me from remembering tomorrow morning all the things I've said tonight, I'd be mortified. "The least important parts about me are the parts you like the best," and—and everything that means the most to me in the world is meaningless to him. He has no idea what matters to me. It's about so much more than the hundred-fifty marks, it's about—yes, if you could explain that, how you're fighting for something, something which exists but which you can't put a name to—.

"You mustn't say that, Martin—these hateful times—it's so mean to complain about your own times!—My times! The only ones I can live in. The times before, the times after—don't interest me at all. The times now are important to me, they belong to me—you shouldn't moan about your own times, and it's not enough to tolerate them—you have to stay loyal to them.

"I do want to laugh, Martin, I am laughing—I'm very happy—very, very happy, you'll stay with me—and I'll—

"Martin—go away from here, you say—with you! I—Martin—I belong here.—What happens here is my business—all of it. A sad country, you say? Martin, even at school I was ashamed when they sang 'Deutschland, Deutschland über alles'—such a revolting song—so oily when you were saying the words, so oily when you were thinking them, your whole mouth full of cod-liver oil.— Those people—who force their love of the fatherland on you—do you understand that—: instead of being quite humble and grateful when they get the chance to love something—they're proud of it as though they'd created it themselves—and they make what they've created into an obligation for other people. Such terrible nonsense.—It's nothing to do with me—but I was born here, and the language, the air, the sounds—whatever else—it's all familiar to me—the everyday things here, the practical things, the

modest things, the gray paving stones—it's all so important to me, and I love it all in my own way. Ugly country!
Maybe. But a mother still loves her child even when it has
terribly ugly bow legs—of course it would be idiotic and
not proper love if then she said that the legs were straight
and beautiful—she'd do better to go to the orthopedic spe-
cialist and ...

"Oh yes, Martin, I know I'm drunk ... I'm so tired—
I'll ..."

"You'll sleep." He carries her to the bed, slips her dress
off, takes her shoes off—her stockings—oh, no other man
in the world can be so soft and good and gentle ... and
don't think about anything, don't think about anything
anymore—no inhibitions now, no resistance—let yourself
fall, deep, deep, down into the unknown, where there's no
tomorrow—firm arms and smooth shoulders—Martin—I
want to keep him ...

Since that night, something in Gilgi has been broken beyond repair.—Oh, liking someone is good—loving someone—is good too. But being in love, really being in love:
an extremely painful condition. There should be a drug
to cure it. How hollowed out you are emotionally, cut off
from people and things, you're not seeing any longer, not
hearing any longer, everything is sinking—everything becomes profoundly unimportant. The effort to retain an
interest in anything is painful and destructive. Olga, Pit,
the Krons, Täschler—names without substance—without
form—far away, inessential. Names which emerge and disappear in a matter of seconds.—You sit at the office—the
memory of a word, a glance, flares up—reality sinks out

of sight, you feel nothing but this painful physical longing in your lips and the palms of your hands. You go to your room—a thin layer of dust covers the little Erika-brand typewriter, and vaguely your index finger traces strange little wave-patterns and circles in the dust. You lie down on the divan—you think, think, think—but what you're thinking aren't thoughts anymore, they're shapeless phantasms, images shrouded in red fog, ideas, events—from the past, from the future—stupid, silly, crazy—you get a revoltingly sweetish taste in your mouth—ach, why should you keep fighting—how, against what? Because you're so tired ...

"Kron," little Behrend says, "Kron, I have to tell you something ..."

"Yes, yes, what?"—

"It's Wendt, Kron—I was in Accounts, I heard everything they were saying in the next room—Wendt was in with the boss. Was supposed to get her notice—so she cried and said that her mother was sick and that—you—you didn't have to support anyone, and you were well-off—and it's all lies, Kron—I saw her with her mother—the day before yesterday, the old girl buzzes around like a bee and is as fit as a fiddle.—And now Reuter wants to give you notice instead of Wendt ..."

Thank God, thank God—now it's not my fault, I can't be blamed.—Thank God, I don't have to come here anymore, no-one will look at me anymore—I can't stand it anymore when people look me in the face. And if I am getting my notice—then why wait till next month, why not let me go straightaway?

And that evening Gilgi is sitting on the side of the bed—completely naked—except that she's festooned herself with all her colorful necklaces, red ones, green ones, blue ones, white ones—made of glass, wood, and mother-of-pearl.—"Martin, I can give you some good news, I'm not going to the office anymore—I've got my notice. Sad? Why should I be? Can't you see how happy I am, quite ordinarily happy? — — — Hey, Martin, do you know how I feel? Like someone who's sitting in a restaurant and eating and drinking and who knows that he doesn't have enough money to pay—so that he doesn't give a damn—just orders more and more—champagne and oysters and caviar—if you're going to stiff them on the bill, then do it properly, and not just for a small lager and a dry bread roll."

And if relentless activity, if a powerful will to live is diverted from its course, then it turns towards its mirror image—not to passivity—but to a kind of rage for self-destruction. Nothing matters now, tomorrow and debts and confusion—nothing matters — —

"Gilgi, my little Maori girl . . ." A thousand words of love, a thousand silly words, you're submerged in them, you're lying under a mantle of words, probably you're making a final feeble effort to find them ridiculous, formulating a cheeky, trivial little remark which promptly loses its way between the brain and the lips.

Warm, blue-sky days follow. They go out walking—"no, Martin, really—I think it's boring to run around so aimlessly, I love walking long distances, but I must be going somewhere."

"We are going somewhere."

"I seeee—so, where is it that we're going?"

"Well, we're sure to end up someplace."

"Yes, but I've got to know that when I set off."

"Martin, I don't know—don't walk so fast, Martin—I mean, you can't possibly think that these ugly, gray, rotting allotments are beautiful!—It's creepy here. Makes me think of sex-murderers."

"Well, that shows they're interesting."

"Martin, in summer—in summer we'll go swimming together in the Rhine—and we'll watch the bicycle races at the stadium. That's lovely, Martin: the guys in their colorful jerseys strewn all over the grass. And the marvelously exciting noise of the rushing wheels—ssssssst—as they flash around the curves—crash-bang, someone's down—you feel like you've fallen down with him. And everything is boiling and itching and glowing with excitement and tension—and a wide peaceful sky above it all, and the air is warm and trembling, and in the dark the arc lights look like stars which have fallen from the sky . . ." "Oh, my little Gilgi is turning poetical!"—"It's only a reflex, Martin."

It's fun to mooch around in Cologne's Old Town. Winding little alley-ways and uneven cobblestones—hot chestnuts, ten for ten pfennigs!—You fill your overcoat pockets with them and warm your fingertips on them.— Odd little cafés . . . "No, Martin, come on—we can't eat here—those cold cutlets must have been in the window for at least six months—if you go in there and order some, the waiter will take them out and dust them off and . . ."

"You can imagine such unpleasant things, little Gilgi!"

Houses twisted by age, tiny shops with windows no bigger than pillows, crammed with old clothes and suits, blocks of chocolate as old as the Bulgarian farmer in those yogurt advertisements, clocks which have taken a sacred

oath never to go again, guitars, children's trumpets ...
"Himioben" is the name over one of the doors. "Himioben," Martin says, enraptured.—"Himioben—such a wonderful name. Gilgi, I could never be completely angry with
a city where someone has that name." And has a vision of
an amazingly beautiful, mysterious Jewish girl with shining black hair and soft round eyes and entrancing lashes—
invents a fantastic story on the spot, he can do things you
wouldn't expect, this Martin—you're standing in the shab-
biest district of Cologne, outside a crooked little house
which looks like it would blow over in the first puff of
wind, and you feel like you're stuck between two pages
of the Old Testament—some vague idea: serving seven
years—something about cornfields and gleaning and—
whither thou goest, I will go ...

"Well, let's go in and take a look at the beautiful Jewish girl," Gilgi suggests, because now she's quite curious.
And it turned out to be a puny little red-headed guy who
shot up like a jack-in-the-box behind all the junk on his
shop counter—nothing like a beautiful Jewish girl. And
Martin bought a pair of suspenders—mauve with grass-
green spots, and Gilgi thinks that even seventy-five pfennigs is too much to pay for a shattered illusion.—"But the
name is still beautiful, and the idea too—but I won't wear
the suspenders—"

The final disappointment!—Gilgi throws the little
package into the Rhine at the Hohenzollern Bridge—"so it
can float into the North Sea and be eaten by a flounder.—
You know, Martin, I could probably forgive my husband
if he punched me on the nose sometime—but if he ever
turned up wearing suspenders, I'd leave him."

"Wives who make such elevated aesthetic demands of

their husbands demonstrate a very lax morality.—Please don't fall into the Rhine, Gilgi—it'll be too cold for me to jump in after you until the end of April."

And they look at paintings, listen to concerts. Wearing a long black lace dress, Gilgi sits in Gürzenich Hall. Tries to adopt a stylishly attentive expression, but turns her eyes again and again to Martin's hard, angular profile. Hears sounds which bore her, and feels a strong desire to give Martin a kiss. Hears sounds which she likes and feels an even stronger desire to kiss Martin. And just can't stand the fact that at the moment he's occupied with something other than her, must at least touch his hair briefly. Wants him to laugh about something with her, to explain to her quickly why so many people have such silly expressions and closed eyes when they're listening to music—and there's a fat man sitting beside them who's breathing so loudly in time with the music that he almost sounds like he's snoring ... "Pssssst!" go the people in the row behind. Like angry cobras! "Please, Martin, just tell me quickly if it's cobras that hiss like that—schschsch ... like a garden hose when someone pushes the air out of it ..."

Literature, music, painting—it's a funny thing, art. One person's Rubinstein—is another's dance-band leader, one person's Rembrandt—is another's commercial artist. What can you do? It's a long way to Tipperary—it's a long way to ... there ...

THAT'S HOW YOU STROLL THROUGH YOUR DAYS—
playful, in love, doing the thousand silly things that add up
to doing nothing. Not thinking much about tomorrow, not
thinking at all about the day after. And it's only at seven in
the morning, when—from long habit—her eyes open like
two curtains falling back, that Gilgi feels the faint little
pangs of a bad conscience before falling asleep again.

Once Olga visits her briefly. Is disturbed and amazed
and not at all approving of the transformation in Gilgi's
life. Even though she used to talk quite differently.—

"It's all well and good, little Gilgi, little pocket-sized
Tannhäuser—but why are you doing such stupid things?
Living together in this compacted, intense way can only
cause trouble in the end. Gilgi—hey—listen to me!" The
girl's eyes are quite glassy. "Surely you must know what
you want! If you go on like this, he'll get sick of you one
day—or you of him. You silly girl—first you go on like a
petty-bourgeois wife, a dutiful Martha—no man alive can
stand the shock of suddenly discovering that he has to be
grateful to a woman. Well, and now—you're sacrificing
everything, and of course you feel uncomfortable in your
own skin. God, why not lose your inhibitions for once!
But then to cut yourself off so completely from all your
previous interests!—And one day you'll realize that it's impossible for the poor man to do for you what you're doing

for him, and then you won't forgive him for your stupid-
ity. Our own mistakes are always the ones which we hold
against other people ..."

"So—what—should—I—do?—I know, Olga, everything I'm doing is wrong. I can't see my way clear anymore. Everything in me is confused—don't know what I
want anymore—so what should I do?"

"Don't make him the foundation of your life, don't bet
everything on one card. How tired you look! You need
your work and your independence, you ..."

"Stop it, Olga, stop it—my thoughts can't follow you
any further." She's standing in the middle of the room,
the little one, holding her hands over her ears—so what
should I do? Sinks, falls, cries out—"I want someone,
someone, someone—don't belong anywhere—why this
one in particular? No idea—but I want—to have him—to
keep him—I want, I want, I want ..."

"Gilgi," Olga says, and her voice is bursting with love
and the desire to comfort. She kneels beside the little one,
puts an arm around her shoulder, speaks words which give
encouragement with her frivolous hands, asks questions
which give sympathy to the mottled, helpless little face,
listens with an attentiveness which unites her to the thin,
failing voice—"and you're together at night and walk beside each other during the day, without a single word that
binds you—you only catch words which are soap-bubbles.
And there's something somewhere that I don't understand—my thoughts hit a wall—and—can—anyone—
understand—that—Olga, understand that you're so
ashamed when you remember all the important things?
And are afraid of something that you don't understand
and that isn't a word? And you're all ripped up, and have

typewriter words and clockwork words and everyday words and don't want to think about yourself and should think about yourself.—I love him so much, Olga—no, don't look at me ..." And the never-tender little girl Gilgi embraces her friend, moves her lips over her face and neck, her lips are hot ... "Silly little girl," Olga says and has to love Gilgi in the way that everyone who turns their face to the sun and is saturated with light has to love sad tenderness.

"My God, Olga"—Gilgi's hand gropes over the floor—"that's a rug, isn't it? And you're the sweet, blond, radiant marzipan girl, and I ..." she jumps up, her firm, bright Gilgi-voice has returned, "I, Olga, I've been stung by a wild hormone—I'm crazy about a man—c'est tout. Nothing unusual, happens in the best families." She sits down on the windowsill, swings her legs—"he'll have had enough of me one day—there it is. Oh yes, tell me, Olga, am I imagining it, or has Houbigant's ochre face-powder really got worse?"

"I think Hudnut's powder is better. And—Gilgi—I know a lot of people in Berlin, I could get you a job there as a secretary—anyway: you know I have the egotistical habit of giving myself absolution for my own sins by helping the people I like when they happen to need it ... there, take some of my powder if yours is no good." Gilgi turns her face away with a hard little jerk—you've become so sensitive, so exposed to every kind word—you have to bust out crying when someone says something nice to you, it's just because—"I'm full of nerves, marzipan girl—c'est l'amour—ah, Martin! Speak of the Devil ... Why do you have to go so soon, Olga?"

"No, kids, you can't blame me for that. When I'm together with people who are in love—firstly I get sick, secondly I turn green and yellow with envy ... so! For the sake of my complexion ... See you!"

Gilgi is lying in bed. She's asleep. Wakes up: one in the morning. Martin has gone out. Why shouldn't a man go out by himself sometimes? That's quite in order. But why hasn't he got back yet? Surely nothing can have happened to him? ... Can it? ... Nonsense, he wouldn't cheat on her. It's not as if they're married.

Gilgi can't stand it in bed anymore. Gets up, walks up and down the room. How can you be so listless and so tired, tired from doing nothing all day? You never used to be this tired. And why can't you be by yourself anymore? You've got a pathological fear of being by yourself. Don't just walk up and down so pointlessly, now, do something, some work. Gilgi pulls on her dressing gown. Switches on the lights in all the rooms, nothing is too bright. Looks uncared-for, the apartment. Gilgi fetches a broom and some rags and a pail from the kitchen, starts scrubbing and cleaning—in the middle of the night. She works until her arms start to hurt, which makes her feel very cheerful and healthy. And Olga is quite right when she says that not working doesn't agree with her.

Gilgi goes into Martin's room—his writing-room, if you like—calling it a workroom would seem just slightly exaggerated, even to Gilgi. There are some pages with writing on them on the desk, Gilgi reads a little of them: they're about the customs and traditions of South Sea Islanders—"it'll be quite a long, detailed job," Martin said once—"and is sure to take at least two years." Gilgi puts the papers back carefully, pointing this way and that—just as they had been. Because you read that somewhere once: how upset men get when women with a mania for tidiness attack their writing desks. Except—presumably you're allowed to pick up what's on the floor. Bills! A whole bundle. All unpaid. Gilgi holds them with her fingertips, just as if they were poisonous. Which they are, really. She doesn't want to look at them, or to talk about them with Martin anymore, either, never again. Don't worry yourself about them—don't think about them at all. But it's terrible when you leave the building together and stroll immediately and without speaking to the other side of the street, just so that you don't have to go past the delicatessen, because ... no, that kind of thing is no fun, and no matter how many times you say that it's a great joke and a big laugh, you're always lying.

Letters, letters. From all kinds of places. Gilgi puts them into a pile. They're all lying around quite openly, the letters. He has no secrets from her, does Martin. Funny habit, chucking everything on the floor. Gilgi feels a kind of housewifely pride well up in her when she sees an Amsterdam postmark on one letter. The little Dutch girl! Oh, she knows the story. The poor child is still in love with Martin. No reason why he shouldn't write her a few friendly words now and then, and of course no reason why he should write her more than that. Gilgi wouldn't dream of reading the letter, because it's nothing to do with her, and anyway it's handwritten. Handwritten letters seem so importunately intimate, so embarrassingly self-revelatory—this one finds its way into the drawer with the others. Right—the floor looks more or less as it should now. There—another letter under the desk. From Zurich—from Martin's brother—from Christoph. Engagingly clear

typescript.— ... and really it's high time that you finally
see reason ... — ... don't know what you think you can
live on if you take your money now ... Gilgi unfolds the
letter, it's definitely worth knowing what Christoph has to
say: ah, Martin wanted his money, and Christoph wants to
hang on to it. That's good! It explains why there's been no
talk of going away recently.

Gilgi is sitting on the chaise longue, with her feet
propped on the edge of the scrubbing pail, and her left
arm wrapped around the handle of the broom. The letter
is lying on her lap. She shakes her head, understanding
less than ever. Looks five years into the future. A grim vision: Martin in rags, Martin wandering around half- or
three-fourths-starved, she wandering with him. Salvation
Army, homeless shelter, confidence tricks—unedifying
words, particularly unedifying ideas. You ought to make a
decision, you ought to ... suddenly she feels ice-cold, her
teeth start to chatter. Where has Martin got to? It's better
not to look at the clock, it'll just make you nervous. Goose
bumps crawl over her back and arms, the bright lights
suddenly hurt her eyes, stabbing at her face. And if Martin
didn't come back ... this completely idiotic thought occu-
pies one second, but plunges you immediately into a world
of gray and cold, ice and melancholy, and everything looks
like the dirty blackish water in the scrubbing pail, and now
your left slipper falls into the pail, to top everything off.
Gilgi fishes it morosely out of the slimy liquid, limps to the
window, puts the slipper on the sill outside: it can dry off
there, and if the wind blows it into the front garden Martin
will have to fetch it up tomorrow morning.

Gilgi lies down in bed again. Pushes the letter from
Christoph under the pillow—it rustles. You ought to make

a decision. When Martin comes, you'll say to him, you'll say to him: quite calmly and sensibly—Martin, my darling, you have to understand—if you like me even a little bit, then you'll want me to feel well and contented, and that's why I'm going to Badstrasse tomorrow, to the labor office—about the benefits and about a new job—later. I'm going to—we're going to—share the household expenses, and after this we won't talk about it anymore. And if this is just a passing mood on my part—well, then there's nothing you should respect more than another person's moods, especially the ones that make lif̲̲ ̲̲̲̲̲̲ for you. I'll say to him—when he comes, when he—my God, why doesn't he come!

And Gilgi waits. Minutes pass so slowly, slowly, the darkness is oppressive and sad, and the silence hums with that disturbing absence of sound that hurts you and makes you afraid. And I'll say to him ... I—my God, he has to come, he has to, he has to, he has to. And there's a magic lantern in the room, images flicker in the dark, imaginings—you don't want to look at them, must look, precisely because you don't want to. Images, images ... Martin in an accident, Martin dead ... And you feel like a criminal and burn with shock because you can imagine such things, and it's like how as a child you were suddenly seized by the idea that your mother had died, and the only reason you can imagine something like that is because you're incapable of believing it. And the smell of Martin's warm healthy skin on the pillows, so much life on the pillows, whispered words and you and me and longing and ... angular images in the dark, and you want to see them, want to hurt yourself. Sooner a hard pain than this soft creeping longing, sooner—Craccck! goes the door. A step and a breath, you fall into the sound. "Ah, there you are!" You can say it quite calmly at the same time as you're overwhelmed with joy, and beneath that joy there's just a very tiny, contradictory feeling of shame and disappointment because this excess of blood-chilling fears was so unnecessary and ridiculous.

There's a rainbow round my shoulder ... Martin whistles and sits down next to Gilgi on the side of the bed. The pale light from the lamp on the night-table brushes over his hands, hands full of tenderness and love for life. And he tells her all about where he's been: at the Rhine harbor, on a freighter with an old Dutch sailor, drinking toddy and playing cards and sinking thousands of meters below sea level under the weight of the man's tall tales ...

Martin—is sitting beside me, with his hat on his knees, it's a kind of miracle that he's here now. And suddenly the waiting seems to gain a purpose. It's so nice to have waited for a man you love. Waiting made you so pleased to see him. And now he's here, that means so much. So much light. And he's speaking with his lips, his shoulders, speaking—and every word is a little human being, has legs, walks around the room—walks up to you, is round and tangible, you can put your arms around it ... speaking with a quiet, soft voice, very melodious, a little hoarse—a little red drop of blood in the word. Bright light in dark eyes. I suppose they have to be dark, his eyes, to show such a silver light. And young dark hair, pressed into funny little curls at the back and sides by the hat-brim. He speaks: "The smell of fish and tar—an enchanted river— smooth water, unyielding and dark. Reflected lights— silver streaks—shimmering promises. Air like cool silk. Tired blue sky—like the eyes of a woman who knows herself so well that she becomes guileless again. An insistent smell of tobacco—and soft, curly clouds of smoke—fairy tales breathed into the air. A little Frans Hals child. An old salt—always drunk as a matter of principle, his nose—a permanent state of euphoria. A little geranium with sweet, silly flat leaves, entrancingly unconscious of their severity of form, every single leaf a professor of mathematics, and their blossoms—so shamelessly red, as carelessly red as a little Mexican hooker—sweet little hooker—a pure red—a color unadulterated by any mish-mash morality. A great, round nocturnal silence—a circle—a shrill yell falls from the bank — — the secret of contrasts, my little Gilgi. A secret in a thousand boxes—when you open the first box, you find the second one hidden inside it—and so on, forever—you know a little bit more each time and—a great deal less."

He's rather drunk, Martin—there's a rainbow round my shoulder . . .

Gilgi puts her hand on his chin, presses his head down towards her—"Oh, Martin, my darling . . ."—teeth which are so hungry for life, probably wants to eat up the whole world! He's so in love with life, loves everything, everyone—that has nothing to do with milksop-tolerance and rolled-oat-kindness—just loves everything because he simply can't do otherwise. And you understand that, maybe it's the only thing you agree about: Life is a fine thing! Its comforts and burdens, its sadnesses and joys. Life is a fine thing. You'll never let anyone say anything different. Never. Anyone.

There's a rainbow round my shoulder . . . Old Dutch sailor! You don't quite understand what it was about him that Martin liked so much. Not that it matters at all whether you understand everything, the main thing is

that Martin enjoyed it. Why? Who cares why. You have
a sacred responsibility. To respect what the other person
enjoys. People are quite happy to see others in trouble,
then often they're pleasant and sympathetic—and mostly
they're so mistrustful and intolerant of the unfamiliar little
joys of those who think differently. The letter rustles under the pillow—you were going to say something—labor
office ... "it was so beautiful down there tonight, little
Gilgi, I wished so much that you'd been with me." Labor
offi ... every word gets stuck in your throat ... wished
so much that you'd been with me ... another second and
you'll bust out crying for sheer happiness. It would be silly,
anyway—there's simply no point talking about such things
to Martin. Quite suddenly, your eyes are opened a little
to the way he's made. You understand a little about Why
and Because. You feel the spell of his refusal to be worried, his refusal to be weighed down, his lovable eagerness
to take pleasure in everything, a pleasure which makes
everything worthwhile, and his eagerness to find everything more important than himself. With his intellect, he
has completed a journey in three stages—from the simple,
via the complicated, to simplicity again. Is clever enough
to have stopped engaging in clever talk, doesn't need to
say everything he knows. Isn't witty—they're so annoying,
witty people—and of course anyone who really possesses
wit has no need to be witty.

He's a proper human being, is Martin—pas grand
chose—but genuine and real, and he's wonderful just the
way he is, you wouldn't want him to be different, not the
slightest bit different.

"But you're not even tired, Martin! Please, do me a favor,
fetch me that big orange from the dining-room ... Peel it

for me, would you? I always hate doing that. — — — Hey, Martin, you know, really people talk such terrible nonsense—for example, if a woman loves a man, she wants to be proud of him and admire him! That's quite untrue. If you love a man, then you don't want to be proud of him, then you just are proud of him, terribly proud—it's impossible for you to be anything else—regardless of whether it's the ex-emperor of China or Willy Fritsch or a hunchbacked guy who sells radishes on a street corner. And admiration! Nah, that won't make a woman look up from her magazine. What good would the most fabulous, most learned university professor be to me if he didn't know how to kiss properly — —"

A miracle comes to pass: Martin works for three days straight—day and night. Gilgi moves around the apartment on tiptoe. Cooks his lunch, puts it silently on his desk—disappears again. A few sentences on the handwritten pages become illegible, because they've got spinach stains on them—so tomorrow you'll cook cauliflower.

Gilgi is left to her own resources. It occurs to her that she doesn't have a thing to wear anymore. She'd rather string herself up than run around sloppily dressed. Her spring and summer wardrobes must be overhauled. It's a good thing you have time for that. In the afternoon she goes to the savings bank, withdraws five hundred of her twelve hundred marks. Firstly you have to buy material, shoes, a hat—gloves—God, suddenly you need all kinds of things. Bath salts, a little perfume, face-powder . . . "first come powder and perfume—then food," Olga always says. This statement contains profound wisdom. And also you're going to contribute to the household expenses, Martin needn't notice. You'll see if you can't straighten things out a little after all, secretly, quietly, and softly.

That evening, Gilgi works like a madwoman at the sewing machine—half the night: a dress like this has to be made quickly, otherwise you lose interest. And the next morning she makes her planned visit to the labor office. You'll get a little over thirteen marks a week. You don't mind taking that! "Don't you see, Martin?—more than fifty marks a month for nothing, nothing at all! That's worth the trouble of picking it up!"

"Well, if it's a kind of pension ..." Martin once knew an army officer's widow who also ... There's no point in explaining the purpose and significance of social welfare to him—he just doesn't get it—so you won't even try.

"Gilgi, I've gotten a friend to send me two thousand marks, shall we go away somewhere?"

Gilgi is shocked. "No."

"But why not?"

"I can't do that, Martin—you have to understand—I mean, everyone has something they can't do. I can't set off into the blue from one day to the next on borrowed money. I'm not a Philistine, and I'm not a coward, either, but I must be able to keep a grip on the things I do, and to take responsibility for them. I can't be completely dependent on someone, even if it's the person I like most in the world—maybe then least of all.

"Send the money back to your friend—or let's pay debts with it—to please me, Martin ..."

A thousand objections from Martin, a thousand more from Gilgi—and there's a thousand-and-first objection too—maybe there is—you can't talk about that one yet.

Great God—this happiness comes at a high price! There's no possibility of holding onto it, none . . .

"Martin, be nice, be reasonable. No-one can change who he is. Look, I wouldn't love you as much if I was being towed along helplessly in your wake. That's a good reason, that is—isn't it? Do you want me not to love you as much?" No, he doesn't want that, he must like the little one more than he thought, because he goes cold all over just at the thought of that happening.

"I do want to respect all your crazy ideas, Gilgi, I swear to God—even when I don't understand them. But as it turns out that your independence complex is incurable, then—why don't you go to your mother—to the one who has so much money—she's shown no interest in you her whole life long—there's every reason why she should give you a few thousand marks—my God, it's the most obvious thing in the world: anyone with money to spare gives it to people who are close to him—and who don't have any at the time. I've always done it like that. Because having money is no fun at all in itself and . . ."

"No, no, no, Martin, I won't do that—go there." Gilgi is offended. "I won't do that, I can't do that, I don't like the idea"—the exalted tone in her voice is making her angry, she throws her arms around Martin's neck—"let's just stay here, let's just stay here, for God's sake. And I don't like that, I can't ask anyone for money—can't ask anyone . . ."

"But, my little Gilgi—of course I'd be a thousand times happier if you didn't go. What's the matter? There's no reason for you to get so upset. I just thought that if relying on me a little disturbs you so much . . ." There's almost a trace of bitterness in his words. What a terribly stupid man! They're all the same. Their minds make them logical, sometimes—their feelings make them illogical, always. "You men develop textbook cases of claustro-phobia as soon as we become completely dependent on you—it's your deepest fear: an obligation which deprives you of your freedom—all right, fine, it's understandable. But then suddenly we're supposed to rely utterly on you anyway, and if we don't want to, then you're even more annoyed . . ."—"My little Gilgi, they don't suit you at all, these speeches in the plural: We women! You men! Come on, be nice and sweet. Will you be happy if I say: we'll stay here, for God's sake?"

"Yes, Martin, yes—and, we'll pay some debts now, won't we?"

"Yes," Martin says. It sounds rather lukewarm, that Yes, and could just as well mean No. Nonsense—pay some debts! There's still plenty of time for that. It's so marvelous to have two thousand marks in your pocket, you simply hadn't realized before how marvelous it is.

And that very afternoon, Martin goes to Olga. He wants to buy a beautiful fur coat for Gilgi—so Olga has to help him choose it—and material for a violet-blue dress, and dark amethyst jewelry in old silver settings to go with it. He saw it the other day at an antique dealer's near the cathedral: ring, bracelet, necklace. That'll be pretty—such a feather-light, pale little girl with such heavy jewelry. Olga is blazing with enthusiasm. Shopping is one of her passions, quite regardless of whether it's for her or some-one else.

"Ach, Martin!" Gilgi's face trembles on the verge of tears as Martin, beaming with pleasure, spreads his trea-sures out before her that evening. If I start crying now . . . no, no, no—it made him so happy, and now I'm happy, too, I'm so happy—so happy today, and tomorrow ... yes, yes, I'm happy. He's so good to me, so nice and so good.

The violet-blue material is duly made up into a dress the next day. Turns out really well. "I've never had such a beautiful dress, Martin!" He's amazed: "You're so good at this, little Gilgi! It's a dream by Paul Poiret, a—what can I say ..." And Gilgi's cheeks glow with pride and joy. And it's so cute—there's no other way of putting it—so touchingly cute, the way these men look at a woman's dress—with one eye for what's in it, and the other for the dress itself—sort of semi-understanding things. And he's so terribly proud of this semi-understanding—holding a bit of the silk in his hand almost reverently, anxiously, as though it could burst into flame between his fingers.

"Right, little Gilgi, we're going out tonight—in the best style—and only eating and drinking things which are appropriate to the dress." And Olga has to come with them, she chose the material with such a sacred passion.

"Right, and if we have the least spark of imagination, then we'll be able to convince ourselves that this old rattle-trap of a taxi is a fabulous Rolls-Royce—or—we're arch-snobs, Martin ..."

"You're as pretty as a picture, little Gilgi!"

"Always like hearing that kind of thing, Martin—please, say it again. What? Say it three more times—can't ever hear it enough.—Martin, the fur coat! Well, it makes me think I'm—absolutely top-class, Martin! Stop it—don't mess up my hair—I'm too elegant now for such backseat fumblings. Stop!!! We're there—go up, Martin—fetch Olga ...

"Wait a second, Martin—how do they do it: left foot on the ground, right foot on the running board—the wife of chairman of the board So-and-So and her streamlined, sporty 17/100 hp four-seater cabriolet with its elegantly customized bodywork—*Elegant World*—back page ... I'm sorry, Martin, but all this provokes me into being uncouth. So now I'll spit, in a first-class, streamlined, elegantly customized three-meter arc over to that wall there. Oh, Martin—Martin—no, you can't do that—in broad daylight on a public street—Martin, let me go—if that's from *Customs and Traditions of the South Sea Islanders*—it'll get you into trouble with some customs and traditions of the Cologne City Police ... Don't, Martin—otherwise I'll have to spend more than the thirteen marks unemployment benefits on my lipstick — — — go on, get up there, Martin!"

The young lady Gilgi stands by herself beside the taxi, dragging her upper lip at a crazy angle down over her attractive white teeth. Suddenly turns pale under her make-up, a shoulder sags back against the side window—it'll all get serious soon, it'll all be over soon ... She puts her brave little-girl face back on quickly. You'll get through it—one way or another—you have courage, and you won't let it get you down, and with God's help—at least it won't be twins.

"Ah, Olga, my dear Olga! Doesn't she look marvelous, Martin! I think it's unnatural that you're not in love with her — — —"

"Little Gilgi, your men are sacrosanct to me."—"Men! Who said anything about polyandry!"—"Yes, we're all hopelessly monogamous."—"Of course, we're decadent from sheer morality ..."

There's a lot to be said for hiding your feelings under chatter. Dear Olga. Gilgi is holding Olga's hand, her knees are enclosed by Martin's knees. Three people are speaking to each other, knees are speaking to each other, and two

hands.—You have to love her, Olga, this frivolous girl.—
Gilgi laughs, draws her fur coat around her shoulders with
a graceful, gentle movement—the dark amethyst glows
on her pale, slender ring-finger—her left hand is gripped
around Olga's, digging her fingernails into Olga's soft
palm. Don't be afraid, little girl—Olga's fingers say—don't
be afraid—there'll be no questions, nothing said—I'll wait,
and when the time comes I'll be here. You can be sure of
that—and is it enough that you can be sure? Thanks a
lot, Olga.

"Where are we going, anyway? Oh, to the Savoy . . ."

"Yes, Chablis first—old Pommery later . . ."

"Oh, Martin, I think most high-class people have a
waiter psychosis. They order only the best dishes, and pretend that they do it all the time—just to impress the waiter.
I suppose that's some kind of ambition!"

They eat, they drink, they laugh. They get on well together and feel good.—"Nothing agrees with me today,"
Gilgi complains after the second glass of champagne. Feels
like she's been KO'd by a heavy leaden tiredness. But soon
she's laughing again, she's kicking over the traces, and she's
just a tiny, tiny bit too loud. "Your health, children," she
cries, with an unpleasant little undertone of mockery in
her voice. Gallows humor. "Your health, children—are
there three or four of us here at the table?"—"Are you already seeing double, little Gilgi?"—"Qui sait?" She laughs.

"Pit came to see me a few days ago," Olga says, "he was
asking after you, Gilgi, and . . ." Pit! Gilgi passes a hand
over her forehead. Pit! "What's he doing, how is he?" Her
questions tumble over each other. If he was looking for
me, then he needs me—Gilgi suddenly feels a senseless
longing for Pit, for his hard solitariness, for the clarity

of his being. She jumps up—"I have to go to him for a
bit—don't be angry with me, Martin—is he still playing in
Lintstrasse, Olga? I'll take a taxi, Martin—I'll be there in
five minutes, and back again in no more than a half-hour."
Martin objects, Olga objects: now—so suddenly—surely
you've been all right without him for long enough—tomorrow will be just as good—but why—why ... "God in
heaven, you're driving me crazy. Does everything always
have to be explained!!! I want to go now—now—try to
understand me—no, I want to go alone ..." She's already
outside in a taxi.

Love Song From Tahitiiii ... "Hello, young man," Gilgi
says, tapping Pit on the shoulder—just like the last time ...
Pit looks up. His face has become even narrower, even
paler, his eyes even more sunken—different—not softer—
no—his gaze is more distant.

"Just take a seat, Gilgi, I'll be with you shortly." He
presses her hand quickly, firmly, and lets it go ... Love
Song From Tahiti ... Gilgi lets her fur coat slip half off her
shoulder. She looks exquisite, very beautiful and elegant.
She'd completely forgotten that she looks like that—she
only remembers again because the waitress asks her so respectfully what she would like to order. She's almost a little
ashamed when she looks at Pit—she finds her elegance so
false. She's ashamed because she loves this false elegance
so much. She even has to give the ring an extra polish,
arrange the folds of her dress more attractively. "Madam."
The waitress with the hopelessly ravaged face sets the glass
of port before Gilgi—you stupid fool, you—stop grinning
so obsequiously! If I was sitting here in my battered trench
coat, with the smell of work about me, I wouldn't impress
you! Hey, aren't you ashamed to be so stupid, so terribly

stupid ... I suppose I should go to the doctor tomorrow—tomorrow or the day after or—whether it's true—
the ... Love Song From Tahiti ... Gilgi closes her eyes, she
never did that—before. When she shut her eyes, she saw
nothing—nothing—now she sees a great deal behind the
closed lids.

"Don't fall asleep, Gilgi!" Pit is sitting opposite her.
"Well, you've made a good job of your clothes—you could
be Al Capone's moll, about to set off for the Metropolitan
Opera."

Gilgi is so tired that her eyes stay open. "Give me your
hand for a moment, Pit—hold on to it hard—harder—
so that it hurts—I've got to feel right down into my heart
that you're holding my hand." Pit presses Gilgi's fingers—if
she says a word like "heart," then there's something badly
wrong with her ... the pulse beating in her fingers, the
bare white shoulder, the tilted-back head—a little red
patch on the white throat ... "it'll be like giving me a gift,
Gilgi, if you let me help you." He'd been looking for her,
wanting to talk to her, been looking for her—her kind little
friend, and now ...

"Pit"—Gilgi's voice comes into the room from a long
way away—"I'm starving for brutal honesty—Pit, I wanted
you to hold my hand differently ... you can't help me by
doing something for me, you can only help me because
you're there. Be tough and angry and clear, Pit, I need that."
Gilgi isn't looking at Pit, her glance is stuck somewhere in
the jungle of red and white paper streamers on the ceiling—but she knows that it's Pit and no-one else that she's
speaking to. "Maybe you already know that I don't have
a job now, that I'm living with a man ..." Pit sits leaning
forward, looking at Gilgi's arm: a diagonal, stiff, white line

which flows into his hand. The corpse-like indifference of that line suddenly becomes a vicious, brutal insult to him. His hand feels like digging all five nails into her soft, pale shoulder, and dragging them down the diagonal line—scoring five bloodied furrows into the unmoved and unmoving white. His brain wraps itself around Gilgi's words. "I don't have a job anymore, I'm living with a man . . ."

"Do you like him?"

"Since when do you ask superfluous questions, Pit! I'd pick out someone to live with that I don't like! I'm giving you some facts just to set the overall picture. Facts don't scare me, facts are something I can deal with. I might be having a baby—this kind of thing happens all the time—to any number of girls. If that's the case, I'll deal with it as well, no reason to go all sentimental or lose my head. No, what's scaring me is something different. Usually people don't talk about it, or if they do, they lie about it and wrap it up . . . and that's why you don't know whether you've suddenly become completely different from everyone else, you don't know whether it's normal and everyone gets through it, or if you're alone with a sickness . . ."

"What—do you mean?"

"Just let me talk, you'll catch on soon enough, catch on to what I mean. You know that I've had boyfriends—two—three . . . we liked each other, we had fun together, and our skins said Yes to each other. That was natural and comprehensible, it caused absolutely no pangs of conscience and no unease. I always felt clean and clear, I was sure of myself and knew what I wanted and the limits I had set, which made such good sense that you didn't need to think about them. And now — — — that I love someone—really love someone, for the first time in my life, so that I feel good and honest and capable of anything—everything should be fine—and right and—but . . ." Gilgi's head falls forward, she grabs Pit's wrists with both hands—her mouth a garish narrow line, her words—falling slowly, unemphatically, mechanically: "I don't know what my limits are anymore or what I want, I can't be responsible anymore for what I might do from one day to the next. I thought that my love had made me infinitely safe and protected—now it's made me defenseless, completely exposed—how is that possible, Pit??? I'm at the mercy of everyone and everything—of a hand which brushes the back of my neck as it's helping me into my coat—of a glance, a voice . . . I had no idea that I could be like this—I'm burning up—I have an agonizing physical connection to everything—when I close my hand around the edge of the table, when I see a flower—when I stroke this fur coat . . . I find myself unspeakably disgusting. Nothing is clean and clear and simple anymore, not even my previous life. Maybe everything the previous Gilgi did and wanted was just a means of running away from—from her own desire. Maybe nothing has value in itself, maybe everything is untrue, and everything is driven purely by that running away . . . Where will it end? What's happening with me? It's stretching on into eternity—I'm scared, Pit."

Pit's face is distorted, his voice hoarse and broken: "Why are you telling me this—you! That's why you came to me—that's why . . . just to tell me . . ."

Gilgi looks at him. "I see, Pit!" Dull mockery appears at the corners of her mouth. "Well, you're right—every man for himself . . . neither of us can complain of a shortage of egotism. And thank you, Pit—maybe the best way for you to help me is by showing me—another glass of port,

Fräulein—quickly ... by showing me that each one of us can rely only, only, only on himself." Gilgi jumps up, stands behind Pit, grips him firmly by the back of the neck. "I believed in you, young man—in your capacity for fairness.— To hell with you and all your Socialism and your schemes for improving the world if you're one of those men who hold it against a woman if, by God knows what accident of biology, she doesn't want to sleep with them. You guys know exactly how to make a woman furious!" Gilgi's hand moves slowly and angrily over Pit's ear, creeps into his hair—"don't flinch, young man—I've known for ages that men and women are animals by nature, I also know that we have a sacred duty to make something different of ourselves, and I still believe that we have the strength and the chance to be more than we are. Through ourselves? Despite ourselves? Doesn't matter, I still believe ..."

Gilgi is standing on the street. Leaning on the gray wall of an apartment building. Haze in the street—hookers screeching. I'm so mean! Better to find yourself mean than to lie to yourself. Gilgi walks, walks—each step an unspeakable exertion—chewing on her disappointment. Stops again. Twists her pale hands together—avoid one thing at all costs: never be cowardly, never be dishonest. That would be the worst thing: attributing your own guilt to other people ... and forgive us our trespasses as we forgive those ... tear the Lord's Prayer to pieces with your hands, tear it to pieces with your teeth—it lies, lies, lies, and deceives. Instill knowledge in our blood, instill belief in our blood—one thing, one thing above all: teach us to believe only in our own guilt—not: as we forgive those ... that doesn't make sense—we have nothing to forgive, nothing—never—no-one. No-one has trespassed against us, there is always and only our own guilt. Yes, that's how it is—Pit didn't make me furious—he only proved to me how angry and hateful I really am. Dear God, what's happening to me ... I want to go home—I want to go to Martin. The elegant young lady Gilgi hails a taxi—"this one's a cutie," the driver thinks, winking with his right eye—she collapses onto the shabby upholstery. Lets her hands hang down over her knees, her head loll forward, has her lips half-open—Martin, my darling, what have you turned me into? Such longing. Longing for you—longing beyond you—longing—you—you've kissed away the firmness in my legs.

It's late at night. Gilgi's head is lying on Martin's chest, she's buried her hands in his armpits. "Martin," she says quietly, "you're much smarter than I am, you know much more than I do—you must make sure that love doesn't destroy my love for you. It mustn't ever happen that one day you're only a man to me—you must always be Martin to me." She lifts her head — — — no answer. Quick, regular breaths. He's asleep. Her unsatiated lips feel their way up his chest, his throat—as far as the mouth—my darling, it would be so nice if you always knew everything that was in me without me needing to talk about it. That would be so nice. But I suppose one shouldn't ask too much.

A functional consulting-room. Shining instruments. Smell of nothing. Self-conscious asepsis. Gilgi sits on the narrow, cool, slippery chaise longue and manages to put a neat, firm knot in her tie despite the absence of a mirror. The little blond doctor stands at the wash-basin, drying his thin, pallid gynecologist's hands with irritating slowness.

"For crying out loud, spit it out, Doctor—what can you tell me? Am I having a child or not? What? In seven months? I see.—Fine, that's all I wanted to know. — — — Please say what you have to say in German, I don't understand Latin." The little blond doctor doesn't know whether to be surprised or offended. In the end he conceals his indecision behind patronizing goodwill.

"You're as fit as a fiddle, young lady. Marvelously constructed hips—"

Gilgi interrupts: "What do you mean, Doctor, marvelously constructed hips." As always when confronted by difficult and unalterable circumstances, she's completely enveloped in ice-cold rationality. You need a strong dose of street-urchin manners for self-protection. No fear of words, no fear of ideas—plain speaking. She feels a fierce and unjust anger against the harmless little doctor. Don't make yourself so important, you pathetic medical-school Mickey Mouse, you ... "What do you mean, marvelously constructed hips! I don't want a child."

The little doctor places his hand paternally on Gilgi's shoulder. —"Young lady ..."

"Enough of the cozy granddaddy routine—I don't want a child."

"You mustn't get so excited now, dear young lady—it would be best if you got married."

"I'd say that knowing what'd be best is somewhat beyond your area of expertise, wouldn't you? And anyway, that's the last thing I'm worried about. I wouldn't have the least hesitation in bearing five healthy children as an unmarried mother, if I could support them. But I can't. I've got no money, the father has no money—I mean, it'll cost less to dispose of the matter promptly. Can you do that?"

"What do you think I am!" The little doctor is shocked, half in earnest, half not. Oh, for God's sake—do you want me to put on the act, you pint-sized idiot! All right, so we'll put on the act. Gilgi stares into space for several seconds, lost in her pain, then seizes the doctor's hand—the script would consider some low moaning appropriate at this point—oh well, perhaps it'll be enough to say: "Help me, Doctor! I feel so safe with you (every doctor likes hearing that), I don't know what—I mean—you see, I—"

Nonsense, it's too ridiculous, I can't do this. Surely you can talk sensibly with someone like this. And Gilgi speaks quite calmly and quietly: "Listen, Doctor, there's nothing more immoral and unhygienic and absurd than making a woman give birth to a child which she can't feed. And there's absolutely nothing more immoral and absurd than making a woman have a child which she doesn't want ..." And they talk back and forth—for a solid half-hour. Gilgi's aggressive energy is already slackening. Ach, none of it makes any difference, just let whatever has to happen come to her.

"So you'll come back in three weeks, young lady, and quite often these things come right by themselves — — — and, well—and in a case like this things could perhaps be helped along." Gilgi nods wearily. Yes, she'll come back in three weeks.

Slowly she goes down the staircase. Suddenly feels so limp and shattered that she has to sit down on one of the steps for a moment. She thinks back over the doctor's final words—what exactly did he mean by them? Maybe a veiled promise. Must have been. What else? Or — — — he wants to string me along until it's too late ... which would mean that I should try someone else—ach, once was enough. I'll come back in three weeks. Three more weeks! Three more long weeks. Three more short, short weeks. Gilgi lets her head sink onto her knees. You won't tell Martin anything—not until there's absolutely no other way. In the meantime you won't say a word. Maybe something will be broken if he finds out. Maybe he'll take it terribly lightly—you couldn't bear that. Maybe he'll be helpless and completely out of his depth—you couldn't bear that. Maybe he'd feel that he had obligations and was forced to rearrange his whole life—that'd make him desperately unhappy, and me as well. The whole thing is revolting. Yes, if you loved Martin just a little less, then everything would be much simpler. But instead you're senselessly and insanely afraid that something could destroy this love, this love that you depend on unconditionally, that you want to keep at any, any, any cost. And you'd bear any difficulty sooner than take the slightest risk that could endanger this love.

Gilgi shakes her head: you still can't really believe it— and you almost want to laugh: at the idea that Martin, the damned fool, has made me pregnant. And doesn't have a clue that right now—he thinks I'm in my room. And he himself is having a great time at that film about Africa. Oh, dear, foolish, clueless Martin, if I wasn't so tired I'd be really angry with you — — — Three more weeks—for the next three weeks I just won't think about it at all.

"Come on, Martin—get up! It's your turn to make the coffee today!" Gilgi punches Martin in the side—without result. He has no intention of opening his eyes. "Old lazybones." She bends over him, gathers a few strands of hair and brushes them over his face. Doesn't work either. So you have to apply "the guaranteed method": tickling the soles of his feet—he can't stand that. Gilgi crawls to the foot of the bed. "Damn it! Gilgi, would you stop that!"—"Kukirol's Plasters Work the Fastest!"—"Gilgi, I'll murder you ..."—"Good idea, Martin, commit a little crime against passion, why don't you?"—"Gilgi, you're playing with fire ..."—Gilgi is already sitting upright in the bed again.—"The gentleman is awake at last? May I respectfully suggest that the gentlemen be so good as to make the coffee at last?"—"Tell me, Gilgi"—Martin rubs his eyes—"and I'm asking quite seriously, tell me, my sweet clever girl, exactly why does the German public have the idea that anyone who stays in bed in the morning is of bad character?"—"How should I know, my darling?"—"They have quite a few curious ideas here. For example—as a child, I was only ever allowed to eat things which I found disgusting, quite unconsciously people had this vague feeling: food that tastes good is sinful."—"Listen, Martin—if you imagine that I feel like philosophizing with you right here and now, on an empty stomach—then you're mistaken—and if you don't get up right this minute, I'll fetch some cold water—get up, you—I think the weather will be beautiful today." Gilgi jumps out of the bed, runs across the room. She's wearing pyjamas of light-blue silk embroidered with little dark-blue swallows. She opens the curtains: "Look at the sunbeams, Martin! You can reach out and take them in your hands!"

At midday Gilgi is standing in the kitchen, wielding a frying pan very expertly and importantly. "Martin, please—you've got no business in the kitchen at the moment."—"Oh, Gilgi, I don't like it when your hands and your hair smell so much of the kitchen afterwards."—"Let me be now, Martin." Gilgi is concentrating devoutly on her fried potatoes. Sunlight flows in through the kitchen window, lies in wide gold stripes on the blue-gray slate floor—and Spain has become a republic, and there's always something happening in the world—really great things are happening, but nevertheless the fried potatoes are the most important thing at the moment. And outside the kitchen window there's a chestnut tree—it's very proud of its brand-new green leaves and doesn't quite have the confidence to blossom yet, a plump blackbird with an orange-yellow beak is singing in its branches—yes, it's spring now, and—I suppose I'm crazy, but actually I'd like to have the child ... the frying pan slips just a little to the side, Gilgi cries out because hot fat has spattered her leg, and Martin starts going on as though a bomb had exploded—"completely ridiculous, all this fooling around in the kitchen"—and carries Gilgi into the living-room, peels her stocking off: tiny red spots on the white skin ... Then suddenly the whole apartment is full of smoke, they're almost suffocated. And the fried potatoes have become as hard and black as heating coal—that's the end of lunch. And right now they're completely out of cash again—it would be nothing short of sinful to eat at a restaurant. But the smoke is intolerable. So they make some sandwiches, like the pettiest of the petty bourgeoisie, and set off, strolling for ages along Aachenstrasse—and in the end they take luncheon on a bench in the city forest.

"Oh God, Gilgi, this terrible sandwich paper! All that's missing now are some hard-boiled eggs, straight from the third-class car on the passenger train ..."

"Oh, Martin, are you an aesthete? May I point out to

the gentleman that there is a corn on the third toe of the
gentleman's left foot? They don't fit so well together—
being an aesthete and—" Gilgi often fails to finish her sentences now, she's simply too lazy to bother. Oh, how lazy
she is. She'd like to put her arms behind her head—much
too much effort. Hasn't a bit of strength left in her joints.
Lets her arms lie limply in her lap, blinks up at the sun—is
so wonderfully tired, completely enveloped in a twilight
cloud of sweet, soft indifference. Doesn't want to break
out of the cloud yet—not yet, not yet—because something has to happen, something has to be done, when you
break out of it. Decision—action—oh, the words hammer
too loudly.

Broad, broad green lawn, shy little daisies, trees, sky,
sun, caressing air—very occasionally a human figure—but
who would be taking a stroll in the city forest at this time
on a weekday? "Don't you notice as well, Martin, how even
a single person can ruin the view for you?" Martin doesn't
answer. Both look into the sunlight for another half-hour
in silence.

"Tell me, little Gilgi"—Martin shatters the silence suddenly—"how was it exactly before we met—who was it
that you—liked? You see, I know so little about you." Gilgi
ignores the soft, insistent, inquisitorial tone which men
can never avoid when asking such questions. "Yes, there
were a few I liked—was probably in love, too—my God, I
can't remember them properly anymore. You know, I suppose the mind remembers, but the feelings have no memory anymore—it's so difficult to reconstruct something
if the feelings have lost the memory." Martin isn't satisfied, wants to know more—how—what—who—why—
wherefore—. For a moment she looks at him doubtfully

from the side—"ach, don't ask so many questions. There's probably nothing that's wiped out more conclusively by the arrival of something new and stronger than old love affairs are." She lets her head fall onto his shoulder—"don't ask so many questions, I really don't think that kind of thing is important"—she has a well-meaning, superior expression around her mouth, as people do who suddenly discover that someone is concerned about something which they themselves consider insignificant.

"You shouldn't go out in this terrible weather, little Gilgi—your cheeks are hot—probably a temperature ..."—

"Heck, it's only a little influenza, Martin!"

"You should go to bed!"

"Later, Martin—later. I just have to pop out to the labor office—because my money is due today!"

A gray room—filled with the smell of humanity, vapors from wet clothes, dust, and noise. You queue up at the counter—for many, many, many minutes. Immediately in front of you a little, destitute woman with a grubby child on her arm. They're pushing behind you—women and girls, women and girls, packed together—you're pushed so disgustingly close to each other ... Gilgi's gaze falls on the greasy hair of the woman in front of her—the yellow-gray scalp showing under the sticky strands. You feel sick in your stomach, your throat—Gilgi closes her eyes. And now everything forces itself upon you—the smell forces itself upon you—the people force themselves upon you—the room forces itself upon you. You're dissolving among a faceless crowd—what's left of you? What's in the room: a buzzing hopelessness, droning like the crying of a

half-starved child—a broken will which has lost its power
to desire—a waiting in which all purpose has died—fum-
bling for the days—resting in yesterday—no strength for
tomorrow—excluded from common experience—forced
out of the circle—forced into another, unwanted commonality. An acceptance of having sunk—an inability to
protest—against yourself—absolved of personal responsibility—no longer supported by your own desire and
ability—leaning on what's outside you, leaning on what's
outside you . . . ach, the breathing around me, and if they
wouldn't stand so close to me in front and behind—I'm
about to fall over, but I can't fall over like this. What's left
of me? Do people ever suspect how completely they can
be influenced!!!! The body's immunity is so disproportion-
ately greater than that of the mind. The slightest concession to weakness, the very least willingness to let yourself
go exposes you to the world—alien thoughts enter through
your pores, alien wishes, an alien desire, an alien hopelessness—alien influences which take root in you—you don't
notice it, you don't know it, but days—weeks—years later
you might feel the pain of inflamed, sick feelings—might
wonder wearily about the incomprehensibility of a wish,
a thought which didn't grow within you yourself, wonder,
puzzling over the motive and the purpose of an involun-
tary action to which you feel no connection—even though
often a mere breath was the cause, a breath of a stranger
whose face you maybe hadn't even seen, a breath that en-
tered you—remained—festered—erupted . . .

Gilgi opens her eyes: still three—seven—eight people
in front of her. The monotonous collective noise of those
waiting is broken here and there by single sounds, a sharp
laugh, the impatient tapping of a foot, words—Gilgi can

distinguish different kinds of backs—shoulders in front of her. Brash shoulders, despairing shoulders, tired shoulders, indifferent shoulders ... ah, why do I belong to them? Maybe misery and poverty aren't the worst thing. The worst thing is that the people here have had every feeling of responsibility taken from them. The worst thing is that quite a few of them almost feel comfortable in their "it's not my fault"—lying down, as in a coffin, in the idea that their misery is exclusively other people's fault. They let their precious, precious knowledge of their own laziness and incapacity be strangled, let their will for life and desire for action die slowly within them—because it's not their fault. And the fact that other people's failure helps to cover the tiny quantum of their own failure—maybe that's the worst thing, that's the end, that shows that you've died ...

Gilgi coughs—her chest really hurts. She shudders with cold. Probably really does have a bit of a temperature—and it's just the right weather now for catching a chill. The woman with the child thinks so, too—and she remembers that her feet are cold. "If it'd jus' warm up properly at las', so that we didn' need the heatin' anymore," she shifts from one foot to the other, the child starts to fret—it has such ugly scurf around its little mouth, and horribly old eyes — — — and one more week—then I have to go to the doctor ...

"Ach, little Gilgi, so you went out in the rain for a lousy thirteen marks! My God, you're such a stubborn, inexplicable girl!"

"Only a little influenza, Martin! There were times when I went to the office with a temperature of 39.4." Gilgi speaks as though it had been great fun to go to the office with a temperature of 39.4. And Martin isn't satisfied until she's in bed. "And do you really feel warm?" Right—and now he'll go to the drugstore and pick up some aspirin, and some elderberry tea or something like that—and he'll make the elderberry tea when he gets back. And Gilgi wants him to buy his shoes at the same time, too—"you know how it goes, Martin! If you put it off, all of a sudden we'll be out of money again, and you need shoes sooo badly. And go to Schilderstrasse—you know, where we saw that pair for nineteen marks, they looked verrry smart. And make sure that the soles are good and tough and . . ."

Martin has been gone for five minutes when the doorbell rings. So what is it now? Gilgi crawls out from under the carefully stacked pillows and blankets, pulls on her black silk kimono with the big yellow sunflower pattern, smooths her hair . . .

Oh God! She got out of bed for this! A door-to-door salesman, sales representative, traveling salesman—with a dusty little suitcase—"What? Floor wax? Don't need any." Gilgi hesitates: it's terrible to slam the door on such a pleading voice.

"Just let me show you, madam . . . but wait a minute . . ."—the man looks at Gilgi in amazement, becomes embarrassed and nervous—"aren't you Gil—madam, aren't you—"

"Ooooh, Hans, is it you? She holds her hand out to him. Looks at him: this hardened, waxy face was once so young and fresh and shining . . . "I didn't recognize you, Hans, you've changed a lot." Gilgi blushes a fiery red, she's said something tactless. Wants to make up for it immediately: "Come in, Hans—come . . . here—sit down, Hans."

The man lays down his hat with its grease-spotted band beside him. Sits stiff as a board on the extreme edge of the armchair. "Oh, what a wonderful place you have here, Gilgi—but may I still call you Gilgi? Shouldn't I say 'madam' and ..."

"What nonsense, Hans—old friends like us!" Gilgi is standing before him—a pampered, well-groomed, well-rested little woman, completely enveloped in expensive embroidered silk ... and he's still got those faithful eyes, old Hans, except they've become tired and sad—now a little spark of genuine happiness kindles in them—"I'm so pleased that at least things are going well for you, Gilgi."

And now they look at each other and don't know what to say—after all, they haven't seen each other for so many years. "Wait a second, Hans—I was just about to have breakfast, so shall we eat together?" Gilgi runs into the kitchen. She has to sit down for a moment. What have just a few years done to the boy? By now he's—yes, by now he's—maybe thirty—that was four years ago when we ... Four years! That's hardly an eternity, four years! That makes you think a bit. Such a lively, cheerful boy, old Hans! You could have fun with him—you could laugh! He had such blond hair and flashing blue eyes and wonderful muscles. Yes, he was always very proud of his muscles. We were together in the swimming club, it started when he wanted to teach me the Australian crawl—he could do the Australian crawl very well—really well. And I was so upset about Jonny— well, I suppose the first man is usually a dud. And I was so utterly sick of Jonny, but it's always the way that you still can't bear it when a creep like that — — — I would've been quite happy at the time if Jonny, that combination of Douglas Fairbanks and a mailman, if he'd jumped off the roof of the club—because of me. It never occurred to him—he took up with Hilde, the redhead with the curls—and Hans was so nice, we were such good friends—just good friends—and if we hadn't done that two-week trip in the Hunsrück hills together, we'd probably have stayed "just" good friends too. Anyway, none of it was a big deal—then I went to Frankfurt for five months, because Mayer & Rothe were opening their new branch there—yes, so then I forgot him. It's funny—how long ago it all is. You just can't believe that all of it was real once. The guy looks quite starved. Gilgi spreads a few bread rolls—and there's a half-bottle of Tarragona left over . . .

"Right, Hans, now tell me a little about yourself."

"Not much of it's good, Gilgi." They both fall silent—the memories they have are—filtered by the passing of the years—still bright, cheerful, light-hearted ones. Were they really so young back then? And now? Surely they must have grown terribly old to be wondering so skeptically about how young they once were.

"And, Hans, do you remember how I stood up there on the ten-meter springboard at the pool and trembled like a blancmange that's about to be eaten?"

"Yes, and then you dived just the same."

"And do you remember how we capsized in the canoe?"

"And a Rhine steamer fished us out . . ."

"God, and they thought we were so interesting—"

"And we thought we were a thousand times more interesting than that."

"Do you remember how Heinz always took his gramophone onto the boat and played 'Valencia' a thousand times?"

"Yes, Gilgi, and then you threw the record into the

water while he wasn't looking. And do you remember how that cute one, Ruth, sang sooo badly to the mandolin that it almost sounded good again!"

"Of course, Ruth! The one who thought she was so beautiful that she couldn't waste herself on any man, and I suppose that every time she looked in the mirror she was sorry that she couldn't be a guy as well as a girl and start a relationship with herself.—And how you made that fabulous profit with the Dutch cigarettes!"

"Yes, and when we celebrated in the boatshed that night it wobbled like a nutshell on a storm-tossed ocean— we were having so much fun. And that fat guy, Conny, was so drunk that he was determined to go diving for coral in the Rhine ..."

"God, yes, I spent a half-hour hanging onto his leg— otherwise he'd probably still be lying down there now among the broken beer bottles and the tin cans—"

"And he wouldn't have been one of those corpses that look so peaceful when they're fished out of the water!" — — —

Do you remember, do you remember, do you remember. And now? That poor gray-faced guy there was once the liveliest of the bunch.— He's no longer the same at all—and—his life now ... you can hardly ask.

But then he starts talking about it of his own accord. Because they're not very inhibited at all, the guys. God, yes, they don't say anything—until the need and the opportunity to say something happen to coincide. " ... of course back then I was working for my uncle in the transformer factory, and working hard—and everything was going well—and I had quite a clear, straight path laid out before me, which went upwards gradually, but reliably.

And then there was Hertha—you remember, Gilgi ..."
Gilgi thinks—oh yes, pretty blond Hertha with the soft,
motherly hips—"of course I remember—she was very
good at the breast-stroke—and a lovely girl ..."

"Yes, she is," Hans agrees whole-heartedly. "We got
married. You know, she had such funny parents, they always kicked up a fuss when she came home a bit late at
night ..."

Gilgi nods: "I know—the usual!"

"Yeah, so we just got married. And I was very happy,
too, about having our own apartment and everything—everything was wonderful—and as a young guy you thought
you were really something when you could say: my wife.
And Hertha was a secretary with Brandt & Co., of course,
with quite a good salary—not to mention my salary—! We
got by really well. And Hertha wanted to keep her job for
another two years, until I was earning enough for both
of us. But then the first child came along, and she had a
nasty chest complaint for a long time. And then our firm
went bust—I was running around for months before I got
another job. And we had to give up the apartment and
moved into a back attic in Friesenstrasse. And Hertha was
so good, Gilgi!—never complained, never moaned. And
the most difficult time was also the nicest—that's when
I learned what it means when someone really belongs to
you.—Then I found something in an insurance company,
as an agent—it didn't suit me at first, you have to talk at
people so relentlessly and intensively—but in our times
you really can't afford to say that something doesn't suit
you. I tried terribly hard—but just when I was starting
to get the hang of it I was fired again. And Hertha had
the second child. But we love each other so much. It's just

terrible, Gilgi, how you only bring each other bad luck when you love each other. Hertha would have got on by herself, and I would have got on by myself too. And together you're lost, finished. But you belong together come what may, and if you wanted to go your separate ways—it would kill you. Shouldn't be such a thing as love in the world, Gilgi."

"Shouldn't be such a thing as love in the world, Hans."

"So I ran from pillar to post, helped out in a garage, and as a waiter in a garden restaurant. I addressed envelopes and delivered newspapers. Once I got a good offer for the Dutch East Indies—but of course I couldn't accept it. Then I was a sales representative again for an underwear factory—then a welfare recipient again for a while. One time I was onto a good thing as a branch manager—if I could've paid a surety of four thousand marks—which of course I didn't have. Then I went from door-to-door again with vacuum cleaners—and now with floor wax.— Gilgi—anyone who hasn't gone through it themselves doesn't know what it's like. Like a criminal, that's how they treat you, like the worst kind of common criminal. You get the door slammed in your face—you get such angry, hostile looks—and you walk and walk and walk, and often the day's earnings wouldn't even pay for the wear and tear on your shoes.—But—damn it, it's your duty— not to lose heart, isn't it?" The corners of his mouth are trembling hopelessly—"and it should get better one day, shouldn't it?"

And he looks at Gilgi, wants to read a Yes in her face— and suddenly his head falls forward onto the table-top, and his shoulders are trembling, his whole body is shaking—he's crying, my God, he's crying—a rasping, sobbing sound is coming from his throat—you can't listen to that, you can't look at that—a man who's crying. And the sobbing—my God—Gilgi has leapt up, she's leaning on the arm of the chair, chalk-white—stop it, stop it, I can't listen to that—he's sobbing so brokenly—it's driving me mad, I'll jump out of the window if he doesn't stop ... And now he lifts his head, the whites of his eyes are veined with red — — — "it—will—never—get—better again, Gilgi—I can feel that it will never get better again. And I can't stand it anymore—just can't—stand it—anymore—when I walk along the street—and see such plump red-cheeked children, and then think of my own two—so pale and miserable—up there in the stuffy attic. If I was only responsible for myself I'd never, ever lose heart—but I can't stand it anymore—I don't know what to do now—can't go on now ...". Tears run down his face, but he doesn't turn away, he's not ashamed—once you've ended up where he has, you're not ashamed anymore.

"Hans, dear Hans," Gilgi says. Because this is one of her group. And you ought to stick together, you ought to stick so closely together. That's much more important than any ideas about being in love: we young ones ought to stick together. We shouldn't let all these things happen to each other, we should all, all of us be such true friends ...

"I'd better get on, Gilgi," Hans says, and stands up.

"It's raining outside."

"Yes, it's raining outside."

"You don't have an overcoat?"

"Couldn't redeem it from the pawnbroker."

"Would you like to leave seven tins of floor wax here for me, Hans?" They'll cost the exact amount of her unemployment benefits.

"Yeah, you see, Gilgi, I wasn't used to talking anymore. And you shouldn't talk, either—it doesn't make things better, it just makes everything more vivid. See you, Gilgi. It'll work out all right. Has to work out, doesn't it? Hey, Gilgi, I'll write down my address for you—visit Hertha sometime, would you? It'd cheer her up—she's always so alone—we have no friends at all ..."

"Yes, Hans, I'll visit her. Goodbye, Hans."

Gilgi watches him as he staggers down the stairs with his little case—then slowly closes the door of the apartment. Walks around as in a dream, clears the crockery away and takes it into the kitchen. Goes back to bed. What's being done to people? What? What? You ought to help each other—that's so important—and there are pale little children who don't have enough to eat—and at the labor office—and—yes, when you love each other you only bring each other bad luck. I'd get on without Martin, and Martin wouldn't run up so many debts without me. And anyway, love isn't important at all—as long as there are people who want to work and aren't allowed—as long as there are people who are prevented from earning money— as long as there are little children who don't have enough to eat ... and always this buzzing desire in my limbs, the sweet repellent desire—I can't stand it anymore, I want to die—I don't want it anymore—I don't want—it disgusts me to be so powerless against my body. And if I could talk to Martin about it! But I can't do that—whatever I say, I'll never strike to the heart of it, I'll just give a fuzzy outline— because words which pass the lips never reveal, they only conceal. And Gilgi thinks of the impoverished, hardened young man and longs for Martin—and she feels ashamed that her thoughts of other people's misery are interrupted

by her longing for Martin—and a tiny droplet of hostility
flows into the longing—and she feels ashamed because her
longing for Martin is paralleled by such a profound sympathy for someone else, another man—and feels guilty—in
her own eyes—other people's eyes—everyone's eyes—her
thoughts go round and round — — — peace, if she could
have some peace for once. You probably don't find peace
until renunciation forces you into its gray prison—when
you've become old and undesired and undesiring ... I'm
so tired ...

Crack—goes the front door—and then Martin is
standing in the room, swinging his shoebox cheerfully.
"Did a great job getting everything, you'll be happy, sweet
girl ... but what's the matter with you?" He sits down next
to her—"Why are you looking like that—so white and—
have you been crying?"

Oh, his dear face and his kind voice! "It's just my cold,
Martin." So tired—you have to dig every word out of
yourself.

"I'll make you some tea, little Gilgi—and you must stay
in bed today—hey, tell me, what are all those yellow tins
out there in the hallway?"

"Floor wax, Martin—I bought them from—a—
poor—man." Gilgi pulls Martin's head onto her chest
with a lightning-fast movement—he mustn't see her fiery red cheeks. Martin, my dear Martin, I've lied to you.
Too tired to tell you it all—no, not too tired—but you
would've asked questions, questions, questions—and if
I'd got the feeling—from a single glance, a single breath,
that something which was infinitely sad for me was just
"an old boyfriend" for you—that poor broken man—if
there'd been just a flicker of some kind of mistrust in your

eyes—I would've slapped you in the face. Martin, I've lied to you—now you're infinitely superior to me. I love you so much, Martin, I'll die if I stop loving you—there has to be something which lasts forever, has to be something which has substance. Martin—have I done something hateful, immoral to you now? How that makes me love you. And Gilgi draws Martin's face up to hers, kisses it all over—everything's dark, everything's spinning around—something has to be, something has to continue—Martin—and puts her hands around his stiff, sinewy neck—Martin—I've lied to you—I've delivered myself over to you because I've lied to you—and seven tins of floor wax—and walking, walking, walking from door to door—no work—little children who don't have enough to eat—that's so important—why is it sinking now, why is it not important anymore—you, Martin—only you—nothing else matters anymore—only you—closes her hands more firmly around his neck—"I could wish you were dead—don't we all wish some day for the death of what we love too much—because it doesn't leave us air to breathe anymore, because it cuts us off from the world ... ah, Martin, don't listen to what I'm saying—because I love you and want you to live" ... digs her sharp nails into his neck—"no, let me, Martin—I want to hurt you—I don't want to be good to you—want to hurt you—I love you so much ..."

The next morning Gilgi is quite fresh and cheerful again, with barely a trace of her cold left. Makes coffee in the kitchen, whistling "The Marseillaise." Olga is sitting at the shiny scrubbed kitchen table, radiating brightness and

the scent of chypre ... "Just wanted to say goodbye, Gilgi—
my train goes in an hour."

"Oh, Olga, are you really going away now?"

"Yes, to Berlin, little Gilgi—now, don't make such hor-
rified saucer-eyes, little one—I mean, you're so occupied
that you really won't miss me ..."

"It was such a lovely, reassuring feeling to know that
you were nearby ..."

"Come here, Gilgi." Olga pulls Gilgi to her, strokes her
soft, wavy brown hair, "here's my address for you—don't
lose it." Olga puts a piece of paper folded to the smallest
possible size down the front of Gilgi's dress. "So, little one,
you know that you have to write to me from time to time,
it would be uncouth and irresponsible of you to make me
worry because I'd heard nothing from you. Look out—
your coffee's boiling!—if it's drinkable, you can give me a
cup. Right—what else did I have to say? I won't give you
any more advice. Everything that you decide and that you
do now has to be worked out by you alone ..."

"Yes, Olga. But—but you should've told me before that
you're leaving today, I ought at least to have packed your
suitcases for you—you've absolutely no idea about packing, marzipan girl. How did you possibly get it done?"

"Yes, it was a problem, Gilgi, but I solved it with a
stroke of genius. First I boldly emptied all my wardrobes
and drawers and threw everything onto the floor—then I
ran out of ideas, and didn't know what to do next. All at
once I had a bright idea: I rang up the would-be Musso-
lini—you know—the Casanova with the black curls, who
loves me with such elegant hopelessness that it'd really be a
pity if we ever—anyway, I rang him up and invited him for

tea—tête-à-tête. You should have seen how he charged in a
quarter-hour later bearing roses and chocolates, and smelling adventurously of Coty—evidently he'd also quickly put
on a clean collar and a provocative tie—and felt that his
boldest hopes had been more than fulfilled. So I led him
into my room—took the roses and the chocolates and
climbed up onto the big tiled stove and declared that I'd
only come down again when all the stuff had been cleared
off the floor. Gotta say, he did beautiful work, and took a
lot of trouble. I sat up there on the stove, eating chocolates, giving instructions about everything, and occasionally calling some very kind and encouraging words down
to him. Afterwards, when it was all done, the room looked
as bare as if a plague of locusts had been through it—I said
I couldn't possibly expect him to stay another minute in
such an unappealing room, and it would probably be better to take tea at the Restaurant Charlott. — — —

"Now—my little Gilgi—it's high time I—come on, give
me a kiss before I go . . ."

"Oh, Olga . . ." Gilgi wants to say something else, tell
her—but better not, better not—once something has been
said, it takes on such a strange life of its own. "When will
we see each other again, Olga?"

"As soon as you need me—for sure, Gilgi. You can always
rely on me.—You know"—Olga's merry blue operetta-eyes
suddenly become serious and thoughtful—"I really do like
men as such—but it's funny and it makes me mistrustful to
see that there's no true friendship among men anymore, no
honest, immediate sticking together, and above all no un-
conditional solidarity. All that's left are 'comrades' or 'party
colleagues'—which isn't much at all. I'd have a hell of a lot
of respect for a man who had a male friend he preferred

to me. Haven't you noticed, too, Gilgi—that we're living at a time where there's more true solidarity among women than among men? That makes us superior. Pity. I don't set much store at all by superiority in itself. Oh well, if that's the way it is!—God, my train!" Gilgi's brown fingers close around Olga's pampered little hand once again.—"All the best, Olga."—"All the best, Gilgi—where's Martin?"—"Still in bed."—"I'll just say goodbye to him." Olga flits into the bathroom, pours water onto a sponge—pulls the bedroom door open—takes a solid wind-up and throws the sodden sponge, hitting Martin on the nose—"It was a lipsmacking kiss, my beloved lazybones, wasn't it? Farewell for a while—I'm leaving town. Be good to my little friend, and don't forget to send me my procuress's fee."

And Gilgi finds that the world has become even darker and gloomier since Olga left. She thinks back on Olga's words: no solidarity among men anymore . . . Could well be right. Suddenly remembers her promise to visit Hertha. Maybe this afternoon? You'll take her some underwear and a few dresses—you'll talk and behave in a way that allows her to accept them without being the least bit embarrassed.

But today's visit comes to nothing. Martin's got money again from somewhere—at midday he goes out suddenly, and ten minutes later he comes back beaming proudly and driving a smart Cadillac—which he's hired for the day.

They drive down the Rhine—past the Siebengebirge hills—it smells of spring, sun, air and wind, earth and folk songs.—"Gilgi, take your hand off my arm—you're one of those women who aren't allowed to touch me while I'm driving."—Oh yes, it's beautiful—life is beautiful . . .

They sit in an old inn on the Rhine, drink old wine

from Rüdesheim and look at the even older mountains and the water flowing in the river. Darkness descends slowly. A freighter rattles and screeches as it throws out its anchor, then sits heavy and black on the deepening gray of the water.—Guelder roses rest their delicate whiteness on a profusion of leaves, a soft wind wafts petals of cherry blossom through the open window, and the smell of the burgeoning lilac is like a love song in the air. They don't say much—from time to time they just toss each other a word—like a brightly colored little ball which is caught by gentle hands.

The silence becomes heavier and fuller—it breathes with secrets, and the knowledge of the earth's eternal harmony with everything that lives.—Silver veils over water and meadows—sweet smell of damp leaves and earth ... Gilgi's hands lie flat and open. A curiously profound knowledge about being here, about being, flows hotly and with a joyful heaviness through her veins—and the sweetness of their shared connection with the moment becomes almost unbearable. Silently she takes the man's hand, puts her hot, dry lips on the blue-veined wrist and feels the pulsing of his warm, living blood in the depths of brain and body and limbs—and the earth says Yes, and the aroma-laden air says Yes, and the darkly glowing colors and trees and meadows and everything, everything that is growing says Yes—and you drink the Yes and are dizzy with happiness—but still you know about the No behind the Yes and know about the pain behind the happiness and know about the transience of hours saturated with happiness. Know about tomorrow, know about danger, about the everyday and the Never-Again. And deep down you sense the purpose of pain and inevitable loss. Part your lips in a foreknowing smile—and feel the deepest and most sensual desire—desire that senses sorrow, desire that accepts pain, desire that fears fever—a foreknowing fear in the blood which transmutes our joys into gold.

After the labor office, Gilgi went to Hertha. It's all a thousand times more sad and more bitter than she'd thought. The sun breaks through the gray curtains, harshly and tactlessly illuminating the poverty of the room: one narrow bedstead along the wall, a smaller one beside it, a wash-stand, a cupboard, a table, two chairs, a small gas stove—and that's all. It smells of people and cabbage and children's underwear.

Hertha is sitting opposite Gilgi—a tired blond woman with heavy, slow movements. She's holding the little twelve-month-old boy on her lap—"didn't want to have him, Gilgi—but now he's here, and wouldn't give him up again"—and presses the child's thick pale head with her rough little hand onto her sagging, heavy breast. Talks in a soft, monotonous voice: "I hated the children so much while I was pregnant with them—do you think that's made them sad? They're always so quiet and hardly ever cry and don't laugh much—sometimes I think that all my love now can't make up for that hate.—Aaaach," she stands up, puts the well-behaved child onto the bed, goes to the stove, and turns down the gas jet under the bubbling saucepan. Embarrassed and clumsy, Gilgi strokes the thin, silver-blond hair of the little girl, who stands silently and stiffly beside her—she has never liked children and doesn't know how to behave with them—the child presses her little head more firmly against the stroking hand—the tiny, gentle, baby animal's movement almost brings tears to Gilgi's eyes. Hertha sits down at the table again. The atmosphere in the room becomes increasingly heavy and oppressive—full of acknowledged and unacknowledged hopelessness. You can see the unhealthy flickering of the air. Far down below on the street an organ-grinder is playing, fragments of "The Volga Song" from Lehár's *Tsarevich* make their way upwards. The little girl chirrups a few incomprehensible words in her high, cheerful little voice—the child is so ugly with her peaked, bloodless little face—and it really gets to you, an ugly child's touching lack of awareness.

"When the nice, warm days come again, I'll take the children to the parks on the edge of town—they'll get some sun there," Hertha says in her soft, slow-flowing voice. "Gilgi, you wouldn't believe how good little Resi looked last summer. And Hans will be earning more money soon, and we'll buy a pram—you see, they're a bit heavy for me, and the little boy is quite a weight. — — — — I'm glad you came, Gilgi—I can talk properly with you."

"You're so brave, Hertha!"

"But what else can I do? I'm not so very brave."

"You're very good—I could never be so good."

"Ach, Gilgi, I'm not good."

"Yes, you are, Hans says it too. He loves you so much."

"Yes, I suppose he does." The blond woman stands up, walks over to the window. Speaks softly and slowly: "I'm not good. What does a stupid man like that know? Oh, Gilgi, sometimes I've had such hateful, hostile thoughts. I hated him so much when I realized that the second child was on the way. I hated him so much sometimes, when I saw in the mirror that my beloved beauty was all gone—faded gray skin, a slack mouth, clouded eyes—oh, don't contradict me, Gilgi—I know quite well what I look like, and I've learned to accept it.—And I felt such contempt for him sometimes, all the times I saw him start something incompetently and clumsily and drift further and further into poverty and misery, taking us with him. I've had very bitter and very ugly and very, very unfair feelings, Gilgi—and I knew that they were ugly and unfair, too—but I couldn't always fight them down. But at least I never directed them outside me, I always let them eat me up inside. Oh, I'll never forget it—with the second baby— how I was lying in the bed there—the contractions had begun too early—they were tearing my body in two—I was screaming, screaming, screaming—and Hans was having a good time with some friends in the back room of a bar, drinking beer and forgetting me. The poor guy! Anything like good times were few and far between for him, and of course he couldn't know how things were for me—but it was like I'd gone crazy. The pain, Gilgi!—I thought I'd go insane—that's when I hated him, you see—I could have murdered him—you pig—was all I could think—you pig, you pig—it's your fault, your fault that I'm lying here like this. Yes, and afterwards, Gilgi—when he was sitting by my bed—then I just stroked his hair and kissed his hand— and that was a kind of asking for forgiveness and wanting to make amends and a tiny bit of lying and dishonesty. No, Gilgi, I'm not good—Hans is much, much better than me. You know, I love the children more than anything—I'd do anything for Hans, too, I'd die for him—but do I still love him?—I don't know. I think I've become too tired to love a man. Of course I know how difficult things are for him and how hard he tries and how good he is—but I can't tell you how much I envy him, because he can do things and try things, while I have to sit here quietly, without doing anything. I suppose what's worn me down most of all are these years of helpless, impotent waiting.

"And, Gilgi"—Hertha's voice becomes even softer—"that—that narrow little bed is where we sleep together—and every evening, every single evening as soon as it gets dark, disgust and fear seize me—my body has become so tired—I can't bear anyone to touch it anymore. It used to be different—but illness, tiredness, and the unending fear of pregnancy—I suppose they've combined to make—that—a torment to me, a horrible torment. And then a man is so stupid and never feels what's going on inside you. Sometimes I think—if he'd wait and leave me in peace, until maybe I started to feel — — — I hinted that to him once—and he almost fell apart on me, weeping: I disgust you, you don't love me anymore. A man just doesn't understand that kind of thing, he assumes with absolute naiveté that the woman feels exactly as he does—well, what could I do—I mean, I had to let him keep his belief in my love, when he's so good and has nothing except his belief in my love, that's what keeps him going—so how could I ever take that from him? And after all I also realize a man needs that. But for me it's so revolting, and such a sacrifice. So then I kiss him and put my arms more firmly around his neck, just so he won't notice how he disgusts me at that moment and how that makes me hate him. And sometimes I want so much just to lie quite gently and quietly beside him, and then I have such good, tender thoughts and stroke his hair and put my face against his and I'm so grateful and happy when he just kisses me quite softly and lovingly on the mouth—but right away I'm afraid again and actually praying: dear God, dear God, not the other thing now, not the other thing—although I know it can only end one way—and then every time I'm so bitterly, bitterly disappointed again and feel like crying and yelling and putting three marks in his hand so that he can go round the corner to a hooker and leave me in peace.—That's how good I am, Gilgi, how horrible I am. Do you see now why I can't stand it when you say that I'm good?"

Gilgi goes to her, puts an arm around her shoulder— "and if you left him, Hertha?"

"Oh, Gilgi—don't get me wrong—I couldn't leave him any more than I could leave the children. I need him the same way I need the children. Whether maybe that's love after all—or what other kind of feeling it is that gives me an unbreakable bond with him—I don't know" — — — —

"Hertha—it'll all get better. I'll see that you get a pram, and we'll go to the parks with the children, and you'll be pretty again ..."

"That's nice of you, Gilgi—that cheers me up. You like me in spite of everything, don't you? That's so nice. I'd really like a friend, a woman who understands.— Listen, Gilgi, I'll tell you something—you still have time— no matter how good things are for you now: make sure you have your own income and your independence—then you can love a man and keep that love alive. See while there's still time that you'll never become as helpless and unprotected as I am ..."

"But, Hertha, it'll all get better."

"Get better!" The blond Hertha smiles wanly—"I'm expecting my third child, Gilgi. Grotesque, isn't it? You almost want to laugh. Get better? Ach, I don't want anything for myself anymore—only the strength to hold out—but everything I want beyond that is for my little children and for Hans—yes, for him too."

"Hertha—my God—you can't have the child, you can't!"

"Looks like I'll have to, Gilgi—or do you think the health insurer will help me not to? Just don't tell Hans anything, he doesn't need to know about it yet—he's already a nervous wreck, and has enough to worry about."

"Oh, Hertha, I'll help you—I'll work out how . . . I want to help you—I'll come visit you often."

"Yes, come visit me, Gilgi. But—tell me—you don't look as though everything in your life was just fine, either?"

"Oh, I, Hertha—I'm not at all important."

"You silly child, as if the most important thing in everyone's life wasn't themselves! Your own toothache always hurts more than someone else's broken leg." — — — —

The young lady Gilgi is walking through the streets—walking, walking, walking—is so tired and keeps right on walking—right on, without a destination. Such heavy feet—and stones on her chest and stones on her shoulders. And you have to help—I used to think it was enough to get by on your own and not accept any help. I wanted to buy my freedom by not accepting any help—but now I know that you have to help—even if there's absolutely nothing left of you at the end. How much money have I got now? Of course I might need it for the doctor and the clinic. Should I give her the money? So that she doesn't have to have the child? Yes, and what about me? It would be completely irresponsible of me. Me with a child! And Martin! We would end up like Hans and like Hertha—oh, my God!—are you really so abysmally egotistical that completely genuine sympathy with other people always leads you back to yourself? Oh, and it's not about me at all—but what would become of Martin? What? And all the love and all the beautiful things and all the good things would be destroyed. And I love him precisely because he's so light-hearted and happy and youthful. And if I stay with him for a long time, then suddenly there'll be no more money—and all the things that make him happy will be destroyed—and then everything will become so awful ... Isn't there any way out? So what should I do? So what should I—do? ... and Hertha doesn't even have that anymore, her complete and total love for the man she's bound to—she doesn't even have that! I'd rather be dead than stop loving Martin. — — But I have to help her—yes, I have to.—

And she lies beside Martin during the night—I could never exist without you. The dark tangle of her thoughts becomes more and more confused. "What's the matter, Gilgi?" Martin asks. He's uneasy. He was cheerful and satisfied while she was still only a toy and a diversion to him—now he loves her, and the stronger feeling brings uncertainty, doubt, and mistrust along with it. "Gilgi, what's the matter—where were you today—don't you love me anymore—am I too old for you—do you like someone else — — —"

"Don't worry, Martin, don't worry—oh, my God—how can you say such things?" He puts a hand on her arm—he only needs to touch her for her skin to start feeling like it's burning—a sharp little flame springs up from every point of contact. She puts an arm around his neck—"but how can you doubt that I love you." Something in the dark heaviness of her thoughts forces its way into him—he

defends himself against it—"I don't have any peace anymore, little Gilgi, just can't stick it out for so long in one
place—let's go away from here, Gilgi—"

"Yes—Martin—yes." She no longer has any idea what
she's saying—she can just feel his hair, his mouth, his
limbs—"away from here—Martin—yes" — — — Words
die.

Gilgi has barely fallen asleep—when she wakes up
again. The room is so hot—and the air is so oppressive—it
could suffocate you. So why aren't I sleeping—I really want
to sleep. And why am I afraid? And why am I so restless? I
can't stand it any longer. Just—what—is—wrong—with—
me? And Gilgi stands up slowly, feels her way through
the darkness into the next room—closes the door quietly
behind her so as not to wake Martin. Opens the window, stares out into the cool black air—presses her hands
against her chest—what's wrong with me? Why don't
I have any words—for Martin—or for myself, either?—
There are two layers in me—and the upper one, it dictates—everyday words, everyday actions—little girl, little
machine girl, little clockwork girl—the lower layer underneath it—always wanting, always searching, always longing and darkness and not knowing—not knowing where
to—not knowing where from. A thinking without words,
a knowing behind the words—a wakefulness in sleep—
behind laughing, a weeping — — — the uncut umbili-
cal cord—a tie to the dark world. And the gray world and
the bright world, you're familiar with them and you know
about them—and you didn't want to acknowledge the dark
world and you're still trying to lie it out of existence. But
it's there—for every woman—every man. And one person says sorrow and one person says pain and one person

says crime—filth—or God—no word cuts right through
to the core. What—am—I—really? All the bad things and
all the good things—that's a human being—and heaven
and hell—that's a human being—the most tragic and most
ridiculous thing—a human being. The most inhibited and
most eager thing—a human being. And war and peace—
that's a human being—and the urge to murder and Mary's
desire to give birth—a human being. The most alien thing
sinks down into you, making what's most truly you rise
up—in you, in you—everything in you—everything, everything, everything in you. And whatever your thoughts
desire, your body loves—and whatever your body loves,
your thoughts desire. It's a sharp flame, the pale girl—has
eyes which speak, eyes which scream—she's like all the
others—knows much about herself, knows nothing about
herself. Burning in the blood, burning in the brain—burning, burning, burning. Restless limbs—longing for flesh—
restless hands—longing for flesh—for flesh that lives, flesh
that breathes, flesh that thinks ...... An identity broken
in two—an identity shattered into a thousand pieces. I—a
transient dutiful wish for We. I—an eternal cry seeking
You—and everything else—isn't true ...... cover your
dark world with the diamond lie of shame—cover your
dark world with the golden lie of the will—cover your dark
world with the silver lie of contenting yourself—cover
your dark world with the iron lie of belonging to the everyday—but don't—cover your dark world with the tarnished copper lie of cowardice ....

Midday concert from the West German Radio Network.
Gramophone records: ... If you're coming to Hawaii / If

the temperature is rising / If your eyes with love are shining … It's a little too much to expect—that so many unusual events will coincide—Gilgi thinks, and anyway she's busy darning Martin's socks. She has to do this secretly, picking a time when he's gone out. "I'd rather walk around barefoot than have you do such a horrible chore," he said the other day. And he shouldn't want her to do it, either—which is precisely why she likes to do it … There's a ring at the door. Gilgi walks slowly over. Opens up. "Hans—you?" He's standing there with a white, distorted face. A torrent of words falls upon Gilgi—she understands one here and there—"… forged a check—for the children—won't prosecute if the money's paid back by tonight—if not—Hertha—doesn't know—jail — — —"

"How much do you need?"

"Twelve hundred marks — — — but no-one—been everywhere—but I wasn't being irresponsible — — —"

He definitely wasn't being irresponsible. Gilgi nods. Feels as though she's been anesthetized. Thinks of the brave blonde woman—the little children—the room—everything — — — It dawns on her suddenly that she didn't say anything about herself, that Hans thinks she's married—that she's well off, that the beautiful apartment belongs to her … and should she explain now? But I'm poor myself, Hans … Always words, always words, always wanting to help with words. No, no, we have to stick together—one day you have to prove yourself, one day you mustn't think of yourself, one day you mustn't. Because even in our times there are still deeds, even in our times there must still be deeds. And she sees the ugly little child, and again her body feels the trusting pressure of the little silver-blonde head against her stroking hand — — — "oh,

Gilgi—I feel—so dissolute—so pathetic—I should leave—
how can I ask you ..."

"Don't talk anymore, Hans, go home—I'll bring you
the money no later than tonight."—

"You—what—are—you—saying — —" —

"Go home, Hans—I'll bring you the money."

Gilgi is standing by herself. What did she say? She
promised something. What did she promise? She has to
keep her promise. — — Twelve hundred marks!—How
can she keep it? She will keep it. You have to help—not
always just think that you ought to help. You have to really
do it. And if Hans goes to jail—then Hertha and her little
children are lost ... And they're such upright, really good
people, you mustn't let them be ruined. And how disgusting, revolting—everyone's eternal, cut-price, glib sympathy—without any deeds behind it. Don't think now—act! I
must have twelve hundred marks by tonight.

And Gilgi pulls on her trench coat—forgets to put on
her hat—runs through the streets—to the savings bank.
Right—she's got seven hundred marks—five hundred to
go. Where can I get five hundred marks? I made a promise,
I have to keep it. To Pit—maybe Pit can think of something.
And Gilgi runs with her coat flying out behind her—has
red cheeks and tousled hair—occasionally forgetting completely the sad purpose she needs the money for. She forgets Hertha, the little children—forgets her own problems
and worries—even forgets Martin—has only one end in
view—I must have the money by tonight. That's a difficult assignment, and carrying it out gives her a positively
liberating sense of sporting enjoyment. All of a sudden,
intermittently, she's the smart little Gilgi of old again, the
Gilgi who didn't bat an eyelid before accepting the most

hair-raising bets, and who wouldn't dream of letting any kind of emotion stand in the way of her winning them.

Running through the streets at a steady pace—oh, that won't make you lose your breath. Really it's fun to have an assignment which is a bit difficult.—Maybe I'll burgle someplace—once when I was fourteen I decided to become a cat burglar's girlfriend—I thought that would be very exciting—keeping lookout on a dark street-corner somewhere and whistling with two fingers when . . .

" 'Lo, Gilgi," Pit says with a surprised, happy expression when she bursts into his room. " 'Lo, Pit," Gilgi says—and she only needs to stand still, only needs to hear her own voice, to plunge from the fleeting lightness of the past minutes—from the brief dream of the old Gilgi back into the dark, alien, experience-freighted world of now. Ach, confidence has become self-deception. You've stepped over the narrow border which divides those who are concerned only with the present from those who are connected to the past and the future. You've been forced away from the thin-blooded, comfortable, supine idea of "people"—and forced to be human. Being human—that means something—you can't hide in the totality anymore—it means being alone. You have to learn how—being human, you have to learn how—learn that one laugh costs a thousand tears—learn that an hour of happiness is paid for with a thousand hours of pain . . . Yes, and right now I have to find five hundred marks.

"Don't you want to sit down, Gilgi?"

"Of course." Gilgi drops onto Pit's bed. "I think I've lost my mind, Pit—I'm going crazy . . ."

Let her talk. So what do you care if someone else

is talking? Pit has his own burden to carry — — so he frees himself of it. "I behaved like a pig, Gilgi—the other night . . ." Again Gilgi emerges from her preoccupation—looks at Pit—listens to him—understands clearly what he wants and what he means. She smiles a little, and her eyes are big and knowing . . . there's a lot of pleasure in saying how awful you are, isn't there, Pit? But how many times do people want to be born? So some guy believes he'll turn himself into a new person by making himself out to be rather worse than he really is. It's our age-old hereditary sorrow that no-one can give himself absolution—and God can't, either. God—this little figment of overworked imagination, God—this pallid lie born of desperation—we say God—and we mean humanity, ourselves and others. The longing for a human being is genuine—a human being is more than God—a human being is a beast and God. Longing for God—damned laziness which costs nothing. Mild, bloodless hysteria. Longing for a human being—you pay for that with your blood and with your self and with your flesh—your longing for God can be settled with promissory notes — — rags—paper — — — A drop of red blood is worth more than three prayers. — — — "Yes, Gilgi, I behaved like a pig—you must despise me."

"I despise myself three times over before I start despising anyone else," Gilgi says in a high, clear voice. "Don't talk such utter garbage, Pit—the things that torment you and make you unjust torment everyone and make everyone unjust—or at least that's what I believe now—and I could be wrong."

"Do you want a cognac, Gilgi?" Pit stumbles about the room with an uncharacteristically hospitable intent—puts a glass with a toothpaste ad on it and an egg-cup onto the table.—

"Pour it out, Pit," Gilgi says, and then picks up the half-filled toothpaste glass—sits down opposite Pit—"you're a decent guy, Pit—sometimes. No-one can be decent all the time—if someone even gets the chance to be decent now and then, that's already something—well, you have the chance. And if you also have the same natural, healthy illness in the blood as I do—God knows I can't hold that against you."

Gilgi's words make Pit more drunk than the cognac does. You might have imbibed self-confidence and world-weariness by the pailful—you still need an authority from time to time—the authority which tells you "You're good" or "You're bad"—"You're in the right place" or "You're in the wrong place"—the authority which can confer the Order of Whiteness or Blackness upon you. You need an authority, so you create one for yourself—and the little, hurriedly devised authority called Gilgi, whose friend is hungering for reassurance, is more than ready to pin the Order of Whiteness on his incessantly self-doubting chest. "Well, you'll sort yourself out, Pit—probably more quickly and easily than me, just you wait." But no-one likes hearing that things will be easier for him than for others. Of course, your own problems aren't exactly pleasant or totally fulfilling, so to compensate at least they should be highly unique, and most certainly they should be extremely difficult. Pit reaches for Gilgi's hand, puts his hard, youthful face onto her soft, cool palm—"a little Oedipus complex, Pit? Male longing for female superiority? Well, Pit — —" the soft palm under his face closes into a fist, hits him lightly on the chin—"it's not about the two of us at all, Pit—it's about third parties. Do you know where I can find five hundred marks right away?" Pit listens closely as Gilgi tells him Hans and Hertha's story.

"... and two little children, and a third one on the way ..."

"Irresponsible, breeding like rabbits. Why do they have children all the time?"

"They've only got one bed, Pit."

"They shouldn't bring the pregnancies to term ..."

"They haven't got any money, Pit."

"There are some people who are too weak to live, and whom we shouldn't hesitate to let die ..."

"Weakness and strength aren't the measure of a human being's worth by a long way, Pit."

"But of their fitness to live."

"But not of their right to live."

"Everyone must earn that for himself."

"You can only earn that for yourself by helping others to earn it."

"You have to think in economic terms when you ..."

"Your miserliness makes you poor when you cut back on helping ..."

"You should only help those for whom it really is help."

"You should help everyone."

"That's not true."

"It is true."

"Wishy-washy do-goodery."

"Obligation. — — Stop it, Pit, maybe your dialectics are superior to mine. Dialectics! How shameful—when we're talking about four living human beings. Sometimes you should find individual human beings more important than the masses ......"

Pit stands up. "I don't have any money myself—as you know—but I'll—I'll—go to my father—I haven't seen him for four years ......"

"Heavens, Pit—you—would—do—that?"

"Well, if you need money—then you need money, don't you?—and if you think it's right to help people, then that's probably the right thing to do." Pit grabs his hat—"wait here for me—I'll be back in an hour at the latest." You can already hear his heels clattering hurriedly down the steep wooden staircase. Gilgi thinks nothing and does nothing, falls onto Pit's bed and goes to sleep. "Wake up, Gilgi—dammit—will you wake up!"

"Pit—you?" Gilgi rubs her eyes. "I'm terribly hungry—what time is it?"

"Five o'clock, I think." God, Martin, what will Martin be thinking—I must get home—yes, what was I doing ...... "Have you got the money, Pit???"

"I was at home—my father was away—giving a lecture in Frankfurt. So I went to a friend's ..."

"Have you got the money?"

"No—maybe by midday tomorrow ..."

"That's too late—my God, there's no time left to lose. What other well-heeled people do we know, Pit?" Gilgi thinks it over. Should I go to the Krons? Impossible. Well, they might give me the money—but when? The day after tomorrow, or next week. Because they're the kind of people who "don't have any cash on hand." Pawn your fur coat? But you wouldn't get anything like enough. And you wouldn't do it anyway. Because Martin gave you the coat—and Martin mustn't have the slightest connection with the whole business. "Wait—I know . . . . . . S'long, Pit . . ." Gilgi bolts down the stairs.

Kaiser Wilhelm Crescent. Greif.—Gilgi rings the bell. The status-conscious maid opens the door. "Frau Greif around?"

"Madam is not at home to callers."

We'll see about that—Gilgi pushes through the door, past the astonished maid—sits down on the little wicker armchair in the hallway—looks at her wristwatch — — — "I'll wait here for a half-hour—I expect Frau Greif to be at home to callers by then."

The maid disappears—comes back a minute later: "Madam wishes me to ask your name—and the reason for your call?"

"They're not for your ears. Just tell Frau Greif that I'm waiting—she should hurry."

Suddenly the maid comes closer—looks at Gilgi with eagerness and a hesitant knowingness—"Are you — — are you perhaps Herr Longin's girlfriend?"

"Am I what?"

"Oh, I thought you were — — but if you're not—then please forget that I . . ."

"Maybe I am," Gilgi suggests, and assumes an enigmatic expression. Because it could be that if you're Herr Longin's girlfriend you get to see this Greif lady sooner. The maid's face shows smug satisfaction and inside knowledge. She opens her mouth halfway—is evidently about to say something—but then closes her mouth again with a visible effort of self-control and departs.

Gilgi sits and waits. Waits for a complete stranger from

whom she wants five hundred marks. Apart from that, this stranger is her mother. That's odd. But what's even odder is her deep, unshakable indifference to that idea. Surely that's not normal—surely by rights she ought to be excited . . . . . . nothing to be done—you're not excited. Is that really such an important thing: mother! Yes, and if you have any feelings at all for this unknown mother—then it's an inexplicable, undeniable aversion. I'll see her in a minute—her heart is beating normally. Hans and Hertha—she has to give me money—her heart beats faster. Martin—Martin will be worried about where I am—her heart stops beating for several seconds, and Gilgi wants to faint. She's suddenly seized by a feverish impatience. She's been waiting for five minutes, and thinks that hours have passed. The money—Martin—little children—jail—and Martin will be waiting. And it seems to Gilgi that she's committing a crime against Martin which can never be made good. The little children—what business are they of mine! Hans will go to jail—let him. Martin's waiting—I'll have to explain—he won't understand—why am I sitting here? I was supposed to go to the doctor today. The child—maybe it'll have the same untidy black hair as Martin and the same dark silver-flecked eyes—I'd like a child like that—Martin, my darling—money—five hundred marks—ach, there it is again, that whole mess. I can't do this anymore—Martin's waiting — — — — —

Oh, I didn't notice that I'd stood up. What am I doing — — — I'm going—to the door—Martin — — — no, I shouldn't—I must have money. But it's not important—yes, it is important. But a moment ago everything was clear—and I wanted something—and I want something now too . . . Gilgi bites into her wrist—it has to hurt

more and more, more and more—riiiight—and now you
remember what you want. Where is the woman? What's
she been doing all this time? I've been waiting for hours—
a glance at her wristwatch: I've been waiting for a whole
six—seven minutes. Why doesn't she come? I'm angry
with this woman. I wouldn't dream of sitting down in
that ridiculous little wicker chair again, like an idiot. Gilgi
goes into the nearest room. A nasty, unpleasant apartment. Such overdone, calculated elegance—so puffed up.
Ridiculous—this showy desk with the obligatory leather
portfolio and such a silly metal crocodile clasp. Martin
was bitten by a real crocodile once—in Colombia. Have I
kissed the scar a thousand times, or ten thousand times?
It's very important to know that. Certainly I haven't kissed
it often enough. Martin, my darling, if only we had as
much money as we have kisses which we haven't given
each other yet! Money. I must have money. If I see money
somewhere now or something valuable, then I'll grab it
and take it away with me—then I won't need to wait anymore and can go to Martin. Gilgi looks closely at paintings and other furnishings, estimating their value. None
of them are what she needs—after all, club chairs aren't
easy to carry away. Let's have a look at the next room.
Gilgi wanders from room to room, grimly determined to
take whatever's worth taking. It all stinks of money—but
of course you can't judge the value of vases and paintings and little sculptures—you can go badly wrong with
that kind of stuff. And unfortunately you can't take the
grand piano away with you, nor the sideboard. Another
locked door—Gilgi hears voices, and stops to eavesdrop—
without a trace of bad conscience.

"Diddy," a sharp and slightly theatrical female voice

says—"Diddy, why must you marry her? Wait, Diddy chéri—listen—you know you can have whatever you want from me ...."—That's my mother, talking with an extra-marital relationship—Gilgi decides. Probably Diddy is Herr Longin, and I'm Herr Longin's supposed girlfriend. Very sordid. So let's hear what this crook has to say. The crook or the presumed extra-marital relationship speaks with boyish resentment and charming exasperation, like an operetta tenor who's dissatisfied with his salary—"I tell you, Magda—I want something substantial at last. The old man is taking me into the business. And even if I marry the little girl—everything will remain the same between you and me—Magda—I beg you—don't make a scene—God, my nerves! You're a sweet woman, but ...." A silence which lasts three minutes, and can mean only one thing. Then the boyish voice takes wing again ... "of course it's her, Magda—the way the maid describes her—I suppose she saw us the other day. Magda, whatever happens you must make her believe that there's nothing between us ... let me leave now—keeping her waiting will only make it worse." That's right—Gilgi nods. "And Diddy, tomorrow you'll ...."—"Yes, yes—only we'll have to stop our excursions together ...."—"Yes, Diddy—Diddy, she's sitting out there in the hallway—you must go down the back stairs ...."—"I know the way.—Thank you, Magda—sweet one—"

As long as she hasn't just given him the five hundred marks which I need. Gilgi sighs worriedly. Because Diddy said "sweet one"—that must have cost a packet. Gilgi has no time to enjoy her spunky, reassuring cynicism before the door opens — — —

As coolly and uninhibitedly as the casting director of a

revue, Gilgi examines the petite, elegant lady who is standing before her. Doesn't impress me. How to classify her
type? Title character in a mediocre magazine serial. Quite
good figure—style a little undecided—half coolly fashionable American girl, half older lady who's kept slim by
dancing with gigolos. A touch too expensively dressed—
the usual tasteful but slightly impersonal uniform of the
traveler in first class. The face! Yes, if you like, you can find
some resemblance to yourself—the same large eyes, the
same high eyebrows, the same short, straight nose and the
slightly flattened oval of the face. An alien face nevertheless—and if you like—with no resemblance to you at all.
With that well-cared-for hennaed hair, she shouldn't wear
such red make-up—that's clumsy. But precisely this clum-
siness fills you momentarily with a certain sympathetic
fellow-feeling.

"Do you want to stare at me like that for much longer?" the magazine-lady asks, with a sharp hotel-terrace
smile. "Please come with me." She goes into the adjoin-
ing room—Gilgi follows her. "Please sit down." I don't
like her—Gilgi decides, coldly and definitively. And what
strange swinging movements she has—like a combination
of a tennis champion and a soubrette on the talkies.

Gilgi sits in a low, uncomfortably soft armchair with a
little table in front of her—and the magazine-lady opposite
her. The room has lots of curtains and hangings, and sub-
dued light—a flattering and no doubt carefully planned
setting for a woman over forty. It smells of good French
perfume and Elizabeth Arden cosmetics. Gilgi has the
feeling, which is both vaguely disturbing and very pleasant, that none of this is actually happening—the feeling of
dubious temporary security experienced by drunks. The

magazine-lady opposite her—with a cool, self-confident and superior attitude. No doubt she plays bridge and can mix exotic cocktails and knows the right months for eating oysters and is terribly cutting about people who don't know when the season ends in Monte ... "Won't you tell me why you've come to see me?" Yes, and she'll be able to converse knowledgeably about modern literature—and sometimes she's stylishly unhappy ... she's the complete magazine serial—those lines on her neck are really ugly — — — I have the honor, dear poor Frau Mother ...

"Why I've come to see you? Oh, I'll tell you ..." Gilgi falls silent, turns very pale, and must suddenly fight against physical nausea. And I thought I wasn't excited ...

"Do you smoke?" the lady she doesn't know says, opening a cute, brightly enameled cigarette-case and holding it out to Gilgi—

"No, thank you," Gilgi says. Runs her hands hastily and pointlessly over her battered trench coat a few times—I feel so nauseous — — "You know, that shocks me—that a human being who has hands and feet and eyes just like me can be so alien to me that I think it's not a human being at all, but something completely different ... Oh, you think I'm crazy? No, I'm quite normal—it's just—right now I have a strange feeling, as if the world were divided into two halves, and you and everyone else were sitting in one half, and I was sitting all alone in the other half. I would never be able to talk familiarly with you ... oh please, please don't interrupt me—I'm making such a big, big effort to speak quite openly and honestly to you—you're a snob, and have a primitive kind of vanity which disgusts me—you're alien to me, and I don't like you—I think it's pathetic, the way you're looking at me with such

mockery and a little contempt, just because you're better dressed at the moment—don't speak yet—oh, surely it
must be possible to get through to someone, even in the
face of mutual antipathy. Of course, I don't let people get
close to me so easily, either—but nevertheless I'm open to
some words and glances ... won't you help me and tell me
what I have to do or say, so that you become a living being
for me? — — —"

"I don't understand what you mean!"

"No, I suppose you can't ... yes, yes, I'll tell you what I
want now. I want you to give me five hundred marks, and
I want to tell you that you're my mother."

"That—I—am what?"

"My mother. At least to the extent that you gave birth
to me twenty-one years ago." Gilgi tells Frau Greif briefly
and clearly what Täschler told her.—"Right, now you
know everything." — — —

There's not a sound in the room—quiet, oppressive
semi-darkness—a small, silent, white spot, the face of
the magazine-lady. Somewhere a door slams, a car horn
blares—noises which could help—you stretch out towards
them—don't reach them. Everyone is dead—I'm all alone
in the world—I'll have a child—I'm happy—I'm so sad
with such happiness ... A fly buzzes, buzzes, buzzes ... I
can't move—the smell in the room here—a thousand rib-
bons which are winding themselves around my body and
around my arms and around my head—there should be
noises, I want to hear my voice, I want to be able to move
my hand. So quiet—the woman over there ... the light-
colored spot, I can hear it thinking, that's how quiet everything inside me is—I'm listening—I have to answer ...

"You're thinking that what I told you isn't true! How can

I prove—maybe it's blackmail—oh, don't deceive yourself. You're only trying to think that because it's how you want things to be—but you felt quite clearly that everything I said is true—we always feel the truth. Why are you fighting it? You don't need to torment yourself or feel any obligation to be shaken now or to have any kind of emotion for me. Don't be surprised by your indifference—that's not a lifelessness which has to shock you—we can't just react by compulsion and immediately—that only ever comes later. — — — I beg you, say something—I can't bear the way you're sitting there like a dead woman—I feel like I'm dying along with you. And when you do speak—please don't lie, and don't try to talk familiarly with me—that would be so shameful and embarrassing, because you can't feel at all close to me yet …" Gilgi falls silent, exhausted, little beads of sweat are forming on her pale forehead. An inexpressible physical exertion, every word of it. The white spot over there moves—a garish red mouth tries to speak—Gilgi leans forward—waits—for a word … I have to help her—it must be terrible for her, not being able to say anything—I feel how terrible that is for her. I have to re-establish her connection with her world for her …

"Maybe you're ashamed and depressed now, because you're simply afraid of scandal and mess in your life—there's no need for that to depress you—it's very natural for you to think about that. But you don't need to be afraid—no-one knows anything, and no-one will know anything. Think sensibly and logically—there was no place for a child in your life at that stage—I was a minor mishap for you—and you removed it from your life, or had it removed, in a most admirable, energetic way—of course with some inner struggles and pangs of conscience. But there's no doubt that you did what corresponded most strongly and definitively with your wishes ... Please don't cry—you've shaped your life according to your own taste—don't disown that now. As much as possible you sought out the things which you considered of greatest value ..."

A tremulous groaning from over there—Gilgi reaches for a cigarette, lights it—holds it out to the little, pale woman—"There, take it—it's good to do something normal right now." I've done something terrible to her by coming here—I have to help her ... Gilgi's voice has an infinite softness: "You should keep on being honest and logical now. Don't exert yourself to suddenly feel something more than indifference for me. Because nothing is changing in how you see life or what you want—and you don't need to think that something should change now. You committed yourself to a particular idea of life and a particular idea of taste long ago. And you can feel quite satisfied and unburdened, too—my life has been very good—I enjoy being alive—and I'm very grateful to you for having given birth to me. It's not every child who can say that to its mother, by a long way, is it? Beyond that you don't have the slightest obligation to me, nor I to you. We're not each other's concern. I'm here for one reason only—I need money. But for heaven's sake don't think that I believe I have the right to demand it from you—I'm only asking it of you ..."

Trembling fingers drop the cigarette—Gilgi stubs it out carefully in the ashtray.—

"People always want money from me, and never anything else," a curiously empty, childlike voice says at last.

"That's quite natural—other people ask someone to give what he has to give—what he has most of—love, sympathy, beauty, ideas, joy—or money."

"And I only have money to give?"

"I can think of—nothing—else—that—you—could—give—me."

"I'll give you money tomorrow."

"Tomorrow is too late."

"I don't have any money right now."

"But I need it right now—my God—now—you must understand that it's not for me—I would never have come here for myself, it's for friends ..." The woman grabs for Gilgi's hand suddenly—Gilgi pulls it away hastily—"don't touch me—please—it's better for you never to touch me."

"You must—tell me—about yourself—yes, you must come to see me—all the time—when?" Gilgi's open hands are lying heavily on the table—you can't lift them—you want to stand up and can't lift your hands. The room is spinning around her—fog, fog—dancing shadows—yellow clouds—shimmering air—

"I'll never come to see you again, I would only be a disruption for you—and you for me. And your world is alien and repugnant to me, I want nothing to do with it. I must go now—I've promised to help—I must keep my promise—I have no more time, I have to work out where I can get money." Gilgi looks at the little, deflated woman—who's raising her tired, empty eyes to Gilgi's face—stretching out both her hands—pulling them back suddenly—and slowly she slips one ring after another from her slender, smooth fingers—puts one ring after another into Gilgi's open hands—the blue sapphire—the green emerald—the two diamonds and the big pearl. A little heap of platinum and glittering stone in Gilgi's hands.

"That was very good of you," Gilgi says with trembling lips—"but—don't you love the rings—I mean, weren't they given to you by someone you love?"

The empty, childlike voice again. "My husband gave them to me—every time he cheats on me he gives me a piece of jewelry . . ."

"I should go," Gilgi says, and stands up. The woman wants to rise, too, suddenly becomes even paler than before, falls backwards—in one movement Gilgi is at her side. Puts the slack head on the arm of the chair—holding the little heap of glittering stones firmly in her left hand . . . she's fainted — — I've—never believed that people really faint—I'd never have thought such a thing possible . . . what are you supposed to do—? Water—yes, water—water—water — — — aach, it's all too much—Gilgi sinks to her knees—strokes the thin, bare arm which is hanging down slackly and lifelessly. The little magazine-lady is my mother—I shouldn't have come to see her. But she'll be all right again soon—she's got a Diddy and a reliable husband whose adultery is so lucrative for her—he'll probably turn sixty soon, and then he'll really start having affairs, and then she'll get lots of nice new rings—Gilgi presses the little hand briefly, it's so bare after all it's given away . . . Magda, little magazine-lady—things aren't so bad for you, Magda—but Hertha—poor Hertha—Hertha! The money! Martin! Gilgi leaps up, runs out of the room—encounters the maid in the hallway—"Madam feels ill, go to her—at once."

Half past six. Hans has until seven to pawn the rings, or sell them. You can be in Friesenstrasse in ten minutes at the latest. You're not going out of your way if you drop in on Martin first. Just to tell him quickly that he doesn't need to worry. You'll explain later. That all seems very calm and sensible. Gilgi sets out with quick, sure steps. All the emotions and events which she has experienced have been extinguished for the moment, only one thought remains: I've done it.

She's hardly even touched the bell before Martin tears the door open. Fear and rage are burning brightly in his eyes. "Where were you? My God—almost seven o'clock— I've been looking for you everywhere ..."

"Oh, Martin, this is hardly the first time I've been out so long."

"Yes it is, and you've never gone out without saying a word, either."

"Don't look so angry, Martin—give me a kiss, do— quickly—I just have to pop out again now—I'll explain afterwards ..." He pulls her into the room, holding her wrist in a hard, angry grip. And he's got every reason to be angry. Oh, my God, he's been so afraid. Once he started waiting, he fell ever more deeply and agonizingly into fear and uncertainty. He thought about thousands and thousands of things which might have happened, all kinds of things, all mixed up chaotically—sad, horrible, terrible—things which finally all combined into a torturing certainty. And suddenly you realize how much the little girl means to you—a hard nut, this realization, by no means entirely pleasant. A dubious benefit—to find out all at once that your own happiness and well-being are dependent on someone else. And you stand there like a helpless idiot, no longer the master of your own joys and sorrows. Purely because this ill-behaved little girl takes it into her head to spend countless, endless hours running around town in a downright irresponsible manner—yes, running around town—you have to endure the torments of hell—yes, I'm really angry with you, because I love you so much. "Damn it all, talk to me—where have you been?" Of course—to be completely in the right now, she'd have to be dead—thank God she's alive. "Where have you been?" The little girl is standing there in front of him—all pale and upset—no hat—her hair tousled—worn-out, looking guilty—has an angry, defiant look about her mouth—

"Let go of me, Martin, I have to go out now . . ."

"But, little Gilgi, I was worried about you, I presume you have a few minutes for me now." He lets go of her wrist, strokes her hair—Gilgi surrenders immediately to the gentler voice and the softer touch. She puts her arms around his neck, opens her hands without thinking—the rings fall onto the floor—the blue sapphire, the green emerald, the two diamonds, the big pearl . . . Martin picks them up one after the other . . . "what's all this—where did you get these from?"

"From my mother."

"Which one?"

"The magazine-lady—she fainted—she's quite alien to me. The rings still have to be sold, or pawned—but will they bring in five hundred marks? Martin—I said, I have to go—they're waiting for me . . ."

"Who's waiting? — — — Come along, Gilgi, rest for a while and then you can tell me . . ."

Gilgi goes into the dining-room with Martin—look how nicely he's set the table—and he hasn't touched anything—only the bottle of Hennessy, which was still full yesterday, is half-empty now. Gilgi drops tiredly onto a chair—"I'll eat and drink something quickly"—yes, drink a lot—then telling the story is sure to be much easier. Gilgi drinks—several glasses hastily—everything is so confused—more and more of her words are sliding back

inside her. Ach, if she could just sleep now. No, she can't
eat anything, she doesn't want to, the smallest bite becomes
huge in her mouth—you have to swallow a hundred times
before it goes down. She'd rather drink, and—"a cigarette."
The rings are lying on the table, sparkling a little, glittering . . . "Martin, do you think they'll bring in five hundred
marks?" Gilgi's eyelids are dropping with tiredness. Such
a heavy scent in the room. Three round black vases with
white hyacinths. Martin loves them so much, those flowers, and Gilgi loves them, too, because Martin loves them.
Martin gets up from the table, walks restlessly around the
room, sits down on the divan, smokes . . . The scent of
the hyacinths becomes mixed with the smell of Virginia
tobacco—a combination which for Gilgi is connected in-
separably with Martin. — — Drink another glass . . . then
you'll probably be able to talk. But really everything's quite
clear, and there's nothing to be tragic about. Really, it's
laughable that you suddenly make the simplest things in
the world so complicated and . . . "Martin, you don't have
to look so angry—no reason at all — — I was at Pit's and
at my mother's—to get money—otherwise a friend will go
to jail."

"What kind of friend?"

"A guy I used to know. Things were going so badly for
him—he was here once—" What Gilgi is saying becomes
obviously confused. Now she'll have to admit that she lied
the other day, that's probably the worst thing there is. She
hasn't lied so very often in her life—but when she did—the
fate of the world could have hinged on it—then you'd have
stuck with the lie. And of course Martin's sure to think
that she's done really terrible things, because she's so red
and uncertain and embarrassed. Although everything's so

simple—laughably simple. Hans and Hertha, they've got real problems ... Gilgi jumps up, reaches for the rings—"I have to go now, Martin ..."

"Stay where you are, little Gilgi—do you think I'd let you go out like that now! If you want to take the rings to someone—well, I can take them there for you later. Come here ..." Obediently she sits down beside him, lets her head fall into his lap ... "So who is supposed to get the rings? What kind of friend is he?"

"I used to know him—he was here the other day—with floor wax—so poor—and the wife—the children ..."

It's hard to work out the right meaning from the confused things Gilgi says—it's all too easy to work out a wrong meaning ... "So this is what I understand now—an old boyfriend of yours was here, and you concealed that from me. My little girl, if someone conceals something, then something's not right, then there's some feeling or other ... or are you such a stupid child that you think I'd be upset because you didn't wait for me—to be the first one? What do you take me for, little one? Don't misunderstand me, little Gilgi, if I asked stupid questions sometimes recently, it was because ... well, if you love a woman very much, then you become childish, then you're not smart, or superior, or perceptive. Then all the stupid primal feelings well up in you, then you're inclined to torment yourself—ideas and images force themselves on you, and it torments you to think that all the dear, sweet caresses have also been given to ... then the evil male urges are awakened, the brutal instincts of the possessor and the ruler ... My silly little Gilgi, my little Maori girl ... how such a little woman can be untrammelled by tradition—how I love you because you're the way you are—ach, a man is a thousand times more tied to tradition, my little one . . ."

How I love you because you're the way you are—how I love you because you're the way you are . . . he's never talked like that before, never like that. You've almost certainly done something wrong, to make a man talk like that. "Martin, Martin—I had lots of new caresses for you—and Martin, don't forget that you've had a lot of women too. But even if a man has had a thousand women—how poor would a woman be whose kisses didn't bring him to say at least one word that none of the others had heard—and that one word is what matters then—that—one—word— you—see"—presses her head more firmly into his lap, closes her eyes—Virginia tobacco—scent of hyacinths— a song, a song—music—the scent sings so that you feel it in your blood—the wakeful tiredness—the life behind closed eyelids—glittering stones, burning stones in your hot hand—but they don't have life themselves, I give them life . . . "Martin, I didn't ask my mother about my father—I simply forgot to, just think. But I don't care—wanting to meet your family doesn't get you much . . . yes, Martin, yes—I know I didn't want to go to her that time—now I've gone—because Hans had to have money . . ." Gilgi leaps up—staggers—stands upright—"I have to go, Martin . . ."

He grabs her arm—he's chalk-white, his voice is hoarse—"You did that for another man! Asked for money! How much you must love him."

"God, Martin, Martin . . ." A merry-go-round spinning in her head—I shouldn't have drunk anything—now I'm drunk—you have to explain, can't explain—confused words which just make everything worse, even harder to understand . . . "I have to go out . . ."

"I want you to stay here, Gilgi—do you hear me, I want you to."

"What you want doesn't matter, Martin"—Hertha—the little children ...

"Yes," says Martin, and lets go of her arm—Gilgi walks to the door with shaky little steps ... Martin watches her, his head resting on his hands—"You're right, little Gilgi— what I want doesn't matter—just go, little girl, just go."

"No, no, no, Martin—I won't go." Gilgi rushes to him, has lost control. "You will understand—it's all so ridiculous—Martin—I'll stay with you, I'll stay here—I love you—it's none of my concern if Hans goes to jail, I hate him, Martin, if you're sad because of him—you believe me now when I say that I love you, don't you? You have to believe me ..." You—the red, hot cloud—the sun—closer and closer—hyacinths, hyacinths in black vases—your hands on my chest—your lips—your eyes in the light, the loving pain in your eyes ... you—the rings—have dropped onto the ground—leave them there—my hands—I need my hands for you now ...

Thin gray morning light creeps into the room. Gilgi wakes up—raises her head. It hurts, feels like a thousand knives are stabbing into your brain. A glance at Martin—he's asleep. Gilgi swings her legs out from under the covers with a quick and decisive movement. Feels tired and shattered. She goes into the dining-room—the rings are lying next to the divan. Gilgi picks them up, holds them in the palm of her hand for several minutes, looks at them silently and absently. Tries to find a connection to her eventful yesterday, without success. Feels empty and pumped dry. Sees the used cognac glass on the table and grimaces slightly with tired distaste. Feels herself to be ancient and half-dead, finds herself disgusting without knowing the reason—and is a thousand times too tired and indifferent to look for a reason. She yawns. Would like to drop onto the floor and stay lying there—forever—gives herself a shake suddenly and goes into the bathroom. Lets the ice-cold shower play over her for several minutes. Then gets dressed quickly, in under ten minutes. Goes to Martin, sits down next to him on the bed and runs her hand lightly over his face, very gently pushing the lids up over his eyes—"Wake up, Martin! Listen, darling, it'd be a good idea for you to get up soon—you're due at the dentist's at nine, and you wanted to go to the library afterwards." She recites the words tiredly—a dull, constricting pressure on her chest almost deprives her of the power to breathe.

"Are you sad, little Gilgi, are you not well?" Martin asks—still half-asleep as he reaches for her hand.

"Ach, I have such a silly anxiety and a bad conscience, Martin—but it'll be better soon. I'm going to Friesenstrasse now and taking the money and the rings—because I won't feel at ease until I do. Do you see, darling, it's got nothing to do now with sympathy and feeling and those things—it's simply that I have to keep my promise—otherwise I'll be ill. I insist and I want so strongly for people to keep their word to me—I wouldn't like to lose the right to want that through my own fault ..."

Martin sits up in the bed.—"Of course, little one—you should do what you think right. How stupid we were yesterday! I gave you a lot of trouble for no reason, didn't I? I'll get dressed quickly, and if you like I'll come with you ..."

"Don't bother, Martin, I'd rather go right away—every

minute might count now. And don't wait for me, I'll go straight from Friesenstrasse to the labor office. And be here punctually for lunch—I'll make something really nice. Bye, darling—don't fall asleep again—and don't forget the dentist!" When she gets as far as the door, Gilgi runs back again, kisses Martin hastily on the neck and the throat and the eyes—"no, don't hold on to me, darling— bless you—see you at lunchtime . . . !"

Friesenstrasse. Outside the building where Hans and Hertha live, people are standing around, evidently excited about something—talking, gesticulating—Gilgi pays no attention to them, opens the street door—a clump of women in the stairwell—a rattle of chatter . . . Gilgi stops, extracts a blue envelope with the seven hundred-mark notes from her handbag, takes hold of the rings—are they all still there? Oh, how happy they'll be, the people upstairs! Two steps at a time, all the way up—how your heart's beating, it's cutting off your breath. But why am I sad? Such an aching sadness in every bone . . . I should have come here last night, then I wouldn't need to feel so oppressed—ach, nonsense, that's just exaggerated conscientiousness—now is still early enough . . .

The door of the attic room is half-open. A man she doesn't know comes out of it—Gilgi almost collides with him. The man has a cap in his hand—the man looks at Gilgi—the man opens his mouth—words crawl out of black gaps between his teeth . . . "Are you here to see the people in there? They're dead. They were taken away a half-hour ago. Dead. All four of them. Gas. The man wrote a letter—beforehand — — — he'd had enough. I'll have had enough soon too. Good morning." The man puts his cap on. His heavy tread on the staircase dies away slowly . . .

Gilgi's grip tightens on the envelope and the rings ...
but you're not allowed to have such dreams—that's revolting—such dreams ... She knocks on the half-open door—
a kind of bony sound ... tack, tack, tack ... everything's
quiet up here. Someone said that I have to knock here for
a thousand hours—tack, tack, tack—I've got red shoes on
and my blue dress—how did I come to wear red shoes
with my blue dress? Because I've never done that before—I
have to knock for a thousand hours ... why is there such a
terrible lot of writing on streetcar tickets—I'd like to know
what all that writing on streetcar tickets means ... tack,
tack, tack—have I knocked for a thousand hours now? The
door-handle is dull and has dark spots—someone should
see about cleaning the handle with ... yes, what's that stuff
called that you clean handles with? What's it called again ...
I know the name ... now the dirty handle is calling out to
my hand—I have to touch it ... Gilgi goes into the room,
closes the door behind her. The window has been torn
open, the beds are in gray disorder. A disgusting, sweetish
smell is crawling across the floor—up to your nose ... I've
got red shoes on—and there's a terrible lot of writing on
streetcar tickets ... I know that I've got red shoes on ... I
know more than that ... I know that they're dead—Hans
and Hertha and the little children—Hans—Hertha—but
do dead people still have names? I'm not insane, I'm quite
alert and clear and cold and not sad at all—I'm not anything anymore. Gilgi steps over to the open window, leans
out a long way ... sees the street far below ... you must decide — — — and you mustn't run away ... I know everything—everything—they're dead—what's that?—they're
dead because I didn't come yesterday—I'll have to think
that right through to the end—I won't be spared that—I

must keep thinking about it—keep thinking—keep thinking—keep thinking—think very carefully—don't leave
anything out ... they died here, while Martin and I ...
hyacinths in black vases ... Gilgi leans further out of the
window ... the pavement down there, that finishes everything—that's something—to know that everything can be
finished—very nice to know that—very, very nice. You
should picture that to yourself in detail: you fall down-
wards—through the air—a soft noise—an extinguishing
pain, a very strong pain—a spread-out mush of flesh and
blood and bone—everything flows out of you—all of the
blood and the brain and the unbearable thing. That's not
disgusting at all—that's very nice—such red blood on the
dirty, gray pavement—and everything finished ... You
must decide—I'm not insane, and I won't faint, either—I
have every part of my free will—nothing is influencing
me—from outside. Lean out a little further—then I'll fall—
then ... I'm not at all afraid ... my head is so heavy—it's
pulling me—down—there—my feet are so heavy—won't
lift from the floor—I've got red shoes on, red shoes—
they're nailed to the floor ... Gilgi falls backwards, bumps
her temple on a chair—blood trickles across her face—
damp and warm. She remains lying there, not making a
sound—her eyes wide open—for seconds, minutes. Then
stands up. Hard and determined. Goes to the little mirror
over the wash-stand—dips a handkerchief in the water-jug
and wipes the blood slowly from her cheek and temple—
the face in the mirror is gray and hollow. Gilgi looks into
the estranged mirror-face for a long time. Presses her lips
together in a narrow, hard line. Start again from the beginning, Gilgi! Four people are dead. The guilt that is mine ...
I'll see how I come to terms with it. The guilt that isn't

mine—I'll reject that, I won't talk myself into it, I won't carry that burden. The truth is difficult enough for me. And I know what I have to do—the most difficult thing. But I'm alive, and Martin's alive, and the child's alive ... I want to live—and I'm happy that I'm living. Gilgi's firm little steps die away on the staircase. Past the chattering women—along the street ... It's nine o'clock, and Martin will have left the apartment. As it should be.

Gilgi's suitcase is under the wardrobe in the bedroom. She pulls it out. Puts in her clothes, her underwear. She works very quickly and surely. Surely? The tiniest question mark, the very slightest thought beyond what's in front of her makes her hands tremble, incapable of moving, of picking up, of holding. Stay hard, stay hard—do the most difficult thing, do the right thing—right thing? Right how? ... Ah, don't think ... She runs her hand lightly over the colorful evening dresses in the wardrobe—you can all stay hanging there, I don't need you—by the time I wear an evening dress again, you'll be long out of fashion. Don't stand motionless—keep doing something, keep doing something—she shuts the suitcase. What now ... a few lines for Martin ... I'm hurting myself so much, I'll kill myself entirely—the air will have to help me and the paper and everything around me—too difficult alone ... too difficult—no—yes, I will write ... firm, hard letters—white paper, black loops, white paper ... red shoes, red ... and the air will have to help me.

"... precisely because I love you. Don't be afraid—not for me. It all has to be like this, you must trust me—Martin—something has happened, I can't laugh anymore,

not for a long time. The way I am now, I'd only be a burden
to you and make you sad along with me ... then maybe
you wouldn't love me anymore ... there's nothing I fear
more than that. Don't forget me—please."

She signs with a long, swerving line like a sob. She puts
the note in the center of the dining table—hyacinths—
white hyacinths in black vases. My sweet life—I'll carry
you in my blood forever. The golden fire ... Kneels down
in front of the divan, little Gilgi, lays her head onto the
cushions—the red-gold silk—the color of the love of your
life—you, and again only you ... I have no tears for others—tears evaporate unshed for love of you ... I am your
creation—I worship you—your red-gold color—I will
have no gray in it—not for you, not for me ... the suitcase
will be heavy ...

Gilgi stands up. Her eyes hollow and unseeing, her
mouth twisted, her skin ashen ... and you walk, walk—
you don't cry, you're not dying—you walk—with your
suitcase—you catch the streetcar ... Frozen world. Why
do you hurt yourself—so much? You're a bleeding scrap
of flesh, disguised by skin ... oh, my head—who is stabbing the needles in—dear God, do you think my head is
a pincushion ...

"Pit," Gilgi says as she enters his room—"Pit, you're
here! Thank God! You have to help me, so that I get on the
Berlin train tonight ..."

They sit quietly beside each other, the two children.
Pit holds Gilgi's limp little hand for a very long time,
very calmly—giving her what it is he has to give—a little human closeness. That's not much. That's a great deal.
And the walls surround two small, insignificant people
with indifferent understanding. A drop of sorrow in the

room—a teardrop of nothing shed behind the eyes—a drop of long-suffering breathing—a drop of sweet, young superfluousness. And so much outside! Nazi guys beating up Communists—Communists beating up Nazis—they're both right—because they both believe they're right. A terrible lot of newspapers writing—right and left—and right and left don't get to the core of things. And the world bends over laughing—go ahead and paint your political colors on my face—a single, tiny raindrop will wash them off ... you can try that with me—oh well—so much purposeful-purposeless racket—and a little cloud opens its mouth and spits in your stupid non-faces—just incidentally. There's a great deal going on in the world, and nothing happening—precisely because so much is going on—sophistry which is bellowed down to the earth and bounces back—try not to choke yourselves ... a great deal going on outside ... And the sun falls in love with the earth again—kisses all kinds of bright, green, flowery toys out of her ... its own game makes its love warmer and hotter—and there'll be a little notice in this evening's edition of the *Advertiser*—reporting and regretting impersonally ... four people dead of gas ... The notice isn't on the front page, and isn't very long—because that kind of thing goes on all the time and isn't really anyone's business particularly ... And in a halting monotone Gilgi tells her friend what will be in the newspaper this evening, tells him a bit more than that ... She wants to look at Pit, but her gaze flows emptily and vaguely down him—it's quite unable to fix on anything tangible ...

"What kind of people are we, then, Pit? Do you think I could be sad now—do you think I could shed a tear—because that's happened ... yes, I know it has, but somehow

I don't know it has—it doesn't get through to me—only that I bear some guilt for it, Pit—the guilt—but—I don't understand it all . . ."

Dumbly she closes in upon herself—a gray little heap of misery. Pit feels quite weird. Is she still alive? If only she'd cry and groan! But she's not fit for anything anymore . . . And while moments ago he was genuinely moved by the terrible story of despair in the back-street attic—now he's seized by obstinate, senseless rage—he's never hated living people as much as he hates those poor dead ones. They've destroyed the girl I knew, the living girl . . .

"Listen—Gilgi!" He's standing in front of her, stiff strands of his rust-red hair are falling over his white face — — — the girl—who means so much to me . . . "Listen, Gilgi—don't talk that garbage about guilt—when someone does something like that, he's at the end of his tether—and how were you involved in it? By going there this morning instead of last night! Don't make yourself ridiculous, don't give yourself a martyr complex, you silly goose. Do you think death and life depend on you—are you so disgustingly full of your own importance? I'm telling you, they'd completely lost their capacity to live, they were subject to every chance—and a thousand rings couldn't have helped them in the end . . . The guilt belongs in lots of other places, not to you . . . And if you start thinking like this now—well, then pretty soon nothing will happen on earth without you feeling guilty about it . . ." You'd like to shake and to hit the little, dead, gray heap of misery, so that life flows into it again, so that it becomes the little person it once was again, figure upright, shoulders thrown back, bursting with energy . . .

Gilgi barely moves—hears Pit talking quite a long, long

way off ... thoughts wander ... "Pit, you'll make sure that, whatever happens, I get on the Berlin train tonight?"

"Of course. I'll make sure." Pit will do anything. It'll be good for her to go away—only—"Why do you want to go to Berlin, of all places?"

Yes, why! Gilgi looks at Pit—as if he'd know why! Why does she want to go away, actually? Martin! But in a half-hour I can be with him ... "Why, Pit? Yes ... I know Pit, I know." She pulls him down next to her. Her eyes are more purposeful, her hands more alive—she sees her way quite clearly ... "Pit, I'm having a child. I want to have it. Because it's a great joy to have a child by the one man I really love. It's a great responsibility, too—which is good. I'll have to gather and use all, all of the strength that's in me—I'll have to ..."

Pit doesn't quite understand—"Yes, but the man?"

"Yes, you see, Pit, even if I weren't having the child—I'd have to leave him—for my sake and for his sake. I can't work, Pit—if I'm with him. I've already tried, and I've seen and lived what happens then. I just love him too much—and in every way, and I only have to look at him for everything else to become meaningless to me, utterly, utterly meaningless. It doesn't matter how much I strive to change things—nothing works. And you see, Pit, I have to work and keep my life in order ... he doesn't have enough money to support me—and anyway I wouldn't want him to, if he did have enough. And he spends so much when he's with me—and suddenly his small capital is gone, and then we're both standing there not knowing what to do next. And he's not at all used to working for money. He doesn't understand it. And you know, someone can probably change of their own accord—but wanting to change

someone else just means making life difficult for yourself
and for them. I think he really loves me now, and maybe
he'd adapt—to please me. But quite apart from the exter-
nal difficulty—the rest of it's terribly hard too. Yes, if he
did it later quite without being asked and quite slowly and
gradually and above all quite, quite voluntarily—then—
yes, then ... But now! Because of the child—suddenly
and from compulsion! And I'd get more and more nervous and more and more anxious and weaker, weaker,
weaker, and I'd come to depend entirely on him ... oh,
Pit, my beautiful love shouldn't turn into a kind of Strind-
berg play ..."

"And you're going to ... all alone with the child ... Oh,
you're so brave!"

Gilgi smiles—a poor smile that splits her face in the
middle. "You can be sure, Pit, that I'm doing what requires
the least amount of bravery from me. I'm not afraid—just
for myself—I'll look after myself, and the child too. And,
Pit," Gilgi's eyes are becoming clearer and clearer, "there's a
real purpose to it all, Pit—without the child, without such
a stark necessity it would've been harder. I would've had
no armor—and so alone—maybe some man or other—
even without love—just with ... you know what I mean,
Pit—and I know myself. But I don't want any other man,
because I know that I only love Martin. And then if I'm
making a living later—a good, secure living—and the
child—Pit, don't you think too that then he'd come to me
and be proud and happy, and everything would turn out
right? Oh, that's a long way off. The hard part comes first.
But, Pit, you understand that I have to leave? And if I try
to run away—run back—then you'll drag me to the station
and onto the train, won't you?"

Pit nods. "You can bet on it. But it will be difficult, Gilgi."

"Thank God, Pit! I'm so sick with longing to at last overcome difficulties again."

"But the child, Gilgi! That's still not the easiest thing in the world—a child without a father!"

"I'll tell you something, Pit, there are so many marriages where the father and the mother have horrible arguments all the time—well, at least a child who only has a mother is better off than that. If the child's healthy, and if I can support it—I don't care about anything else at the moment. Because you see I'm terribly immoral, Pit. I'm lacking something—where other people have a morality, I have an empty hole. I simply don't understand why an unmarried mother's child is supposed to be something immoral. And, Pit—there's one good thing: I'm so unshakably certain in myself on this point that I'll take other people along with me."

"Yes, but—will you even find a job?"

"Olga will help me. Remember, I can do all kinds of things, Pit—I'm really competent. And I have a very strong will. I've seen so many people who looked for work and didn't find it—but most of them only half-wanted it, they'd already given up on everything. There's a whole heap of people I can beat, because my will is stronger and more durable. Speculation à la baisse—sad—but that's just the way it is."

"But if you got sick . . . a birth can be . . ."

"Got sick! Why should I worry about that? I'm very healthy, and the odds are a thousand to one that I'll stay healthy. Of course I can get sick, I can also be run over by a car or fall out of an elevator ... Those kinds of possibilities don't enter into my calculations—that just costs energy."

She stands before him—her shoulders thrown further back, her eyes clearer. Pit looks at her—he's got her where he wanted her to be. She'll make it, you can see in every line of her body that she'll make it. She knows what she wants, she'll see it through. She's got some damned difficult hours ahead of her—poor little one—she's got mountains of pain and darkness to overcome—she will overcome them. "Ach, Gilgi, I'm damnably in love with you—may I give you a kiss—it's one of the sort that's all right for you to take."

"It's all right for you to give me several, Pit, if it means anything to you."

A drafty railway platform. Cold-black iron of locomotives and hazy gray of stones and dust. Gilgi and Pit are sitting beside each other on a big suitcase. Gilgi is staring tiredly in front of her. Clever, straight tracks—a big, black locomotive—purposefully connected metal. Small wheels, big wheels—all fitted together, belonging together. A little orange has rolled off the platform and is lying out of place, stupidly and purposelessly, between the straight, smooth, clever rails. Hurrying gray sounds fill the air. Gilgi grips Pit's hand more tightly. Trembles a little in her freezing aloneness. Feels the damp, dark evening coolness forcing its way through her thin dress ... Sees how the big hand on the platform clock drops with a jerk to the next minute. An urge to weep balls itself up hotly and chokingly in her throat. So many iron wheels ... there's a little, yellow orange lying in front of the locomotive—but how did the little orange get there ... a silly little melody which hums in her head and sticks there ... in front of the locomotive ... Maybe I'll never see Martin again ... she presses her hands to her face—"leave me alone, Pit—leave me alone"—buries her head in her arms—"please, Pit—surely people must be able to be left alone ..."

If I never see him again ... oh, why aren't you allowed to be only a woman—only, only, only! Is the day more important than the night then—why are we split up into nights and days. Why is the law of the night in our blood—the eternally desiring womb—I'm split up into a thousand pieces—my reason says Yes to order and day and light. And my hands don't know what to do, or where they belong—my thighs, my knees are waiting ... I only need to think hyacinths, and a scent divides the oneness of my lips ... light flashing and searing across white pillows—your dark head—your mouth—don't close the lids over your eyes—most beloved pain—you—I—we—cursed torment—desired torment—God help me—I don't want—but I'm burning up with longing for you ... my fingernails in your flesh—your teeth, which make my lips bleed—as we let the world perish—people, people, people are dying—you, you, you—God help me—"Pit, I must go home ..."

"The Cologne–Berlin express is your home ..."

"Martin is my home."

"Gilgi—you should be ashamed of yourself!"

"I don't know how to be ashamed of myself anymore."—He grabs her arm—he's a great guy, old Pit—poor, little Gilgi, you'd surely be lost on your own. Fold your hands obediently and piously and say "Thank you very much," because he's helping you—in simple humanity. For you being human means being human and being a woman and being a worker and being everything, everything. Asking a lot? Each of us is asked only for what he can give. Woe betide us, if he doesn't give it. "Pull yourself together, Gilgi!"

She looks at him—blind, not understanding—sighs tiredly: "Yes, you're right." She sits beside him again without a word. . . . there's a little, yellow orange lying in front of the locomotive . . . A tiny spark of happiness is kindled—flashes for a second: you'll belong again—have your place in duty and in the system of wheels which fit together—you'll be safe again in the desired compulsion of the days which you conquer by work, in the self-imposed law of what you build up yourself — — there's a little, yellow orange lying in . . . oh, you'll belong again. Because you belong in the overall structure, you're not created to stand outside it—and you happen to believe profoundly in the obligation incumbent upon young, healthy hands . . .

Hissing and steaming, the locomotive begins to move. The track is only clear for a moment—then in the distance two lights are seen coming nearer—nearer . . . The people start to move, the confusion becomes more hurried and more tense. The noise becomes louder and heavier . . . "In you go," Pit says and lifts Gilgi up. For a moment she sways—a thin, trembling little nothing under the huge vault of stone, glass, and iron . . . Scared, Pit grabs her arm—"Don't worry, Pit, I won't faint—that kind of minor anesthetic won't help me, I have to be fully conscious of everything I'm fighting . . ."

She gives Pit her hand once more through the lowered window—wants to say something like "Thank you very much"—can't utter another word . . . there's a little, yellow orange lying in front of the locomotive ... Clenches her hands over her chest ... Martin, you will be with me again one day—and I have to believe—won't be able to stand it otherwise—oh, I know that one day you'll be mine again—forever ... imaginings—Flight from reality? Flight to a better reality? ... there's a little, yellow orange lying ...

"Farewell, Gilgi—farewell!" Pit is running beside the moving train. "Farewell, farewell," he calls in a shaky, childlike voice.

"Dear Pit," Gilgi says softly, trying to produce a last, little smile for him, and half-succeeding.

AFTERWORD:
A WRITER IN THE
SHADOW OF NAZISM
BY GEOFF WILKES

The way Irmgard Keun told the story to the journalist Jürgen Serke decades afterward, once she had finished writing *Gilgi, One of Us* she took a train from Cologne to Berlin (as Gilgi does at the end of the novel), rented a room in a church-run hostel, chose the nearby Universitas publishing house from the telephone directory, delivered the manuscript to its publisher Wolfgang Krüger personally, and asked him for a decision within two days. The next morning, Krüger summoned her back and said: "We read through the night. Are you satisfied?"

Although Keun's accounts in old age of her earlier career were not always reliable, the history of *Gilgi, One of Us* was nevertheless remarkable. Keun was completely unknown and completely unpublished when she wrote it, but when Universitas released it in October 1931, it was an immediate bestseller. It was filmed in 1932, with a cast including Brigitte Helm (who had starred in Fritz Lang's *Metropolis*), and with a radically altered "happy ending," in which Gilgi's lover Martin pursues her train to Berlin in a car and they are reunited. Like many novels in Germany at the time, *Gilgi, One of Us* was also serialized in various newspapers, most notably in the Social Democratic party's daily *Forward*, which also published numerous letters from readers hotly debating whether Gilgi was indeed "one of us"—that is, whether her views and actions were consistent with Socialist principles. As the serialization was drawing to a close, *Forward* invited "its female readers" to submit short literary or descriptive pieces loosely related to the novel (a "sketch of someone's life, a day in the office, an especially typical or significant scene from life and work, and experiences outside the realm of employment too") to a competition; the prizes included a typewriter, a "lady's bicycle," and cosmetics, and Keun was a member of the judging panel.

Keun followed *Gilgi, One of Us* with *The Artificial Silk Girl*—which was also a bestseller—in 1932, less than a year before the Nazis came to power. On November 30, 1933, the German Book Trade Association sent Universitas a form letter headlined "WORKS WHOSE SALE IS NOT DESIRED," which announced that: "With the agreement of the Fighting League for German Culture, we inform you that for national and cultural reasons the offer and the sale of the works named below is considered undesirable, and must therefore cease." The "works named" included both *Gilgi, One of Us* and *The Artificial Silk Girl* and, incidentally, three titles by one of the fictional Gilgi's favorite authors, Jack London (see p. 86).

The "national and cultural reasons" that prompted the prohibition of Keun's novels were not described further in the Book Trade Association's letter to Universitas. However, many aspects of *Gilgi, One of Us* were obviously contrary to Nazi sensibilities. The association's reference to "national" reasons probably includes Gilgi's distaste for demonstrative patriotism:

"Martin—I belong here.—What happens here
is my business—all of it. A sad country, you say?
Martin, even at school I was ashamed when they
sang 'Deutschland, Deutschland über alles'—such
a revolting song—so oily when you were saying the
words, so oily when you were thinking them, your
whole mouth full of cod-liver oil.—Those people—
who force their love of the fatherland on you—do
you understand that— . . ." (p. 100).

But Gilgi's clearest divergences from Nazi ideals origi-
nate in her self-concept as a woman, which encompasses a
commitment to a professional career, sex independent of
marriage, an acceptance of abortion for economic reasons,
and a resolve to support her child as a single mother. And
Gilgi's attitudes are shared at least in part by her friends
Olga and Hertha, and her colleague Fräulein Behrend.

It is perhaps worth noting in passing that although
the Book Trade Association made no detailed criticism
of *Gilgi, One of Us* in November 1933, at least two specific
complaints were laid out later. On December 12, 1934, the
police in the Silesian city of Opole wrote to the Gestapo
in Berlin seeking advice about suppressing a copy of the
novel that had remained in a local library, and quoting
Gilgi's words about "Deutschland über alles" as evidence
of the narrative's "hostility to the state." And on September
19, 1934, the Reich Office for the Promotion of German
Literature had also consulted the Gestapo about a copy of
Gilgi, One of Us in a Berlin library, complaining on behalf
of the Reich Federation of German Civil Servants that "the
reputation of female postal workers" was "insulted in the
crudest way" by the narrative's incidental comment that if

a group of street prostitutes "weren't wearing make-up and using belladonna you could take them for unemployed telephone operators" (p. 31).

As I have explained in my afterword to Melville House's edition of *After Midnight* (1937), Keun never entirely recovered from the damage which the advent of Nazism inflicted on her creativity and her career. She published nothing more of substance until she had left Germany in 1936; she struggled with financial difficulties, psychological strain, and professional self-doubt while producing three novels and a volume of short stories after emigrating; she necessarily fell silent once she was overtaken by the invasion of the Netherlands in 1940 and, for sheer lack of other options, returned clandestinely to Germany; and she wrote very little in the decades between her sixth novel in 1950 and her death in 1982, although she did live to experience the belated recognition which was accorded to her work when critics and scholars began extensive study of writing by women, and writing by anti-Nazi exiles, in the 1970s.

GILGI, ONE OF US

The identity which Gilgi asserts places her at the center of the Weimar Republic's debates about the so-called New Woman. *Gilgi, One of Us* was of course only one among many novels of the period in which New Women played important roles, though arguably it can be located more precisely within a kind of sub-genre which featured female typists, and which included works such as Vicki Baum's *Grand Hotel* (1929) and Rudolf Braune's *The Girl at the*

Orga Privat (1930; Orga Privat was a brand of typewriter). In fact, Gilgi references Christa Anita Brück's 1930 contribution to this sub-genre when she tells Martin that she tries to deflect her employers' sexual advances "without starting some great drama of outraged honor, like in that novel, *Tragedies at the Typewriter!*" (p. 81).

Despite Gilgi's comment here, "great drama" is a constant and significant element in her own story. Gilgi's initial self-concept is founded on a fierce commitment to material and emotional self-sufficiency. Her meditations during the first scene in her attic room are about professional success through her own efforts, whether through her skills in office work, foreign languages, or dress design. She is equally self-contained when she decides that the departure of Olga's brother after their brief romantic interlude is "as it should be" (p. 5), and that spending time as a family with Herr and Frau Kron "is always a pointless waste of time" (p. 26). But simultaneously as the narrative communicates all this, it also suggests that Gilgi's autonomous persona is somewhat self-conscious and exaggerated, as when she "assumes her best woman-of-the-world expression" (p. 18) while discussing with Olga how to divert her boss Herr Reuter's sexual advances without endangering her job. Moreover, the narrative notes how Gilgi avoids showing her admiration for Olga by criticizing the "dirty marks" (p. 17) on her blouse instead, and how "if she didn't have such a distaste for the word 'romance,' you could say: for Gilgi, Olga represents romance" (p. 15), as though Gilgi's studied self-sufficiency will eventually face challenges from circumstances and emotions which she cannot disregard forever.

When these challenges duly emerge, they do so in a

greatly dramatic manner. Firstly, the Krons reveal that Gilgi is adopted, and when she seeks out the woman whom the Krons believe to be her birth mother, Fräulein Täschler, the plot thickens still further: the impoverished Fräulein Täschler explains that she passed Gilgi off as her own child because she was paid by a well-to-do family who concealed their unmarried daughter's pregnancy to preserve their reputation in society. These revelations encourage Gilgi to reflect on how much her career success so far owes to her middle-class upbringing with the Krons as well as to her own efforts ("Just don't stick your nose so high in the air, just don't always think it's so completely your own doing," p. 45), and to sympathize with those who are less successful than she is, such as the unemployed "pale woman" who also applied for the casual typing job which Gilgi secures with Herr Mahrenholz (pp. 65–66). Secondly, Gilgi falls suddenly and tumultuously in love with Martin, with the narrative characterizing her attraction to his bohemian, exuberant personality as the more or less inevitable reflex of her rationality and self-containment:

> Gilgi's imagination was always a well-behaved child: it was allowed to play in the street, but not to go beyond the corner. Now the well-behaved child is venturing a little further for once. Martin talks, and Gilgi sees: oceans, deserts, countries—but that's not the essence of what she's seeing, she'd like to make an accounting to herself—as she always does—to record her feelings in her own words. Oh, my little, gray words! That someone can speak so colorfully! She's sitting on a sphere that's damp with

rain—there's a sun far, far away in the sky—with
each hand you grab a sunbeam, [...] you're getting
closer and closer to the sun's hot orange-red ball.
(pp. 60–61)

As her emotional dependence on Martin increases,
Gilgi abandons her material and professional ambitions
almost entirely, for example by doing "something [...]
disorienting and momentous" (p. 90) in absenting herself
from work on a false plea of illness, and later by actively
welcoming the loss of her job when the hard-pressed Herr
Reuter reduces his staff: "Thank God, thank God—now it's
not my fault, I can't be blamed" (p. 112).

Gilgi's story reaches its peak of drama after she encounters her former friend Hans, and undertakes to save
him from jail by repaying the twelve hundred marks he
has embezzled to feed his destitute family. This leads her
to contact her affluent birth mother Frau Greif for the first
time ("I want you to give me five hundred marks, and I
want to tell you that you're my mother," p. 185), Frau Greif
hands over several rings which were gifts from her husband ("every time he cheats on me he gives me a piece of
jewelry," p. 189), Gilgi is then diverted from delivering her
own money and the rings by Martin's jealous demands
on her ("I want you to stay here, Gilgi—do you hear me,
I want you to," p. 195), and the next morning she discov-
ers that Hans, his wife Hertha and their two children have
committed suicide. Gilgi reacts to this dénouement by re-
solving to seek work in Berlin (where she intends to bear
her child and raise it by herself), leaving Martin immediately. For Gilgi has decided that her love for Martin is
destroying her autonomy completely, but that she should

not expect him to adapt his life to hers in any way, as she explains to her friend Pit:

> Even if I weren't having the child—I'd have to leave him—for my sake and for his sake. I can't work, Pit—if I'm with him. I've already tried, and I've seen and lived what happens then. I just love him too much—and in every way, and I only have to look at him for everything else to become mean- ingless to me, utterly, utterly meaningless. [...] And you see, Pit, I have to work and keep my life in order ... he doesn't have enough money to sup- port me—and anyway I wouldn't want him to, if he did have enough. [...] And he's not at all used to working for money. He doesn't understand it. And you know, someone can probably change of their own accord—but wanting to change someone else just means making life difficult for yourself and for them. (pp. 204–205)

Thus at the end of the novel Gilgi reverts to and in- tensifies one of the attitudes which she demonstrated at the beginning. She does not simply reiterate that profes- sional success is purely a matter of individual effort ("I've seen so many people who looked for work and didn't find it—but most of them only half-wanted it, they'd already given up on everything. [...] My will is stronger and more durable," p. 206), but she expects to succeed notwithstand- ing that she is now unemployed, without any support from the Krons, and intending to assume sole care of a baby. Gilgi also reverts in a significant sense to her emotional self-sufficiency, regarding her baby as a kind of insurance against further romantic entanglements ("without the child, without such a stark necessity it would've been harder. I would've had no armor—and so alone—maybe some man or other—," p. 205), though presumably she feels a connection to the baby, and through it to Martin, and she has a confused hope that she will be reunited with Martin eventually: "And then if I'm making a living later—a good, secure living—and the child—Pit, don't you think too that then he'd come to me and be proud and happy, and everything would turn out right?" (p. 205).

In characterizing Gilgi's initial self-concept as somewhat overwrought, and then showing how it fluctuates through dramas of abandonment, passion, jealousy, suicide, and "flight" (p. 210), the narrative maintains a measure of detachment from her, and it extends this detachment by signaling doubts about Gilgi's ultimate plans, particularly in the final scene when she boards the train to Berlin. The most obvious signal is when Gilgi tries to smile, to convince Pit that she is confident about the future, but only "half-succeed[s]" (p. 210). The repeated image of the orange lying in front of the locomotive (which clearly invokes Gilgi's love for Martin; see p. 207) is similarly ambiguous, as it is uncertain whether the orange is crushed by the departing train or lies far enough below the machinery to survive unscathed. And there is a more subtle double-edged allusion in the description of how Gilgi "gives Pit her hand once more" (p. 209) from the train, as this recalls the song—known in German as "Reich mir zum Abschied noch einmal die Hände" and in English as "Good Night"—which is in Gilgi's thoughts earlier in the novel (see p. 4), and which is sung by the lovers Victoria and Stephan in the operetta and film *Victoria and Her Hussar* (1930 and 1931) immediately before they are separated. This reference could ridicule Gilgi's decision to renounce Martin in the hope of an eventual reunion by linking it with a kitschy popular drama, but that reunion could also be foreshadowed by the fact that Victoria and Stephan are married at the end of their story.

There are also some short passages earlier in the novel which have implications for Gilgi's plans after she leaves Cologne. The first is when Herr Kron reads out a newspaper report about a woman who killed her child by jumping with it from "the Treptow Bridge" (p. 8), which is in Berlin. The second is when Fräulein Täschler recalls that many of her customers "didn' want anythin' to do with me anymore" (p. 40) when she was passing herself off as Gilgi's unmarried mother. The third is when Gilgi reads a letter from the "little Dutch girl" who is "still in love with Martin" (p. 121), and who still writes to him. All three passages are bad omens for Gilgi's ideas about supporting herself as a single mother in Berlin, and perhaps one day returning to Martin, though of course these omens are of no account if Gilgi really is as exceptionally competent as she believes, and it is possible that she would encounter less prejudice than Fräulein Täschler suffered twenty years previously.

The narrative's slightly detached presentation of Gilgi's frenetic present and her ambiguous future is complemented by its account of her difficulties in expressing herself verbally. Although there was some justification for the dismissive remark of Keun's great contemporary Kurt Tucholsky that the characters in *Gilgi, One of Us* too often speak "as though they'd just been eating Freud for breakfast," later commentators such as Ritta Jo Horsley

have shown that the issue is more complex than that. For
the novel emphasizes what Horsley has termed "Gilgi's crisis of language" repeatedly, most often by describing her
relationship to "words" ("Worte" in the German text). For
example, the difference between Gilgi's psychology and
Martin's which is apparent at their first meeting is encap-
sulated in her sense (in the passage quoted above) that she
has only "little, gray words," and her wonder that Martin
"can speak so colorfully." When Gilgi tries shortly afterwards to clarify her feelings for Martin, she thinks that
she "should probably talk to someone, but there wouldn't
actually be any point. Because she doesn't have any words,
to make herself understood" (p. 68). She does talk to Olga
later, but only to reiterate her linguistic deficiencies:

> And you're together at night and walk beside each
> other during the day, without a single word that
> binds you—you only catch words which are soap-
> bubbles. [...] And you're all ripped up, and have
> typewriter words and clockwork words and every-
> day words and don't want to think about yourself
> and should think about yourself. (pp. 118–119)

And nothing changes in the remainder of the narrative.
When Gilgi is preoccupied after visiting Hertha, and Martin worries that she no longer loves him, she asks herself:
"Why don't I have any words—for Martin—or for myself,
either?" (p. 170); and when Martin's possessiveness flares
again as she explains why she is giving Frau Greif's rings to
Hans and Hertha, Gilgi feels "more and more of her words
[...] sliding back inside her" (pp. 191–192).

However, there are few indications that, if Gilgi were

ever to articulate her thoughts and feelings more clearly,
Martin would listen to her. When Gilgi leaves the Krons
and goes to Martin's apartment, she is still debating aloud
whether to live there or in her attic room when he—
"ignoring these words completely" (p. 93)—starts unpack-
ing her suitcase. On a subsequent occasion when Gilgi
talks to Martin in bed, it turns out that "he's asleep" (p.
139). And in the conversation about Frau Greif's rings
mentioned above, Martin's interpretation of Gilgi's sympathy for Hans is shaped by jealousy: "So this is what I
understand now—an old boyfriend of yours was here, and
you concealed that from me" (p. 193). Martin's failures to
listen to Gilgi are paralleled for most of the narrative by
Pit: for instance when she seeks him out after her first encounter with Fräulein Täschler, but he delivers a political
monologue while she waits in vain "for a moment when
she can interrupt him and tell him about the things which
are more important to her, and have more to do with her,
just now" (p. 46), or when he refuses to discuss her relationship with Martin because he is attracted to her himself: "Why are you telling me this—you! That's why you
came to me—that's why ... just to tell me ..." (p. 137). It
is also worth noting that Gilgi's relationship with Martin
meets with blank incomprehension and uncompromising
rejection from the Krons: Frau Kron can only account for
it by wailing that "some man has hypnotized you" (p. 87),
and Herr Kron can only deal with it by "laying down the
law" (p. 88) and forbidding Gilgi the house, leaving her
to conclude that "there just isn't any common ground" (p.
91) between her and her adoptive parents. But those in the
older generation who claim to empathize with Gilgi and
her peers leave her unmoved, as she complains to Martin

about "those old people who have thrown themselves into the new era. The ones who write about sport-oriented modern youth, driving cars, short skirts, short hair, and jazz, and have an amazing ability to hit the nail right next to the head" (p. 83).

Gilgi's recurring struggle to express herself adequately, Martin's and Pit's repeated failure to listen properly, the Krons' complete inability to understand her unconventional morality, and other older people's misguided belief that they do understand "the new era" indicate one important reason for the great drama of Gilgi's life in Cologne and the obvious uncertainty of her prospects in Berlin. Gilgi's identity as a New Woman seems highly colored and somewhat unrealistic because neither she nor the society around her has yet fully assimilated that identity intellectually, has yet fully described it verbally, or has yet reached the point where the language required to discuss it has become "everyday words." The melodramatic element in *Gilgi, One of Us* reflects and underlines how significant personal challenges and vigorous social controversies are associated with Gilgi's claim to emancipated femininity, rather than (as Tucholsky suggested) unwittingly betraying Keun's inexperience as an author. After all, Keun asserts the legitimacy of popular artistic styles when Gilgi, bored while attending a classical concert with Martin, muses that: "Literature, music, painting—it's a funny thing, art. One person's Rubinstein—is another's dance-band leader, one person's Rembrandt—is another's commercial artist. What can you do?" (p. 116). And for evidence that Gilgi was a highly unsettling character for the society in which she lived, we need look no further than how the film version of her story changed the ending to foreclose her vision of a consciously chosen and self-supporting unmarried motherhood.

The most visible obstacle to Gilgi's development as a New Woman is the attitudes of men. Martin demeans her not only by ignoring what she says and suspecting her motives for helping Hans, but also by addressing her constantly as "little Gilgi," by remarking patronizingly that "there are less intelligent and less sensitive people than you" (p. 94), by regarding her as a "doll" (p. 103) which he can manipulate physically and dress in clothes of his choosing, and by urging her to leave Cologne with him because "when we're somewhere else you'll belong to me more than you do here" (p. 109). Martin's, Pit's and Herr Kron's condescending treatment of Gilgi is paralleled by other men's treatment of other women: by Gilgi's unnamed father, who "disappeared" (p. 39) when he made her mother pregnant; by Fräulein Täschler's unnamed fiancé, who "got a thousand marks out of me" (p. 41) before she broke off the engagement; by Herr Greif, who gives his wife jewelry "every time he cheats on me"; by Frau Greif's lover Diddy, who says—"speak[ing] with boyish resentment and charming exasperation, like an operetta tenor who's dissatisfied with his salary" (p. 182)—that he will continue to see her after he marries another woman whose father "is taking me into the business" (p. 182); and perhaps even by the impoverished and hard-working Hans, who cannot understand the exhausted Hertha's loss of sexual appetite: "I disgust you, you don't love me anymore" (p. 166). Of course, Gilgi's spirited handling of sexist and patronizing men provides some of the novel's most vivid moments, particularly when she contrives with Olga to divert Herr Reuter's sexual advances (see pp. 18–21), and

when she tells the doctor who diagnoses her pregnancy
that she doesn't want the child:

> "You mustn't get so excited now, dear young lady—
> it would be best if you got married."
>
> "I'd say that knowing what'd be best is somewhat
> beyond your area of expertise, wouldn't you? And
> anyway, that's the last thing I'm worried about. I
> wouldn't have the least hesitation in bearing five
> healthy children as an unmarried mother, if I could
> support them." (p. 140)

But Gilgi reacts against Martin's sexism and patronage
not by outwitting him as she did Herr Reuter, nor by chal-
lenging him as she did the doctor, and not even by asking
him to alter his behavior in any particular ("wanting to
change someone else just means making life difficult for
yourself and for them"). She simply leaves him, with great
reluctance, and with a vague hope that one day "he'[ll]
come to me and be proud and happy."

I would interpret this glaring anomaly in Gilgi's
thoughts and actions—which I believe reveals Keun's view
about the New Woman's immediate prospects—by exam-
ining how Gilgi's situation is replicated in Olga's. Olga is
a different kind of New Woman from Gilgi, because she
is much less career-oriented: "When she needs money,
she works; when she has money, she travels" (p. 18). She
is also different because she leads a bohemian existence
largely beyond the realm of "everyday words" in which
Gilgi struggles; indeed, Olga sometimes communicates
with Gilgi non-verbally (see pp. 119 and 131–133), and she
luxuriates in the escape from the problems inherent in

words which is afforded by her visits to Majorca: "The people there talk a language that I don't understand. Can you imagine, Gilgi, how magical it is to hear just a melody of words, without understanding all the nonsense that lies behind them?" (pp. 54–55). However, Olga is very like Gilgi in having experienced a relationship with a possessive man, Franzi, whom she married, whom she left after six months because he was "as jealous as a touring-company Othello" (p. 54), whose story she has told Gilgi "a hundred times" (p. 53), and whose photograph she "slobbers on" (p. 53). Thus there is a profound tension in *Gilgi, One of Us* between how (on one hand) the characterization of the male figures suggests that if the New Woman is to find a settled and undramatic place in her society, then that society will need to produce a New Man, and how (on the other hand) Gilgi barely recognizes Martin's sexism, Olga fights Franzi's sexism and fails, and both the white-collar and the exotic New Women still feel attracted to the unsatisfactory lovers whom they left. This tension indicates that Keun had little confidence that—and little idea how—the Weimar Republic's New Men could emerge anytime soon.

TRANSLATING *GILGI, EINE VON UNS*

This is the first complete English translation of *Gilgi, eine von uns*. I have followed the first edition of 1931. My three major challenges were the novel's strong links with the era in which it was written, Gilgi's use of the German pronoun "man," and other characters' use of *Koelsch*, the Cologne dialect.

Gilgi, eine von uns is a novel of its era—the late Weimar

Republic—firstly in the general sense that it is set explicitly in 1931 (see, for example, p. 33), and that it refers to things which were common at the time but have been largely superseded today, such as gramophones, typewriters, and of course Gilgi's professional skill of stenography. With this in mind, I have endeavored to use only vocabulary appropriate to the era, such as "talkies" (p. 183) for "Tonfilm." *Gilgi, eine von uns* is also—and, for the translator, more challengingly—a novel of its time in its numerous topical references: most frequently to popular songs, but also to contemporary personalities, public events, advertising slogans, and so on. As the song references in particular often resonate with the wider story, I have translated them fairly literally in order to preserve any wider resonance. The best example of this is the line from the song "Reich mir zum Abschied noch einmal die Hände" / "Good Night" which I mentioned earlier.

The German "man" (like the French "on") is an ungendered, third-person pronoun used for making impersonal, generalized statements, and it is most often translated in English by "one" or a non-specific "you." Gilgi uses "man" constantly when talking and thinking about herself, which creates the impression that she finds her feelings and ideas confusing or even unwelcome; this aligns with the problems about "words" which I discussed previously. Given that repeated use of the English pronoun "one" tends to sound artificial, I have usually translated Gilgi's "man" as "you," as if she is apostrophizing herself, although this meant that occasionally I had to paraphrase a "you" when Gilgi was actually addressing someone else.

Koelsch is spoken intermittently throughout the narrative, most conspicuously by Fräulein Täschler, but to a limited extent also by the Krons, and by very minor characters such as some of the Carnival revelers. As attempting to render all these characters' words in some variety or dialect of English (New York slang, Cockney, Australian English, or anything else) would have been grotesquely inappropriate, I have limited myself to marking *Koelsch* with some non-standard pronunciations ("Jilgi," "twenny-one," and so on), and with a few malapropisms, most obviously "cheese lounge" (p. 40) for Fräulein Teschler's "Scheselonk."

I would like to express my gratitude to Dr. Andrew Bonnell (University of Queensland, Brisbane), who enlightened me about some of the novel's more obscure topical references; to Dr Stephan Atzert (University of Queensland, Brisbane), who clarified various linguistic points for me; and to the Mac/Eddy Club (the Jeanette MacDonald / Nelson Eddy fan club, New York), which I consulted about "Good Night." Any deficiencies in the foregoing translation of *Gilgi, eine von uns* are entirely my responsibility.

EDITORIAL NOTE

Keun's interview with Jürgen Serke is in his *Die verbrannten Dichter: Berichte, Texte, Bilder einer Zeit* (Frankfurt am Main: Fischer, 1980). The translation is my own.

The quotations from *Forward* are taken from the section on the serialization of *Gilgi, One of Us* in Stefanie Arend and Ariane Martin's *Irmgard Keun 1905/2005: Deutungen und Dokumente* (Bielefeld: Aisthesis, 2005). The translations are my own.

The letters from the German Book Trade Association to Universitas, from the Opole police to the Berlin Gestapo, and from the Reich Office for the Promotion of German Literature to the Berlin Gestapo are in the files of the "Stiftung Archiv der Parteien und Massenorganisationen der DDR" of the Federal Archive in Lichterfelde, Berlin. The first letter is in the file R55/684, and the other two letters are in the file R58/914. The translations are my own.

Kurt Tucholsky's review of *Gilgi, One of Us* appeared (under his pseudonym "Peter Panter") in *Die Weltbühne* on February 2, 1932. The translation is my own.

Ritta Jo Horsley's article about "Gilgi's crisis of language" is "'Warum habe ich keine Worte? ... Kein Wort trifft zutiefst hinein': The Problematics of Language in the Early Novels of Irmgard Keun." *Colloquia Germanica* 23 (1990), 297–313.

Geoff Wilkes
University of Queensland
Brisbane, Australia

THE NEVERSINK LIBRARY

THE NEVERSINK LIBRARY

THE NEVERSINK LIBRARY